Paying to Play

In

HONG KONG

香港

Paying to Play

In

HONG KONG

John H. McKoy

Abolet Publishing

Washington, D.C.

Claviers, France

3

Abolet Publishing

1348 East Capitol Street, N.E.

Washington, DC, 20003, United States of America

(202) 543-0406

European Office

Impasse du four vieux

83830 Claviers, France

04 94 47 28 75

www.ronkoshes.com

Cover photos by Steve Gay

Cover design : Tom Monteleone, Borderlands Press

The Library of Congress cataloging-in-publication data on file with the publisher.

ISBN-13: 978-0-9818984-5-2

ISBN-10: 0-9818984-5-9

Printed in the United States of America on recycled paper.

First printing, 2009

This book is dedicated to John, Helen, and Paul whose memory and perpetual spiritual presence bring joy and learning to this pilgrim's journey. It is also dedicated to Andrea in whose debt I will always remain for accompanying and supporting me on the ups and downs, the twists and turns of life. They have all given me love, wonder and wealth beyond measure.

PAYING TO PLAY IN HONG KONG
Glossary of major characters

Masterfield Consulting
- **Harry Morton-** Main character and retiring international management consultant
- **Don Bartram-** Chief Executive Officer of international wing of company and a peer of Morton's
- **Ellen Kwan-** Young Stanford-educated management wiz
- **Peter Burke-** Experienced, Harvard-educated financial wiz
- **Roberto Higgins-** Young NYU-educated organizational development expert
- **Hazel Marsh-** Harry's indispensible Executive Assistant

Harry's friends and associates
- **Mary Stokes Morton-** Harry's wife and successful labor economist
- **Mark Morton-** The Mortons' ten year old son
- **Pierce Morton-** Harry's brother
- **John and Lena Morton-** Harry's parents
- **George and Mabel Birch-** Close friends of the Mortons
- **Bobby Boyd-** Antagonist of Mark's
- **Max Dupree-** Old colleague of the Mortons; current friend of Mary's
- **David Lee-** Childhood football opponent of Harry's

Silk Road, Inc. (SRI)
- **Wong Xi-** Main character and Chairman and President of the main acquiring Hong Kong company
- **Ho Duan-** Executive Vice President and right hand partner of Xi's
- **Ying Yi-** Xi's young Administrative Assistant

Xi's friends and associates

- **Wong Shi-** Xi's father, former Tai-Pan and brilliant banker
- **Katherine Harris Wong-** Xi's mother; British journalist who died young
- **Bao Li-** Xi's husband, who's another successful banker
- **Wong Jianying-** Xi's aunt, who raised her in Hong Kong
- **Margaret Schultz-** Xi's business school friend of mixed Indian-British parentage, who's a successful international banker

South China Apparel

- **Xiaobin Li-** Former Red Army General, now CEO
- **Yao Lanxin-** Xiaobin's Executive Assistant and old army friend
- **Yi Li-** Xiaobin's Chief Financial Officer
- **Rip Drake-** Financial advisor from the Bank of England
- **Wang Ren-** Xi's ambitious cousin, who goes to work for her competition

CHAPTER ONE

香港

As he threw his suitcase onto the bed at Hong Kong's magnificent Peninsula Hotel, Harry Morton was glad to finally be heading home to Washington. He loosened his tie, took a slow sip of bourbon, and gazed across the harbor to the hills climbing away from the business and residential density on the Hong Kong side. To him, twilight over Hong Kong's Victoria harbor highlights the most majestic urban scenery in the world. The thick windows muffled the sounds of cars and boats, but Harry had spent enough time on the streets below to be able to imagine precisely what the early evening sounded like ten stories below. Street hawkers pressed pedestrians for one final purchase; double-decker buses sounded warning horns as they quickly shifted lanes; tugs, sampans, barges and ferries honked within the harbor's traffic lanes; and the general din of Cantonese, English and Hindi clashed together in a cacophony of conversations.

"What a wonderful chaotic swirl down there. Business Hong Kong style," he thought. His deal completed, Harry breathed deeply and relaxed fully. He let the bourbon sit on the back of his tongue, leaned back in the swivel chair, turned towards the harbor, and closed his eyes.

Harry was awakened by a rapid tapping against the hotel window. As he slowly opened his eyes, he looked straight into terrifying eyes set in a monstrous head that pulled a flagellating worm-like body. Red, gold and green spiraled in the wind as the dragon attacked the hotel again and again. Bolting upright, he rubbed his eyes in disbelief. Backing away from the window, he tripped over the stand and onto his bed. Panicked, he stood up. Then, he smiled to himself. Harry realized what was happening.

"It's a damn kite. Probably lost by some kid playing on the marina," he reassured himself.

"A dragon," he thought. "This could mean rain and fertility. The deal concluded? Maybe my marriage" He knew the east was full of myth and signs. One only needed to know how to read them. He was wise enough to know that the correct interpretation was often elusive.

The clock atop the lacquered ebony bedside table read eight p.m., already nine a.m. the next day in Washington. It had been a week since he had spoken to his wife, Mary, or to his ten-year-old son, Mark. Harry pushed the speaker button and dialed his home number, thinking he might catch his family before they left for work and school. The answer machine triggered Mary's soft voice, saying that none of the Mortons could come to the phone. He left a message that the assignment was all but wrapped up and that he'd be back sometime Monday.

He looked around the room, opened the chest's drawers and laid out new silk ties and two lightweight wool suits next to his garment bag on the bed. Next, he packed the silk dresses he'd bought Mary and the sports watch he'd gotten Mark. Harry always looked forward to returning home after his long foreign trips. He eagerly anticipated hearing about Mark's activities, his hobbies, and his friends. He missed not seeing every change as his son matured. Returning to his wife was different. The sexual spark was still there with Mary, but they didn't seem to have much to talk about other than Mark. Harry assumed it was one of the normal phases of married life.

He decided to try to get a good night's sleep. Changed into boxer shorts, he pulled back all covers but the thin top sheet on his bed, and lay down. Although his eyes closed, his mind continued to operate at remarkable speed. Only partially conscious, Harry began to review "the deal" just closed.

"Mr. Morton, I don't know how we can thank you. The management team is working better than ever before," said Ho Duan with an enthusiastic smile.

"Well, Mr. Ho, I'm sure payment of our fee will be sufficient thanks. It really has been a pleasure working with Silk Road, Inc. You have a talented group of people," he said. "I'll be in town until tomorrow afternoon. So, feel free to call if you have any questions about the report I've outlined," said Morton. He and the Silk Road, Inc. (SRI) executive vice president exchanged bows.

His brain finally let him rest.

In the morning, Harry rolled out of bed, pulled on his jogging clothes, descended in a quiet and otherwise empty elevator, and trotted out into a light fog. Conducting a little loop past the Star Ferry docks, he saw that two of their green and white boats, bobbing to and fro in the tiny waves from passing cargo ships, were being washed down for the first morning runs across the harbor. The sounds of water slapping on the dock receded as Harry jogged up Canton Road and through Kowloon Park, past the History Museum creeping out of the fog, beyond the aviary whose occupants were chirping about the new day. The fragrance of peach, red and yellow roses; the beauty of ever abundant white Bauhinia (Orchid Trees); and the sprinkling of purple Bougainville countered the grittier street aesthetics along his route. As he turned down Nathan Road, he carefully stepped by street librarians posting the day's papers, journals, and novellas on building walls. He almost ran over a man squatting on the sidewalk reading his morning paper. The only vehicles he noticed were a few taxis and the ever-present red double-decker buses. Forty minutes after he left the Peninsula Hotel, Harry had returned. When he stepped out of the shower, he saw the message light blinking on his phone.

"Mr. Morton, would you please call Ms. Wong of Silk Road, Inc. before eleven thirty this evening; or by eight tomorrow morning? It's very important. Thank you." Harry didn't recognize the voice, but knew of only one Ms. Wong at SRI. Wong Xi was the thirty-eight year old CEO.

Harry looked at his watch. 7:45 AM. The message must have been left late last night, and he realized he must have slept right through the ringing. "Well, I might as well see if she's in yet," he sighed. He dialed and got a recording on the main number. The prompts conducted him through to the CEO's office.

"Wei," answered an alert, alto Mandarin voice.

"Hello, this is Mr. Morton returning Ms. Wong's call."

"Oh, thank you for calling, Mr. Morton. I hope I didn't disturb your morning."

"Not at all, Ms. Wong. How may I help you?"

"I was wondering if you could possibly stop by my office before you leave this morning? I'd like to discuss something in your final recommendations."

"I suppose so, but I haven't written the final report yet."

"I know, and I realize it's an enormous imposition, but I would very much appreciate your stopping by. I will have Mr. Mai, my driver bring you over. Afterwards, he'll cart you straight off to the airport."

"All right, how about eleven? That will still give me time to get my plane." Morton kept the exasperation from his voice.

"That would be perfect," she said.

Harry was puzzled. Why the last minute interest by the CEO? Wong had reportedly paid little attention to the issues Harry had been working on for ten months. She certainly had not spoken to him about anything. Ho Duan had handled all of the top-level discussions. In fact, Harry barely recalled what Ms. Wong looked like, since she had only been present during one of the meetings at which he had reported on the project. She had sat in the middle of the large, mahogany conference table hiding behind black-rimmed glasses and saying nothing, as far as he could remember.

Harry read a Hong Kong paper, the *International Herald Tribune*, and a couple of Asian business journals that he had been carrying for a week as he nibbled on toast spread with mango jam and sipped Chinese green tea. He finished packing, checked around the suite, and headed for the elevator. Even at this early hour, the elevator carried other foreigners in business attire. But Harry Morton stood out. He was a six foot two, medium build African-American man with high chiseled cheekbones and reddish brownish complexion. A gregarious high-tipper, he was a fixture of almost celebrity status with the Peninsula staff.

"You be returning soon, Hong Kong, Mr. Morton?" asked the doorman as Harry stepped towards the car sent by SRI.

"As soon as I can, Mr. Ding." Harry insisted on calling the staff by their family names. He still remembered how insulted and angered black bell hops, doormen and waiters used to get in the States when whites half their age addressed them by their first names. That had been in Philadelphia in the 1950's, but the scenes and stories made a lasting impression on him.

The mist was clearing, so the view of the harbor with its early morning boat traffic was spectacular. "Mr. Mai, would you drop me at Star Ferry? It will be faster to boat over. I would appreciate if you'd meet me in an hour at SRI to take me to the airport."

"Certainly, Mr. Morton, if you wish," responded the chauffeur. Morton knew his bags would be perfectly safe with SRI's corporate chauffeur.

He hopped out of the black BMW sedan at the ferry terminal, dropped coins in the turn-style, and strode to the gate and down the wood-slatted ramp to the next boat. Harry loved the fresh feel of sea air. Outside the Star Ferry building on the Hong Kong Island side, he took a quick cab ride to the Admiralty Centre complex and rode the elevator to the top floor, SRI's headquarters suite. The guard outside the ornately carved teak doors had clearly been expecting him and escorted him into the CEO's office.

She had just put away a briefing memo on her guest.

Team Management Inc.'s president and top international consultant, he was one of the few chief executives that Masterfield Consulting has tried to keep after purchase of a firm. When Morton had sold Team Management in 1993, he made enough money to retire, but stayed on in a consulting capacity to work on assignments of his own choosing. Since then, he has accounted for $800 million in new business for the giant management consulting firm. He has been particularly talented at helping dissimilar business cultures adjust to merger situations.

For decades, Masterfield has built its infrastructure by recruiting from the top US business schools and middle managers from Fortune 500 international companies. More recently, it has been purchasing firms with boutique or niche practices in foreign markets. All new associates and partners are exposed to a rigorous training in the Masterfield approach to problem-recognition, utilization of the firm's many internal subject-matter experts, and the company's core principles of teamwork. Emphasis on client satisfaction, as opposed to the "most brilliant business solution," is heavy. By the 1990's, Masterfield was recognized as one of the world's preeminent firms advising companies involved in complex mergers and acquisitions.

"Please, come in and sit down, Mr. Morton. I must apologize for my inconsiderate intrusion into your plans. Please, forgive me." The five foot four Eurasian with short cropped raven hair and a perfectly creased emerald green silk, Hong Kong-cut business suit bowed. As Wong Xi straightened to her full height, Harry maintained a straight face, and politely acknowledged her apology.

16

"Ms. Wong, there is no need to apologize. I am happy to be of service. Silk Road Inc. has been a gracious and generous client." Harry realized that he had never really looked at Wong Xi. They had never actually been introduced. She was an extraordinarily beautiful woman. Silhouetted against the open view of Victoria Harbor, seated erect facing him at a round gold-fluted tea table was one of the most captivating women he had ever seen. Had he met her in Washington, Harry might have assumed she was Latina, African-American, or Asian. In Hong Kong, she was clearly part Caucasian and totally gorgeous. But, Harry knew this was and had to be about business.

"How may I help?"

"Ho Duan has been extremely impressed with the way you have helped us solve the personnel issues in our financial department. In fact, we didn't even know we had serious personnel problems until you submitted your first report."

"I appreciate your kind words, but I still have to submit a final report. And, with all due respect, I must catch a plane."

"Mr. Morton, I'm sure you're aware that SRI is considering the purchase of a mainland apparel company, South China Apparel."

"Yes, Duan and I have talked about it."

"Well, we are very much aware that corporate cultures can clash and destroy the business benefits of a merger." Her eyes caught a flash of morning sun and Morton saw they were not jet, but coffee colored with splashes of green. He said nothing.

"Mr. Morton, we need your help."

He could think of no reason to turn down a contract extension. Still, he hesitated. Experience had taught Morton that most apparently straight forward requests turned out to require complicated and elaborate solutions. No need to hurry.

"Mr. Morton?"

He knew that there was more to the request than appeared on the surface; else Ho would have asked him to stay. "Could you give me some more detail on South China?" he asked.

"Certainly. They are a mainland company that has an outstanding supply system for gathering the finest silks from hard-to-reach places in rural China. It's run by an ex-Army general with fairly tight discipline, but with no sense of modern business processes or western human rights sensitivity. They have been surreptitiously seeking a buyer for about three years. They generate about twenty million pounds less than we do a year, and have substantial up-side potential. That's a quick sketch. Will you help us?"

"Yes, sorry. Of course, we'll help. May I call you once I'm back at my home office?"

"What will you need as background? I have only a vague idea of how you might go about analyzing this sort of merger or purchase. I know you need to dig into both companies, but---"

"Well, let me think about it a bit. Generally, the process is fairly routine. We assess how you make decisions, how authority is delegated, the way in which you both plan, your tolerance for risk, the reward systems, and of course how change is managed."

"And then, you try to assess where the difficulties might arise in merging the companies and how to best handle them?"

"Exactly. See, you really don't need a consultant."

"You're joking, certainly. I know enough to understand how difficult the analysis and the right recommendations can be. No thank you. I need Masterfield. Naturally, I'll maintain control and some information may remain off limits."

"Such as?"

"Such as some detailed financials and certain personnel documents. Fair enough?"

Harry maintained eye contact, but didn't answer until the CEO moved a muscle to speak.

"Fair enough," he said.

"Good, then you'll have materials waiting for you in Washington. I look forward to working with you, Mr. Morton."

"The pleasure will be mine; I'm sure, Ms. Wong."

They shook hands. As he pulled away, without facial expression, she said, "This will not be straight forward, but if you can absorb, or handle the unexpected as much as I suspect, it should be a fertile opportunity."

He smiled and left. At least, this won't be a boring assignment, he thought.

Outside, it began to drizzle ever so slightly.

CHAPTER TWO

香港

Mary Morton was the sort of woman disliked and schemed against by the most sinister female characters on soap operas. She had a perfectly smooth light brown complexion, a bathing beauty figure, a soothing mid-western speaking voice, and a razor sharp mind. From a distance, one would assume that she would succeed in anything she attempted. Mary had spent much of the week preparing for her husband's return. He'd been away a month this time, and she had missed him, missed the occasional evenings out, visiting friends, and the support Harry provided with their son Mark. He adored his father, and Harry seemed most happy spending weekends doing the "guy thing" with Mark. Mary loved Harry, but recently, she sat up in bed, her arms wrapped around knees drawn up to her chest, trying in vain to picture Harry's face.

She didn't feel particularly distressed, since many of her friends felt the same or even more distant from their husbands. Professional couples experienced these long periods of emotional separation, she reasoned. Based on the examples she had grown up with –her parents, relatives, and friends who married early – Mary thought one worked hard, raised kids, tried to talk to one's husband through the tough times and leaned on one's girlfriends when necessary. Those times always passed. She knew not to expect her husband to remain as attentive as when they were younger, but by and large hers was not a life about which Mary felt she had a right to complain.

Mary was a labor economist at the Brookings Institution in downtown Washington. While her pay was not close to her husband's, she was held in high regard in research, government and academic circles. Her life was quite rewarding. Mark was apparently a normal, well adjusted, happy, and bright ten-year-old. They lived on a quiet tree-lined street next to Rock Creek Park in the District's stylish northern tip. Portal Estates was home to doctors, lawyers, business executives, and some high up federal government appointees.

This particular Saturday night, Mary permitted Mark to watch a video until he fell asleep and she ushered him up to bed; after which she slipped into bed and opened the latest Terry Macmillan novel. The phone rang at about 11:55 P.M.

"Girl, what you doin'?" whispered her friend Mabel Birch.

"I'm falling asleep. What I normally do at this hour. Girl, what are you doing calling at midnight?"

"I had to share this with someone. The finest thing just left my bedroom, and I don't mean George."

"Mabel, are you crazy? George will kill you,"

"Only if he knew about it, but he's out of town. And, then he'd have to explain Miss Lapino, that Filipino in his office he's been screwing. No, sister girl, I don't think Mr. Black Man will have much to say, if he finds out."

Mary was taken aback, yet not shocked, for this wasn't the first time. They talked about the current Mr. Beautiful for half an hour, when Mary said she had to get some sleep, and hung up. Before she drifted off to sleep, she sat erect in bed and again thought about her relationship with the husband she feared she didn't really know that well, any more. She wondered if he was ever unfaithful on his long business trips. The subject never came up, and Harry certainly never gave any indication of other love interests.

"What if he did sleep around a bit? Would I care that much?"

Thoughts raced through her mind. "There's AIDS. But if he's careful, do I care? Stupid, of course I do. It would hurt and I'd be furious. But, it wouldn't be the end. I'm mature enough to handle the jealousy, if they were flings, and not serious," she told herself.

Her alarm went off at 5:45 Monday morning. She rolled out of bed, shuffled to the bathroom, and began to brush her teeth as if caught between dreams and consciousness. She wouldn't really gain full consciousness until she had halfway downed a cup of warm coffee and was preparing Mark's breakfast.

"Mommy?"

"Yes. Finish those Cheerios. You can't leave a bowl half full."

"Doesn't Daddy get home today?"

"Yes, he does. Have you missed him?"

"Yeah, I guess so. And last weekend, we could've gone to the Redskins pre-season game."

Mary often wondered why nobody made the owner change the team's obnoxious and bigoted name. Sports… She bit her tongue, however, and let it pass.

"Well, your father will be here tonight, and you two can catch up on all the sports. Okay?"

"I like it when all of us are around the house," Mark said as much to himself as to his mother.

"Me too, precious. Me too."

After dropping Mark at The Washington Day School, Mary drove down 16th Street towards the White House. By the time she turned right onto Massachusetts Avenue, she tuned out the interview being broadcast on NPR, driving on automatic pilot, and day-dreaming about what life would have been like if Harry had pursued his political ambitions. Would they have left Pennsylvania under different circumstances? Possibly, with Harry as the second U.S. Senator of African American descent? Life takes funny twists and turns. When, as a local resident, you observe the daily stupidity of what passes for government, it's distressing and scary. She used to think Harry's integrity and commitment to values they shared would have made him a refreshing change. She now held a more cynical view; that bad systems chew up good people more often than not. And, the U.S. Congress can mangle the best of them.

Mary pulled into her regular underground spot at Brookings and cleared her mind of everything but the recent labor statistics out of California. Rising in the elevator she entered a world she loved, in which she was a shining star. It's a world that Mable Birch didn't understand and that Harry didn't fully respect. None of that mattered, because this was her domain.

The elevator door opened and Mary almost ran into a tall graying man, who looked like a latter-year Gregory Peck. "Good morning, Mary. Great piece in the New England Journal, last week.

Keep it up and you'll have to crank out at least a couple of books next year," said Robert Pitcher, the Institution's chief economist.

"Thank you so much, Robert," she said as she moved around Pitcher and towards her office. "Good, morning, Ms. Morton. What are you grinning about," asked Crystal Dodge, her assistant.

"Oh, nothing. It's just such a lovely day. How was your weekend, Crystal?" Mary asked as she gave Ms. Dodge a friendly tap on the shoulder.

The Washington workday was winding down when Harry awoke, as the big Airbus touched down at Dulles Airport in suburban Virginia. It was late summer. And so even at seven o'clock, the sun still bathed every building and tree along the main highway from the airport into Washington. The forty minute cab ride into the District's northernmost section gave him time to refocus and readjust. As he rode along the Dulles Toll Road, he absorbed the growing number of high glass-fronted suburban office buildings that seemed to increase every week, eating up open green space. His focus, however, was on Mark and Mary. Returning home always raised excitement and recently, it generated uncertainty.

"Did you see that fool cut in front of me?" the driver asked over his shoulder.

Harry, who had seen nothing, said, "Drivers get worse and worse, don't they?"

He could follow several ideas simultaneously and react appropriately in many settings, like a chameleon.

"Here we are sir. That's forty dollars."

Harry gave the driver a ten-dollar tip as he clutched his bags and mounted the stairs to his Victorian. Almost before he could withdraw the key from the opened door, his son was running toward him.

"Daddy's home. Mommy, Daddy's home."

Harry lifted, kissed, and swung around the 80-pound young mass of energy.

"It's only been a month and you've grown more, Mark? What have you been eating, son? Speaking of that, have you started supper?"

Harry recognized physical features and characteristics of all four grandparents in his son. He often marveled at the process of gene pooling. How much would he be able to teach his son and how much was predetermined by genes, for good or bad? All of these thoughts in seconds.

"Same as always, Daddy. We held dinner, and we're starved."

Harry looked up and saw Mary. She looked fabulous, smiling; apron half-on, and walking straight into his other arm. They kissed.

"How are you, Miss Latte?" He never tired of looking at her smooth coffee and milk colored skin.

"We missed you, Dad," she said.

"Me too," returned Morton, bending to put down his son.

They went into the dining room for a chicken and mashed potatoes dinner, relaxed and restitched family seams. Later that evening, in each other's arms, Harry and Mary caught one another up on job events, Mark's school activities, and the anticipated obligatory social events of the coming month. Harry didn't want to tell Mary that he probably would be going back to Hong Kong within the next few weeks because he felt so comfortable. The job truly seemed half the world away, almost in a different period in time.

CHAPTER THREE

香港

Harry was at the Team Management home office early Tuesday morning typing out a fairly standard proposal for the next phase of work with Silk Road, Inc. After a couple of hours' work, he had finished his detailed outline and had begun to review his accumulated e-mail.

The first item shocked him. It was a copy of a note to his boss, Don Bartram, stating that Silk Road appreciated the contract extension, was wiring a $3 million dollar extension and needed to see Harry Morton back in Hong Kong by week's end.

Harry wasn't sure whether he was more stunned or angry. Wong Xi's aggressiveness was out of character for a Chinese client, and felt like a clear attempt to preempt Harry's reporting to the company CEO. He hadn't even had a chance to run the deal by Bartram. At 8:30, Don Bartram rang on the intercom.

"Welcome back. Must have been quite a trip. Come on in, Harry."

Morton walked swiftly into his graying seventy year-old boss's office and warmly shook his hand. Although they worked closely together, their backgrounds seemed to prevent this "redneck from rural Alabama," as Don called himself, and the Ivy-league African-American, "United Nations Morton," as Don joked, from ever getting personally close. Yet, they worked well together.

A few years back, on their first trip together, Don and Harry were in Sao Paulo to sew up a proposal with a Brazilian timber company. At dinner, Don had been talking up the soccer prowess of Brazilian immortal Pele; assuming every Brazilian was in love with the game and immensely proud of their contribution to sports idolatry. The executive, however, offered perfunctory broken English responses to Don, while making derogatory Portuguese side comments to a Brazilian colleague. As they sipped strong coffee over dessert, Harry, having perfectly understood the side comments, startled the host. "We're both very aware of the various cultural and literary contributions of your countrymen. While we all love futbol, we're particularly appreciative of Jorge Amado."

The Brazilian's tone brightened, as he turned to face Harry to further engage him in a half hour discussion of Brazilian literature. Two hours later, after the deal had been signed and the Americans had been deposited at the airport, Don spoke privately for the first time since his Pele debacle.

"Whatever you said saved our bacon. That was incredible."

"He was a bit of a snob. His side comments confirmed, for me, that he didn't like sports, hated that foreigners thought of Brazilians' as a backward people distinguished only by ex-slave peoples. He was a piece of work."

"But how did you know he liked literature? And, where did you learn Portuguese?"

"The literature was a lucky guess. Portuguese is close to Spanish, which I took in grad school."

"Man, I thought everybody loved Pele."

"Well, a lot of people do, just not our new client."

Now, back in the office, the two men faced each other.

"What did you tell Silk Road? Man, this is some advance," Bartram grinned broadly.

"Don, I don't know that I told them anything terribly profound, but as you know, it's invaluable to have an outsider' eyes look over any operation. That's what keeps us in business, right?" Harry thought for a couple of seconds about their new opportunity.

"You know, I can't figure it out, but something's strange. Wong Xi is just about the only female Chinese CEO of a major company in Hong Kong. There are plenty of Chinese or Chinese-Americans who could help them. Why us? I can't put my finger on it."

"Well, let's pull out the stops. Use whomever you need. Find out every possible piece of background: financial, operational, market competition, family, whatever. This is major, my friend." Bartram moved back to his desk, signaling the end of the meeting.

After Harry left, Don Bartram leaned back in his swivel chair, spun around to face the picture-window view down K Street in the heart of the nation's capital.

"A long way from Mobile, Alabama. Who'd have thought I'd be running this international consulting wing of Masterfield, dealing with Chinese businesses through a black man. No way". Don smiled, but didn't let himself dwell on the irony of the means to his success. His father, a local Klan leader, would not have believed or liked it.

"Boy, dealing wid niggahs and chinks, goin' ruin your reputation and our family name," old man Bartram most certainly would have said.

Don had gone north to business school at Wharton, University of Pennsylvania partly to escape his roots. He was no civil rights liberal, but was never very comfortable with blatant loud racism. Although he certainly held some of the old man's prejudices, they were now buried under years of education and professional interaction with a rainbow of highly successful individuals. "Maybe, I've lost Daddy's views fully," he mused.

He didn't pretend, however, to understand his complex ace consultant, Harry Morton. He just knew that Morton had an uncanny ability to understand different cultures and people, and could empathize with them, visualize and feel how the other person would view a business situation. He knew that Morton read a lot, networked constantly, and went out of his way to get behind people's masks. None of this fully explained Morton's ability. He could have been a priest or social worker, but thank God he was as profit hungry and business-oriented as the next MBA. The fact that he was African American was important and had to be factored into the client match analysis, but rarely ended up being the determining factor with deals. After watching Harry handle a number of situations like that Brazilian deal, Bartram had been clever with his hunches, pushing Harry into situations that appeared ill suited for a black man. Most of the time, the hunch had paid off big. Morton didn't take bullshit, but he didn't lay out some heavy civil rights agenda either. Don often felt the only strange thing about Harry Morton was that he didn't seem to crave recognition from Don or any of his superiors.

"Go figure. He's complex as shit. But I ain't complaining," he'd say to his best friends over bourbon after Saturday golf.

After only a few moments' reflection back at his desk, Harry asked his assistant, Hazel Marsh, to summon a team to his office for a meeting. Harry had asked Don's executive assistant to clear emergency assignments for Peter Burke and Roberto Higgins with the VP of Finance and VP for Human Resources. Hazel was to also call Ellen Kwan from Harry's staff.

Once they were seated around Harry's conference table, he took a few seconds to ask what each had had to drop to work on this assignment, to make sure he wasn't incurring too many major IOUs. Then he quickly laid out the opportunity, gave them a draft outline of his report to Silk Road, and laid out the potential issues as he saw them.

"Roberto, I need you to develop a draft merger analysis approach. Look back at the job we did for that company in Guangzhou and Hong Kong United two years ago and check the files for anything on that disastrous merger that Camden and Lybrand worked on with that British trading company and Hong Kong Goods, last year."

Roberto Higgins took rapid, neat notes on his laptop and looked up intently to absorb the rest of the team's assignment. Higgins was the youngest of the group. He was two years out of NYU B-school, where he had concentrated in organization development and graduated near the top of his class. But his initial impact on the firm was the stir he created with the young female associates. Roberto, from a black Puerto Rican family, looked like a cross between one time Calypso idol, young Harry Belafonte and Spanish actor Antonio Banderas. Like most ambitious associates, however, he had little social time.

Harry knew that he couldn't take the whole team to Hong Kong without making it appear as if he was making some political statement about multi-culturalism. But, together, their talents covered every business situation he could envision coming up. He turned to Ellen Kwan, a twenty-nine year old Stanford Law graduate who had passed up attractive financial offers with West Coast law firms to join Masterfield after hearing a spell-binding campus address by Don Bartram about the future of Pacific Rim business opportunities. She had grown up in Arlington, Virginia, in a family of Korean storeowners and attended the University of Virginia before going to Stanford. She had been the first of three children the Kwans had sent to college in their adopted country. They were happy to have their eldest back in town.

"Ellen, we've got a short period to build a full biography on Wong Xi, Ho Duan, the other top executives of SRI, and their board members. Then, prepare the same for the other company, South China Apparel. The initial file prepared is dated and not detailed enough for this next job."

"But, Mr. Morton, I mean, Harry, some much more junior associate could do that research."

"Wrong," Harry cut off Ellen's complaint. "We need to uncover both the pitfalls and the opportunities embedded in the culture and the personalities of these two companies. You know British and Chinese commercial law and you're a keen observer of cultural patterns. That's why I need you,"

Ellen made some notes, realizing that unanticipated details beneath the surface implications of previous assignments had often provided useful insight into the problems of client firms. She had observed that the way to the top at Masterfield was through excelling on tight timetable team assignments. She also knew that "details, details, details" was the firm's mantra.

Harry turned to face the senior member of the team and the only white, Peter Burke. He was only thirty-four but had distinguished himself as one of Masterfield's brilliant up and coming international financial analysts. He breathed spreadsheets and Harry enjoyed working with Burke, an enthusiastic admirer and observer of other cultures, primarily Latin. He had spent a year traveling in Colombia and Ecuador after business school. His family money made the jungle adventures and river trips possible, but deep beneath the Connecticut highbrow exterior, Harry found a genuine curiosity and compassion for the less fortunate of the world.

"Peter. Welcome back. You've done this drill before, but pretend this is your first merger financial analysis. I don't want to miss some obscure issue just because our focus will be on the people side."

"Got it, Harry."

"Okay, if there are no questions, let's meet back here in three days. That should give you a chance to establish a break point on current assignments. If you can't get me, go through Hazel."

Harry loved having the resources Masterfield Consulting brought to any job. The TMA of the old days couldn't have competed for long against firms like the Masterfield, Touche-Ross, or McKinsey once they identified this niche. But now, he was competing with the best in the world.

CHAPTER FOUR

香港

"Hi, Daddy. You're going to be late. Mommy's already ready to go. Don't forget we go to the Wizards tomorrow," Mark frowned as his father entered the front door.

"How's my little man? School okay?" For the first time since returning from Hong Kong, Harry was truly able to focus on his son.

"Hello, Mr. Morton," said Kwasett Gilmore, the 14 year old sitter from up the block.

"How are you, Kwasett? How's everything with your brother?" Harry realized, as an afterthought, that he shouldn't have immediately been concerned about the welfare of Kwasett's All-American football player brother. "I'll bet you're glad the week is over," he quickly added.

"Yes, 'cause Saturday's when the fun begins." She smiled at the attention.

"I'll bet it is. So, what do you have planned for the weekend?"

"Nothing. Just chillin' with some friends," she said.

"Well, nice to see you. I better go and change." Harry mounted the stairs with an ease that displayed the athletic gate of a younger man.

Later that night, after a heavy dinner at *B Smith's* restaurant in Union Station near the US Capitol, Mary and Harry sat listening with Mabel and George Birch to a trio featuring pianist Herbie Hancock. They were playing songs from a new jazz album in a crowded *Twins Lounge* in northwest Washington. Harry enjoyed chewing the fat with

George. Had it just been the two men, Harry would have paid more attention to George talking about his latest golf trip. But, he often felt slightly uncomfortable when the two couples were together. Harry pretended to listen to the conversation and the trio while actually going over work.

"George, don't be obvious, but there's a group of Japanese at those corner tables. Looks like Twins has been discovered," Mabel pointed out to her husband as a topic of idle curiosity.

"Yeah, but they're with each other. You can't have a problem with Japanese being with Japanese," George responded a little too loudly.

Harry and Mary exchanged looks, as if to say "Here we go again."

"You know, jazz is really more popular in Japan than many places here," Harry chimed in hoping to steer the conversation in a respectful and what he would find more interesting direction.

"Yeah, man. I wonder why Asians dig our music." George turned to face Harry.

"Not all Asians, mainly Japanese. I'm not sure why. Nowadays, there are a bunch of bad, I mean nasty Japanese players."

"I bet Filipinos looove jazz. Don't' they, baby?" Mabel tried to get a rise out of her husband, to no avail.

"Y'all international musicologists, quiet. I want to hear this `You've Got It Bad Girl,'" Mary offered quickly in a friendly stage whisper, as she turned to the bandstand trio.

Harry went back to thinking through the Hong Kong deal. His mind reeled through the list of non-financial reasons why mergers tend to fail; most related to corporate culture clashes.

South China may take longer to make decisions and they probably delegate less than SRI. Xiaobin Li definitely isn't going to take well to dealing with a female counterpart. The Hong Kong company may have an upper hand in understanding the culture of South China, but it may also get frustrated dealing with a potentially slower and more bureaucratic company. I wonder which one will be more prone to ignore "agreements?" This assignment will be interesting for us, since I'm anything but an expert on Mainland Chinese business. By the end of next week, however, I know Ellen's research will turn up any relevant issues I need to understand before we actually start interviewing South China Apparel executives.

A magical interplay between Hancock's syncopated rhythms and the cymbal and brush work of Jack De Johnette snapped Harry back to the present. Everyone at the table popped fingers, bobbed head, or tapped toes to the intoxicating beat.

The night ended pleasantly as the friends allowed the music to fill them and didn't try to make serious conversation.

Saturday was a trying day. Harry was at his desk at the office by 7:30, reading first stage reports from his investigative team. Burke's financial reports were adequate, but showed no extra-effort research and revealed no hidden concerns in the analysis of either company. Harry knew that companies rarely were devoid of blemishes and wondered if Burke was slipping, or just not interested. Higgins's analysis really had to await Kwan's assessment of key staff and board members before Roberto could design a project plan. It was Ellen's biographies, however, that were so antiseptic, pro forma and uninformative that ejected Harry out of his chair and had him pacing down to her office.

"Of course, no one's here. No one is invested in this project," Harry said to himself standing outside of Kwan's empty office.

Back in his office, Harry spent an hour cleaning up matters on old accounts and correcting a draft of the final report on the last SRI assignment so that he could devote most of the day to preparing for the merger. By nine o'clock, none of his young team had arrived. He reached only voice mails when he called each residence and left searing messages that he wanted to see them by 11:30 to discuss what had to be prepared by Monday. He spent about a half hour making notes on each report and then went to work out in the building's gym.

When he returned to his office, relaxed and clear-headed, the team had assembled and was milling about his office. Harry decided to stay on the "no prisoners" course.

"I thought I had some Masterfield-quality professionals on this job. The crap you each turned in was embarrassing. Ellen, didn't anyone ever tell you that a business bio explores events that might measure determination, deal documents that reveal tendencies, and personal habits that divulge preferences? These are not captions for *People Magazine*.

Peter, your analysis could fit the profile of twenty different Hong Kong companies. I'd like a little digging. I can read the *Journal* articles on Hong Kong companies myself. You're supposed to bring brilliance. Let me see some. Damn.

Berto, I know you have to get the others' work before you can really tailor the plan, but for Christ's sake, these aren't New York companies. Why the hell would your outline start off with some heavy interrogation? Hello…this is Hong Kong, China. The first part of any approach has to build relationships, doesn't it? Come on people, this isn't a term paper; this is the real thing. Work with me on this, all right? I want some depth by 4:30 this afternoon. Then we'll go 'round again. Get to it." Harry's eyes followed the stampede from his office.

After a quick sandwich from the grill across K St., Harry spent the afternoon polishing off more edits to the SRI report for Hazel Marsh to finalize on Monday. At 4:30, he got outlines reflecting the level of quality analysis and thought that he could use in preparing for his next round of meetings in Hong Kong.

"Thank you all. This is very useful, and I think the insights you offered on each other's drafts have been first rate. Can we keep this effort at this level, team?"

Together, the memos analyzed five years' of corporate mergers and identified key reasons driving the deals. Sometimes corporations wanted to deepen their niche and reduce competition. In other cases, they wanted to link with a group that extended their depth in the cycle from raw materials to finished goods, to product distribution. They found nothing unusual, nor foreign to Western examples. Chinese companies were without exception, however, concerned about appearance or propriety and business decorum—as perceived by them. There were no `hostile takeovers' in the Western sense.

Harry's antennae told him that all three were back on track, but deep down, he had now developed a caution about how to deploy his team. Saturday's session was healthy, he told himself. But he still wondered why they all had had to be called on the carpet at the same time. He filed the question in his subconscious and followed a visibly more cheerful group out of his office and to the parking elevator. Tuesday, he'd have to decide who made the Hong Kong trip, but for now he could focus on his son and the evening's basketball game.

CHAPTER FIVE

香港

That evening, in downtown Washington's tiny Chinatown, Harry exited the subway with Mark, walked to the MCI arena, and opened yet another world. Mary thought that sports played a disproportionately large part in Harry's life and in his relationship with his son. But playing or watching a game together provided Harry the best opportunity to make up for time missed due to long meetings and longer trips. He felt that these times allowed him to cement his relationship with Mark in ways he never could with his own father.

John Morton was a serious and caring man who died before Harry could really appreciate him. He couldn't get to afternoon activities for Pierce and Harry, because the family didn't own a car to carry him quickly from his work to their school. He spent time around the house after his own day teaching 10th graders from 'the projects' in Philadelphia's tough north side. Friends and acquaintances all knew his interests ran from household chores, classical music, to English literature. What brought joy to his life "up north," having escaped a cruel and segregated North Carolina childhood, was being with Lena and his 'boys.' He had little interest in sports, but provided the gloves, balls and other equipment and access to coaching that enabled his sons to flourish as young athletes. On reflection, Harry the adult realized he missed a great deal by spending so much adolescent time with his peers and so little with his father, or with his brother, for that matter.

By the time Harry recognized his father's strength and became curious about his childhood, John Morton's heart had given out. What Lena told Harry about his dad's youth in the south and his escape to Howard University and later to graduate school in the Big Ten filled him with pride, and with sadness in recognizing a relationship missed. He didn't want Mark to have to wonder about his father, and he hoped their relationship would deepen as his son matured.

"You and me, baby. Take it to the hole. That's it. That's what I'm talkin' 'bout," Harry heard himself yelling above the din of other fans at the arena. He looked over at a relatively subdued Mark Morton.

"Hey, son. I thought you wanted to see this game. You're not enjoying it?"

"It's not that Daddy. School stuff."

"Is it grades? A teacher? Something seem too hard? What?"

"Daddy. Yesterday, some of us were talking about basketball. I said that next to the Wizards, I liked the New Jersey Nets because I liked Keith Van Horne, and Bobby Boyd said that was because I wasn't really black. He said I was an Oreo."

"Son, what does he mean?" Harry knew very well what the young Boyd meant.

"I guess he means I'm white inside. I got too many white and Latino friends, and don't hang with the black kids like he does."

"So, why are you upset? You want to be like Bobby Boyd?"

"No way. But I don't like being called a name. I have plenty of black friends. It's not fair."

Harry knew that there must have been more to the incident to have his son remember the emotions a day later in the middle of one of his beloved basketball games.

"Mark, you remember I told you once how people who don't feel good about themselves sometimes pick on others who are different?"

"Like a bully?"

"Yeah, like a bully."

"But Daddy, I'm not different. Me and Bobby are both black. Why do I have to do what he wants? He's not a teacher. He's---"

"It's Bobby and I. You don't have to do what he wants Mark; you stick to what you believe. You are free to like any player you want. In fact, son, you are free to like anybody you want."

Harry watched the game for several more minutes, but continued to ponder his son's predicament. "Mark, do you remember the video you enjoyed watching about famous African Americans?"

"You mean the one they showed during Black History Month last year?"

"That one. Yes."

"Sure, how could I forget? They were great."

"Well, that video didn't point it out, but people like Martin Luther King Jr. or Arthur Ashe took tremendous criticism from other blacks during their lives."

"Come on, Ashe? But he was good and strong and tough. I mean, they showed him in segregated Virginia, and going to South Africa."

"Right, but during the 1968 Olympics, he didn't join the other black athletes in protest. Many called him an Uncle Tom."

"So what are you saying, Daddy?"

"That as you get older and decide what's worth standing up for, do it because you feel you are right. Don't expect to be congratulated for it." Harry let the words sink in below the din of the crowd.

Mark seemed to return his attention to the game and didn't say anything about what his father had offered.

"Look at that shot. I told you Van Horn was bad."

"Yeah, son. He's bad." Harry smiled and put his arm around his son. He knew, however, that this was only the beginning of Mark's finding out who he was and what he believed. He also knew there was no way to know, for certain, how his son would emerge.

The Wizards won and Harry and Mark took the subway to Silver Spring, where Harry had parked his car. During the five minute ride to Portal Estates, Mark slept and his father reminisced about the last time he and Mary had invited Robert and Mavis Boyd over for dinner.

"We'd like to come, Morton, but are you having white folks too? I see enough of them at work," Robert had said on the phone.

"Tell you what, homie, why don't you stay where you'll be comfortable?" Harry had steamed as he hung up the phone. He then turned to Mary and they agreed they would never invite the Boyds, no matter who they were having over. That had been twelve years ago, before either family had children.

"Like father, like son." Harry smiled to himself as he woke his boy from the short car ride home.

Sunday, after the three Mortons walked along a well-worn path in nearby Rock Creek Park for a relaxing hour, Harry and Mary lounged about the house. Mark visited a group of neighborhood friends.

After a few hours sleep, Harry drove to the office and spent a fairly quiet Monday morning catching up on his domestic projects. Before lunch, he opened his door and leaned out of the office to speak with his assistant. "Hazel, would you ask Kwan and Higgins to come by at 5:45 this afternoon for a few minutes, please?" When he finally revisited the plan for the SRI- South China merger, Harry had decided that he needed the young duo for the first few meetings back in Hong Kong. Ellen possessed a useful background in Chinese culture and history that Harry didn't think was being used by the firm, while Roberto evidenced an astute sense of group process and uncommon instincts about individuals' strengths and weaknesses.

During the week, Harry was either out at night meetings, receptions or reviewing China reports late in the office. Thursday offered a break from the late night routine. He got home early that night, hoping to spend some time with Mark.

"Son, you haven't said anymore about Bobby. What's happening with him in school?"

"He's a chump, Dad. He's not worth the time thinking about him," Mark responded while focused on the `Washington Post' sports section.

"Could I get some male help with the table?" Mary called from the kitchen.

"Right there, babe. Mark, you go wash up."

"How does Mark seem to you, baby?" Harry asked his wife when they were alone for a minute.

"Fine, dear. The boy's growing up and finding out who he is," Mary smiled approvingly.

"Seems to be early for all of that. I hope it's not too fast: he needs to enjoy childhood."

"Listen to who's talking. `Mr. LET'S TRY TO GET ALL A's, SON.' Let's always try to be the best, son. Sometimes, I wonder that he's not a nervous wreck." Mary thrust a dish of potato salad into her husband's hands.

"You think I put too much pressure on the boy?"

"I think you do, sometimes. But, right now, it would be nice if you could finish setting the table."

Later, after Mark had gone to bed, Harry looked up from the easy chair next to his and Mary's bed. He half turned to his wife, who was lying on her back in bed reading some economic papers for the next day.

"Mary," Harry said, half talking to himself.

"Yes, sweetheart." She kept on reading.

"I keep vacillating between wanting to make Mark's decisions for him and letting him learn through his own mistakes. You know there's no right answer to most of these issues. I remember how Dad gave me my lead, but Momma would advise Pierce and me. No, she'd tell us what was right. But scary as some of those years were, because they were pretty wild at times, it all fit together…church, school, scouts, etc."

"Baby, your parents, like mine, gave up much more than our generation does for kids. We can't maintain this life style; with both of us working, and do the same as they did. We cope pretty well, and Mark is fine."

"Yeah, but I want him to be better than fine; he's got great things to accomplish. Things most blacks don't even think are possible."

"Harry, remember what your wonderful Momma said late in her life?" asked Mary, not waiting for a response. "'You will find your potential and your joy only through a deep and profound communion with your inner self.' Momma was so wise"

"Yeah, I sometimes wonder how she went through all she did in segregated 1920's Philadelphia and came out without bitterness. I miss the old folks. You know, I wanted to be on my own so badly…I always had to do it my way, prove my independence. I don't think I fully appreciated their wisdom while Daddy was alive. I always thought our world, our generation, was so different. As your poppa said so many times, 'People are the same. The clothing, language, customs change, but folks are folks.' Sometimes, that sounded so naïve, but…"

"So, Harry, do you have your answer for our son?"

"No, baby, but I guess we keep giving him the basics and hope he absorbs the love and support. I pray he keeps his curiosity and gets the luck he'll need." Harry shifted his focus from Mark, opened another compartment in his mind, and returned to his book— "Corporate Cultures- The Rites and Rituals of Corporate Life."

"Harry, Harry."

"What? What's wrong, baby?"

"Nothing's wrong, but don't you want to do it before you go away?" Mary's warm legs were wrapped around her husband's calves, as they both lay in bed.

Harry looked at his watch. Two A.M. He noticed the soft piano of the Ellington Suites now drifted over the bed from the recessed speakers of the bedroom stereo. No music had been playing when he had climbed into bed an hour ago. He pushed the button off on his bedside lamp and turned towards his wife. She was still gorgeous, he thought. He loved touching her smooth skin and holding her warm body close. Making love, however, often lacked any passion for him.

"I'm going to miss you, baby," Harry finally said as they aroused one another and made love.

Harry slept, but Mary lay in bed thinking. She felt that Harry had scarcely spent any time with her alone, nor had he exhibited real interest in her work during this home stay. She assuaged her annoyance with the knowledge - the assumption- that he was consumed by this current major deal. She knew, however, that her satisfaction was temporary, since she too had significant work and considerable issues of her own that would command some real attention.

"When will I again get his full attention?" she thought as she drifted into sleep.

CHAPTER SIX

香港

"Sometimes, I think Western education only diminished excellent Hong Kong schooling you left here with as young lady. You engage foreign firm to help with merger, and lead foreigner is black? What sense does this make to my esteemed daughter?" Wong Shi had placed his chopsticks down and was staring wide-eyed at his daughter across the Sunday dinner table.

"Father, with all respect, I have built a successful company, negotiated the purchase of excellent mainland partner, and---"

"*Duibuqi (Sorry)*. My daughter is highly intelligent, has a keen eye for good deal, works very hard, and possesses extraordinary sense of timing. But this makes no sense, to me. Most honored son in law, what do you say?" The eighty-year-old former Tai-Pan of China International Bank turned to Wong Xi's husband, Bao Li.

"Well, Tai-Pan, I would be in possession of universal secrets of momentous proportions if I disagreed with you. However, my wife is one of only two major company female Tai-Pans in all of Hong Kong. She is most capable. I have learned not to underestimate her gifts." Mr. Bao returned to the stir-fry in his bowl.

The elder Wong almost smiled, "Well stated, my son-in-law. As for you, my daughter, I only wish your dear mother were still alive. She could talk sense into your stubborn head."

"Father, Mother was very wise, but she knew nothing of business, and certainly didn't try to advise the great Tai-Pan of China International. Mother, as I have been told, displayed her significant Westerner independence. She might not have advised me as you wish."

"Such stubbornness." The old man resumed his meal with feigned annoyance.

"Besides, you both know that Masterfield Consulting is not just a Western firm. They have absorbed excellent firms worldwide and enjoy an outstanding reputation globally. You don't achieve executive status there unless you are talented and, of course, make your clients money. Father, with greatest respect, you dealt only with British foreigners through the bank."

"At least you could have picked a British consultant. An American and a black? This new age, I don't comprehend."

"So, did my honorable father not mean it when he used to advise me to regard all people with proper respect?"

"I do not suggest that you disrespect anyone. Besides, I had been speaking of Chinese, not foreigners. Anyway, enough of business. Let us enjoy this excellent meal. The baked fish is next." With a warm smile, the Tai-Pan tapped the table with the forefinger of his right hand to signal for the waiter. The fish was presented on a large porcelain platter smothered in green onions and Chinese parsley, garnished with pieces of ginger. Aroma and taste silenced any thought of debate.

Xi wondered how successful her father would have been had his British wife, her mother, lived to raise her. Chinese double standards might have forgiven a white concubine, but not a full out-in-the-open wife. After her mother's unexpected early death from smallpox, her father's sister, Wong Jianying, raised Xi. Her aunt often intimated that only her brother's pride led him to marry a foreigner after a casual "mistake." Her father, however, spoke only in loving and devoted terms of the woman Xi remembered only vaguely. Her mother came to life in the stories and pictures of her parents in Shanghai in the late 1950's. Katherine Harris had been a Far Eastern correspondent for the `Daily Telegraph' when she met and fell in love with the dashing and fiercely intelligent Wong Shi. Her perfectly erect posture, curvaceous figure and full mouth were passed on to the child she and her husband created.

Like most Chinese babies of the time, Xi had her hair shaved a few months after birth to ensure growth of a full head of rich jet-black hair. Her mother's brunette coloring, however, blended well with Shi's Asian hair to produce a dark brown that made her olive skin even more striking. The adults who spoke to her saw her as a pretty child, but she was teased mercilessly as a "mongrel" by her early school mates. In Shanghai, Wong Shi could not find more than a few parents who would welcome his daughter as a playmate for their children. His brother's family was more accepting, but Wong Shi knew that his daughter was not a truly happy child. She often spent whole weekends in her room reading about Chinese history and about foreign adventure many years earlier than her counterparts at school. He knew, however, that he had little choice but to leave his daughter's up bringing to his sister. Despite her disapproval of the marriage, Auntie Jianying doted on the bright and irrepressible niece as if she were her own.

By 1965, Wong Shi no longer felt he could prosper in business with China tightly controlled by Mao. Sensing the clamp downs that would define the « Cultural Revolution » for the next decade, Wong considered escaping to Taiwan but accepted the advice of his sister, who felt that the child would do better in Hong Kong. His brother, Wong Fu, cautioned against the move, saying, "Hong Kong is full of Westerners and Hong Kong natives who are too enamored of the West. They worship newness, money, and chaos, but they are no more than a cast-off island."

Shi had met some Hong Kongese through business and had been favorably impressed with their love of China, yet their undaunted trading vigor. Some of the Westerners with whom he dealt in Shanghai also suggested that the future for China lay in Hong Kong. So after a few weeks' reflection, he made up his mind. And so, at the age of seven, Xi moved into a densely populated hillside area of the "borrowed" British colony and began to blossom. Many of her new classmates seemed to be of mixed parentage, but they were not universally ostracized, because prosperous Chinese learned to accommodate and even accept the British. All students learned English and Xi also had to learn Cantonese. She continued to be more studious and a quicker learner than others her age. No mother visited her at school, took her to parties, or could be photographed with her father, one of the island's most brilliant and quickly ascending Chinese bankers. People accepted that her mother had died and that her aunt brought her up. It was in those early years, as Xi began to grow intellectually and physically, that Jianying grew fond of saying with newfound pride, "Even if a tree grows 100 feet, its leaves fall back to its roots."

In the mornings, Jianying would take her niece on the ten-minute walk to the main road to wait for the city bus. The children of other rich families were chauffeured to school, so a headstrong Xi asked her father why he didn't have his driver drop her off.

"My daughter must never forget that she is from humble mainland beginnings. You must understand what it is to be Chinese in this city, even though you will have many choices in life denied children in other schools. You are not just 'one more girl mouth to feed' as your uncle Fu may say. You will be part of the new China, as I am part of the new China for my generation. Probably there will be few girls and women like you as you grow up. But, you must always be Shanghainese," Wong Shi insisted.

One morning, as Wong Jianying pulled Xi from her father's study and out the door of their flat she cautioned the little girl.

"You must learn to accept your difference and your privilege. Your father is going to be one of the most powerful men in Hong Kong. You must be an honorable daughter."

"I already accept my difference. My hair isn't even black like my friends'. Why didn't my head get shaved like other families do their babies to get full black hair, auntie?"

"Your parents did shave your head. They did it twice. Your mother, however, had beautiful brown hair and thus the lighter color of your hair. You must try to be proud of your full background, Xi. You are Han Chinese, but you are also English. Your father has excelled in traditional business, but he has always chosen his own path. Your path will also be different, but I have no doubt that you will excel. Now, let's hurry to the bus."

Jianying walked and worried. She worried about how far her brother would drive his only child, a girl. She worried about how the young lady would learn to deal with the slights in store for a mixed race Chinese. Later that morning, back in her room, she burned a joss stick for good luck, hoping the gods would watch over the development of young Xi.

And now, even her aunt had been surprised at how far her niece had climbed. In their chauffeured limousine, driving back to their hillside estate, Wong Xi asked her husband, "How do you really feel about my using this Western firm?"

"Xi, you know I try not to enter into your business affairs. You are extraordinarily successful."

"Li, thank you for a husband's deference. But, as Tai-Pan of China International, as one of Asia's, if not the world's most respected bankers and businessmen, as my best advisor, what do you think? I need your business advice."

After a long sigh, Bao Li answered with measured words, "Masterfield is an outstanding company, and this Mr. Morton is one of their bright stars. I don't have your father's lack of experience with Americans, so I am sure this man is very capable. Masterfield paid top price to acquire his company. But a black foreigner handling a sensitive deal between a Mainland company and SRI will add complications, so I don't think I would have accepted him as project lead. However, I recognize that it would be difficult to ask that they put someone else on this, particularly after his outstanding first SRI assignment."

"I'm a bit embarrassed to tell you this. In strictest confidence?" Xi opened her eyes to their widest arc so that the man she respected most in the world could see the depths of her sincerity. Li was fifteen years his wife's senior, and had known many women prior to their marriage. He never knew anyone, however, as skillful at disguising her feelings as Xi. So, he stared into her eyes, but he was not sure of her motives in prefacing this next bit of information as she had.

"My wife, this whole conversation is, of course confidential."

"Well, Mr. Morton did team-building work with some of my managers. Not only did he smooth out problems we had, but he also discovered some financial problems that we should have caught that will save us over two millions yuan. If you don't see this Westerner while listening to him, you cannot tell that he is not a native-born Cantonese, or when he changes dialect, a native-borne Mandarin speaker. Duan says he appears comfortable even when people are openly expressing disdain for foreigners. His talent is extraordinary, not just for a foreigner. You know how tough old Ho Duan is? He thinks this American is one of the sharpest at sizing up people he has seen since the old Tai-Pans."

"It sounds to me like you have investigated this resource fully. I hope you are right, because this deal needs to work for our family. Using this Mr. Morton will be seen as another brilliant move by the Bao-Wong family if the merger succeeds."

"We must be positive, Li."

"Perhaps, but we must certainly be prudent, my wife." Stately and stiff, Bao Li gently touched his wife's arm and turned to the passing road illuminated by yellow street lamps as their limo climbed the hill to their estate.

"Man, I didn't realize how long seventeen hours can be. This is a long flight, and that electronic map on the monitor says we're not even beyond Shanghai." Roberto Higgins stretched his lanky frame as tall as he could, while standing in the aisle of first class. Immediately, a Singapore Air attendant was by his side asking if he wanted a drink or snack. He laughed in politely thanking her.

"Okay, let's go up to the deck so we can spread out and go over our plan once more," Harry grabbed his brief case and mounted the red carpeted steps to the swivel chair and table accommodations nine feet above the main cabin. As he settled into the deep seat and peered out the porthole, he imagined bustling life in the many countries whose shores touched the South China Sea. He began to get the electric tingles in his hands that often accompanied a sense of adventure, an anticipation of unknown challenges.

"Harry, are you with us?" Ellen Kwan's question snapped Harry's spell.

Harry began reviewing his mental notes out loud. "While one might assume that South China Apparel is likely to be more risk averse and more top-heavy than SRI because it's a mainland company, remember all of the major players, save Xiaobin Li, are Cantonese. They are as hungry for greater markets as our Hong

Kong client. So, the cultural clash will be different than that between a new Beijing company and a typical Hong Kong outfit."

"Ellen, can we start with the highlights of South China's CEO, what's his name Chow?" Roberto asked his colleague.

"Berto, it's Xiaobin Li. You have to at least get his name." Ellen looked a bit exasperated.

"Okay, Mr. Xiaobin. What are his plusses and minuses?" Roberto swung his seat towards the bar and picked up a Coke.

"What we know is that Xiaobin Li is a sixty-five year old ex-military official, who parlayed his party contacts into appointment of Guangzhou's state-run fabric factory. When the party began selective privatization in the early nineties, he was in position to put together enough capital and IOUs to lead an investment group and take over the company. He has recruited very able operations people, but the company is still learning about big league finance and marketing. He has three grown boys and a typically supportive wife, who is still a practicing physician. While he is perfectly cordial, he's known not to be fond of Japanese or Westerners. Apparently, no major problems with Koreans. But given a choice, he'd select Chinese origin for a business partner." Ellen paused.

"Any hot buttons or unusual traits?" Harry's eyes bore into the young woman.

"He has at least two mistresses, one in Guangzhou and one in Hong Kong." Her almond complexion began to redden.

"So, what's unusual about that?" Roberto was almost laughing.

"Apparently, it's taken some coaching to get him to deal with Wong Xi as an equal," Kwan replied. "Also, he is fond of gambling, but never drinks liquor."

"That's unusual, and perhaps useful," Harry remarked settling back in his chair.

"Okay, Roberto, any ideas on initial activities to break the ice?" Harry turned his attention and intense stare to the other team member.

"We could play the new parlor game--"It May Not Be Heaven in '97."

"Very amusing. I don't' think, however, the return of Hong Kong to China in two years is likely to effect this deal one way or the other," Harry said.

"I bet all parties want to be counting their yuan, however, by the time of the national celebrations, just for insurance sake," Ellen chimed in.

"Ellen, you might find out if our assumptions on this are correct," Harry said. "So, no real ice-breaker ideas, Roberto?" He redirected the group's attention.

"I'd suggest we take the South China team to the race track and dinner, for starters."

"Excellent. You have done some homework." Harry knew that the rest of the details for the first few days were well enough laid out that they could now relax. "Berto, this trip ought to give you a break from the hard work of choosing who to date around the office," he chuckled.

"Hey, I don't play that office stuff. Well, at least not immediate office." Higgins seemed a bit relieved that Harry had lightened up the conversation.

"Is this going to be boys' talk now?" Ellen smiled and settled back in her seat to enjoy the rest of the flight down the China coast.

Hours later, the boat to Yulan Island Restaurant cut through the chilly obscure water that occasionally sprayed Harry and Xiaobin Li, who were talking about the changes in China as the group was ferried to dinner in Hong Kong's Victoria harbor. The breeze brushing over the deck of the ferry was much warmer and more soothing than the intermittent splash of salty water.

During their first day in Hong Kong, the consultants had spent two hours getting to know the top managers from the two companies, and only a few minutes covering the rudiments of the merger. Roberto Higgins now pushed his face into the wind as he stood in front of the bow side of the cabin listening to South China's Chief Financial Officer (CFO), Yi Li, describe the delicacies made famous by Yulan's cook. Yi watched the eyes of his young guest carefully as he described in halting English the hearty taste of cooked dog. Higgins's expression never changed. Good training for a Westerner, thought Yi, who knew that Higgins would find such a dish appalling.

Inside the sheltered cabin, Ellen Kwan was gaining confidence with each Cantonese sentence as she discussed the benefits and hindrances of International Finance Corporation loans with Yao Lanxin, Mr. Xiaobin's executive assistant.

"Permit me to interrupt you, but I wish to point out magnificent view of hill towns as we approach floating restaurant," Mr. Xiaobin said, as he descended from the cabin and approached the other groups, Harry at his side.

"Wow, those lights are spectacular. Is this still part of Hong Kong?" asked Roberto.

"Yes, Mr. Higgins. Hong Kong territory covers several islands and much continental land," informed Yao Lanxin pointing towards the distant hillside lit by blue, green, and red lanterns behind the floating restaurant.

The engine on the ferry was thrown in reverse, slowing the craft to a rocky drift. The smell of sweet perch, sautéed garlic, and plum wine was carried on the fresh breeze that surrounded the craft.

"I am sorry that Ms. Wong and her managers could not join us tonight, but I am delighted to have the opportunity to dine with you and your staff, Mr. Morton." Xiaobin Li spoke in a genuine tone.

"The pleasure and honor is certainly ours, Mr. Xiaobin," responded Harry Morton.

Several hours later, Harry sat with his feet up on a little coffee table in his favorite room in the Peninsula Hotel, debriefing his young staff.

"Boy, these dudes are good at hiding feeling and at postponing business talk. I know what my briefings say about doing business with the Chinese, building relationships and all, but it feels weird taking all this time just to get to know someone. Not a single word of the deal." Roberto scratched his black hair as he sipped bourbon and looked out at the quiet harbor that seemed to define Hong Kong.

"They were taking it all in, Berto. They weren't wasting time. Mr. Yao, for example, was trying to decide how we would handle a Chinese merger. Would we mistake business peculiarities for cultural differences between Hong Kong and southern mainlanders? For quite awhile he watched Harry and didn't eat," Ellen responded.

"How did I do?" Harry smiled over a scotch.

"Well, Yao and Yi seemed impressed. I couldn't tell with Mr. Xiaobin."

"Berto, did you pick up anything interesting? Or any reason to change the opening day plan?" Harry swiveled to look at a tiring Roberto Higgins.

"Not really. Except that I might have to chill the humor. These guys, although focused on relationship, are very serious."

"They just have a different sense of humor," Ellen said.

"Excellent. Let's get some sleep. See you all at seven for breakfast in the restaurant," Harry said as he rose to usher out his lieutenants.

For the next several days, the Masterfield team met with the South China executives at the New Harbor Hotel and with the top team from SRI at their offices. They absorbed nuances about each company culture, while discussing marketing and operations options facing the merger. At the end of the first week, Wong Xi arranged for a young SRI financial aid, fresh from her MBA at Oxford, to play guide and to chauffeur Ellen and Roberto around Hong Kong Island.

The full consulting team planned to meet Xi, Ho Duan, and Xi's husband Bao Li for dinner later Saturday evening.

Harry arrived on time at the Golden Dragon Restaurant to find Wong Xi and Bao Li already seated and issuing instructions to the waiter. As he was escorted to the table, Harry noted that Bao Li stood only about five feet six, was slightly bald, and had an indistinguishable Han face- slightly angled eyes, no facial hair, small nose, and flat cheek bones. The smiling older gentleman in a well-tailored Hong Kong navy silk suit could have been any southern Chinese businessman one sees rushing to work along Prince Street early in the morning. Average looking, except for his eyes. They were intense and rich hazel, suggesting some non-Chinese heritage.

"Mr. Morton. It is indeed an extraordinary pleasure to finally meet you. My wife describes your work as quite exceptional," Mr. Bao partially gripped Harry's hand and smiled genuinely.

"Mr. Bao, the pleasure is mine," Harry responded in fluent Cantonese as he shook the couple's hands. "You and your wife are too kind. It is your impact on modern Asian ventures that is truly increasing standards of living all over Asia,"

"Shall we be seated? Please, call me Li, Mr. Morton." Bao gestured to a seat facing the door. Harry had almost taken a seat facing the picture window opening onto a wide expanse of Hong Kong harbor, but he quickly accepted the traditional position for honored guests.

"Thank you, and you must call me Harry."

Morton noted that Xi played "the wife," not the business tycoon, keeping appropriately quiet as the two men told a bit about their backgrounds and offered general information about their companies. Each knew of the other's taste for horse racing and for golf, and made appropriate overtures to play a round as soon as schedules cleared.

Harry recognized practiced charm and deeply appreciated the skill of the man sitting next to him the way a bullfighter appreciates even subtle head movements of a snorting stationary bull. Appreciation tempered by the utmost respect and caution, none of which did Harry reveal in his conversation, look, or demeanor.

Roberto, Ellen, and Ho Duan arrived in a rush and, after introductions; the exuberant Americans regaled the table with tales of the day's tour.

"Wu Heng is a magnificent guide. She knows about gardens, ancient temples, and great shopping districts we'd never find in a tour book. Thank you for allowing her to be with us, Ms. Wong," Roberto said. He took a bowl of clear soup from the waiter who was dipping the initial helping of the first dish onto plates of the earlier guests.

"The cable car ride up to Victoria Peak is spectacular. I'm envious of the residents who live on the sides of the hill on the way up. We could see into some of the flats on 'mid-levels,' and they look fabulous. To have that view out of my living room window all year round, I'd never go to the office. I'd telecommute day and night. Awesome," Ellen said. The table broke out in grins and laughter at her uncharacteristically girlish jubilance.

By dessert, all members of the dinner party were freely chatting about the weather, scenery, East-West cultural differences, and the world economy. Not a word was exchanged about the South China merger.

Towards the end of a dessert of almond tofu and fruit, Harry spotted an old friend across the restaurant, excused himself, and walked around several elegantly draped tables to greet Johnny Burns, known as Johnny X.

"As I live and breathe, what are you doing here, Morton?" X exclaimed loudly and enthusiastically embraced his old college pal. Johnny Burns had left the States in the 1970's and moved to Kenya. He had become a trader and political consultant, primarily to developing nations. His fierce scowling visage, medium height Afro, tribal cloth robes, and harsh language enabled him to remain a feared but respected figure in the Western press. He had been credited with arranging one of the longest Angolan cease-fires through skillful single-handed shuttle diplomacy.

"Man, how long has it been?" Morton asked of his one-time close friend. Their politics had long since diverged, but the two men still enjoyed each other's company when their paths crossed over the years. "Look, I'm at a business dinner, but where are you staying? We can get together."

"Next time man. I'm out of here early tomorrow. I'll e-mail your home office next time I'm going to be here. It's good to see that the colony is getting some heavy black capitalist advice." X rocked back and laughed deep from his baritone throat, and the Chinese guests at his table, as well as those at the one next to his, sneaked quick glances. Back at his table, Harry rejoined the still lively conversation. As Wong Xi was looking over the bill next to Harry, she asked, so no one else could hear, how he knew Johnny X. Harry could easily detect the disapproving air to the question. He thought for a second of responding under his breath so that the exchange would go unnoticed, but uncharacteristically, Harry responded in full voice, "We're old friends from college. We're part of the great African Diaspora. You know, like overseas Chinese, we maintain our roots." Harry's tone and smile were engaging and warm, but Xi examined every facial line of her foreign consultant. Did she really know enough about this man?

Duan, Ellen, and Roberto continued discussing the day's tour. Li, however, flashed a quick questioning look at his wife.

The gathering broke around one o'clock with warm handshakes and good wishes exchanged by all. Wong Xi and Ho Duan remained in the restaurant a few minutes, while the others gathered for transportation on the sidewalk. They were pleased that the American team was capable of helping complete the SRI-South China deal. They now knew that they would be a competent fit with the attorneys and financial experts working on the merger.

Boa Li chose not to discuss the evening in the car, but waited until he and Xi had returned home and undressed for bed before he opened the subject.

"My wife was correct. These are very competent foreigners. And Harry Morton is exceptionally perceptive and skillful. He is also interestingly mysterious. College friend?" Bao Li knew his wife was focused, at some level, on the enigma she perceived Harry Morton to be. He was more amused than concerned and smiled to himself. He kissed her on the cheek and turned over in bed.

Harry Morton spent the rest of the weekend close to the hotel, working out in the gym, reading reports on his other projects faxed from Washington, and brushing up on the political issues surrounding the return of Hong Kong to China in 1997. He was not prepared to leave this investigation solely to his young associates. Two points were concerning him about the merger. The first was the distinctive work cultures of the two firms. Wages were low and working conditions in South China's Guangzhou factory were primitive compared to the relatively modern SRI Hong Kong New Territories shop. The second involved the flexibility of Xiaobin Li.

Xiaobin had missed much of the ten year « Cultural Revolution » (1966-1976) while advising the North Vietnamese army. When China's policy changed and they supported Cambodia's Khmer Rouge against the Vietnamese in about 1970, he swallowed his feelings and advised Pol Pot. He survived domestic political changes from Mao, the Gang of Four, Hua Guofeng on up to Jian Zemin in 1989. During the period after Mao's death in 1976 through the early 1990's, Xiaobin benefited from the supreme political godfather, Deng Xiaoping. By 1989 and the Tiananmen Square revolt, Xiaobin was comfortably retired from the military and preparing to run South China.

South China's 65-year-old CEO had been in business less than five years when he was given the opportunity to purchase the factory. While he might be an astute manager of people, he had barely adjusted to the ways of the fast-paced south, let alone to business. Now he would have to acclimate himself to working for a younger, foreign-educated female. While his surface attitude seemed to easily embrace the change, Morton wondered about Xiaobin Li's real feelings.

Harry also knew that he would have to learn much more about his employer. He set a meeting for late Wednesday afternoon with Wong Xi at a local restaurant on the far side of the island.

"The *dim sum* is excellent, Mr. Morton. I had not known about this restaurant---"

"I would appreciate you calling me Harry," Morton said. The two business-clad executives stood out from the more casually dressed clientele seated in the noisy restaurant. But Morton knew that they received more than the usual stares from other patrons as they entered. Once seated, however, they attracted scarcely more attention than other patrons. Harry had eaten at the 'Green Garden' for years, knew its owners, and usually came here at least once during any Hong Kong visit.

"I want to be sure that you are comfortable with the next step of our process, now that you have some feel for my team and you also know Mr. Xiaobin better."

"Perhaps, you're wondering if I am prepared to face his resentment to my being a female executive." Xi smiled.

"Well, I see we're adopting the Western style direct approach today. You realize this is not going to be easy for him, no matter how much he stands to gain financially?"

"Yes, and he'll have many ways to try to test my will. He'll find out, however, that I was not handed this position. I earned it like any man would have had to. I know how to play the game, Hong Kong style. I may have been trained at Harvard, Harry, but I am Chinese. Very Chinese."

"You can say that again," Morton let slip an uncharacteristic hint of admiration. Xi smiled and briefly broke her fix on Morton's eyes.

"Mr. Morton, such direct flattery. You surprise me. Most of the time you are almost Cantonese in your approach to business. Every now and then, you slip into *waiguoren* habits."

"Xi, I plead guilty," Harry smiled broadly.

A waiter rolled a two-shelved pushcart up to the table. It contained round dough-covered sweet meats, pork dumplings, barbeque-glazed shrimp and a variety of vegetables encased in flat noodle. Harry leaned back in his chair to point to the delicacies he knew to be the house specialties.

"Oh, I haven't had these dumplings before," Xi said as she finished sampling a few items. She dipped each in a dish of soy sauce and hot bean paste. After another few minutes of silence while they focused on their meal, Xi pushed back from the table. "I'm quite full," she said.

"Let's discuss working conditions, then, for a moment." Harry noticed the edges of her eyes tighten. "Mr. Xiaobin's workers live primarily in Panyu, because he pays them too little for them to afford Guangzhou housing. Your Hong Kong workers, while not getting much by Western standards, are fairly compensated for the industry on the island. The discrepancy is almost a dollar per hour. That's substantial."

"Harry, are you concerned about workers' rights or about helping me make this merger work?" The cat-like hardness had returned to Xi's gaze.

"You're my client. I'm only trying to see that you reflect on all issues that might cause problems later, such as business culture and differences in practice."

"Thank you for your concern, but wages are a financial issue. I'm well aware of the ramifications and have fully taken them into account."

"If I might Xi, let me raise one other issue."

"Surely."

"I can see no reason to feel that China will do anything to undermine this deal in a year or two. After all, they'll---"

"They'll collect handsome taxes from the strengthened firm. Is that your thinking, Harry?"

"Quite. As your British colleagues would say."

"I don't think 1997 is in play on this one. No," she concurred.

"Okay, well, I think we've dealt with my immediate issues." His pleasant tone and smile masked his disappointment at not being able to pursue a number of potentially related issues, like educational and health status differences between the two labor forces. Once production processes were merged, Harry feared the status and rights of worker differences would lead to slow downs and other costly actions.

"Sorry, it's after seven. I need to get back to the office," she said.

"Well, thank you for the time. I appreciate your being able to get away. And thank you for your candor. It's a big help."

The lights of Hong Kong were red, blue, and copper as the limo sped beneath the streetlights of the "mid levels" section on its way back to SRI headquarters at the Admiralty Centre. Neither Morton nor Wong noticed the steel blue Toyota Cressida trailing their vehicle through the traffic.

"So, what entertainment does SRI recommend for special foreign visitors?" Harry almost regretted the straightforward question before the final syllables had left his mouth.

"That makes two very Western questions tonight, Mr. Morton. Most unlike you." She smiled ever so slightly while holding her consultant's eyes.

"Please, Xi, forgive my indiscretion in presuming our team to be special. I wasn't thinking."

After several long moments of silence, she spoke.

"Frankly, I think your knowledge of our city is quite comprehensive. I don't really think that I can expand on your choices."

"Fair enough," Morton said.

The car pulled up to the Star Ferry terminal and the driver got out to open Harry's door. "At the end of this week, we'll return to the States. I think we all need time to digest the progress of the last ten days, before moving to the next stage," Harry said.

"I agree. Your people have been very thorough and professional. Xiaobin, Yao, and Yi have all commented positively. We also feel more comfortable at this point, despite the distance left yet to travel between the companies. And, Harry, don't worry about me handling Mr. Xiaobin. As you American males say, I'm a big girl."

"I would hope that wouldn't become necessary. Anyway, it's my job to worry. In this case, it's also my pleasure."

As Harry bent towards the door of the car facing his client, and extended his hand, Xi grabbed his hand with both of hers and gave an enthusiastic shake.

"Was that in Asian or Western custom?" he grinned as he shut the door.

After the Jaguar pulled out of the turnaround, Harry noticed the Cressida, parked with dimmed lights in a bus bay several car lengths behind the spot where Xi's car had stood.

He wondered if it had followed them and stared for only a millisecond before the vehicle pulled out, turned around and sped off.

Sun rays bounced brightly off the water and building surfaces around the harbor early the next day as the Masterfield team sat around the sitting room table in Harry's suite. The heat and humidity lubricated the hustle and flow of commuters, merchants, gawkers, and strollers on the waterfront plaza across from the hotel. The temperature had no effect on the strained eyes and taught lips in the room inside. Few of the sweet rolls had been touched on the Limoges porcelain saucers next to delicate coffee-filled cups.

"You know how you tell me to trust my instincts, Harry?" asked Roberto. "Well, I think Yao and Yi are too comfortable with a deal that just doesn't seem to be financially good enough for South China. They're up to something."

Higgins hadn't waited for Harry's response.

"Yeah, and I think they're all too casual about the changes they're facing in work processes." Ellen added, looking up from her notes.

"I'm not sure I agree with you," said Harry, although he then remembered the car that seemed to have followed him and Xi the night before. "Well, we have one more set of individual interviews and one group meeting before we head home. There may not be much more we can do until we return."

Roberto stood. "It just feels too easy for what should be an extremely difficult merger."

Several miles away, on the northern outskirts of the island, a set of freshly developed photo prints was spread out on a heavily lacquered hard wood table.

"These are worthless, Heng. An innocent goodbye handshake between colleagues? It will take more than this to do the trick. Stay with it." Yao Lanxin turned from the table, dismissing his chauffeur and the pictures and returned to the stack of legal documents about the merger planted on his desk.

An hour later, a knock at Xiaobin Li's door drew him out of deep concentration.

"*Hue*," he signaled for the intruder to enter.

Yi Li, the company CFO entered the spacious executive office, closed the door, and sank into the deep canvas covered chair facing his boss's desk.

"I wish to speak as your friend, not your CFO," he carefully said to the older man across the desk.

Xiaobin placed the fountain pen down next to the unused Pentium computer.

Yi Li had served with Xiaobin Li twenty years earlier, providing military strategic support to the North Vietnamese during the American war in Hanoi and then the Khmer Rouge in Cambodia. Yi had a knack for lightning quick calculation, while Xiaobin was a master of conceptualization and long range strategy. Together, they had helped devise some of Ho Chi Min's most successful campaigns. Li was more able to put the war behind him, fold the desk and field experience into a "case closed" folder in his mind.

Although Xiaobin didn't particularly like serving the Cambodian rebels, his family experienced no negative repercussions. On the other hand, he had had close relatives killed during US bombing raids over North Vietnam. He recognized, at an intellectual level that deep bitterness clouded and might hamper strategic judgment; yet his animosity towards things Western persisted. He was, therefore, usually thankful for his friend pointing out when Xiaobin's prejudice was impairing his decisions.

"This merger could very well work out for us, if we let it proceed, without additional efforts to derail SRI."

"Yes, my friend, it could. But, as we know, it could be even greater, if we can extract control from the obnoxious Hong Kong clan, Bao and Wong. Impudent young brats," Xiaobin said gruffly.

"I fear my friend may be letting his pride influence his financial judgment," said Yi, maintaining eye contact.
"Only a dear friend can utter such a charge," said Xiaobin, returning the stare.

Nothing was said for minutes, which felt like hours to Yi.

"My friend, I will take your observation into consideration."

"Thank you, Li. I think I shall retire now." Yi bowed slightly and left the room.

In a skyscraper over fifteen miles away, across hills, hamlets, and urban landscape, Wong Xi finished rereading the folder on Harry Morton. She focused now on the summary bio. It read like an All-America twentieth century Horatio Alger. And his Asian stoicism seemed too genuine, as if he'd grown up in China. Too perfect, she thought. Was he ever passionate about anything? Would he maintain SRI's interest when the inevitable ploys from South China were discovered? The African man that Morton referred to as X in the restaurant was not in the bio. A person like Harry Morton is likely to know thousands of people, so clearly the various intelligence services would miss some of them. Still, someone like this X person should have shown up. Xi made a note to check later for more information.

Wong was used to knowing all of the details. She now had as much background on this Masterfield team as on her other consultants. Something about Harry Morton didn't fit. A smile crossed her face as she swung the desk chair and looked over the harbor, beyond the Hong Kong Yacht Club and into the midnight blue sky. She could use an ancient way to find out what she needed to know about Harry, she thought.

Xi pondered for a few seconds about where she might have gotten this idea? Had it been some western movie, impressions from her time at Harvard, some Hong Kong trash novel, or some other source? Probably one of the aunts that used to fuss about the house while her father was out making money. Most likely Auntie Heng, since she was the one always telling stories about concubines, forbidden travel, and lands of foreign princes. Aunt Heng had been Xi's favorite. On the other hand, it could have been one of those Western girls in college or business school. Xi paused for a second longer, for she realized that she often blocked out many details from her adolescence.

She never regretted returning to China. Staying away from home had never been a serious thought. Yet there were many overseas Chinese who supported family on the mainland, but never thought of returning. They remained Chinese-American, or British, or Singapore-Chinese, or whatever. How disturbing to carry your cultural identity inside you while immersed in another culture for most of your life, she thought. Disturbing, yet also intriguing. Her appetite for cultural diversity had always been keen. Xi's well-honed intellectual discipline had been so nurtured and reinforced in school and in business that it necessarily submerged some of her curiosity. It never, however, fully buried it. She would have to find some way to learn more about this Harry Morton, she thought.

When Harry got to the SRI headquarters the Friday prior to their scheduled departure for Washington, he found e-mail from Wong Xi.

"I would enjoy hosting you in our box at the races tomorrow night. Unfortunately, there is not enough room for the rest of the team. It would be our pleasure to have the whole team some other time."

Harry had planned to take the two junior members of his team out for a last night's celebration. He thought for a moment about what Xi might want to talk about, but decided that it could wait. He graciously declined and put in one final day of report writing and final meetings with the SRI brass. Xi gave no indication during their meeting of having sent the message, nor of having received Harry's reply.

The night was humid, hazy, and heavy as the three Americans relaxed on the short ferry ride back to the Kowloon side of Hong Kong. Barges, ferries, tugs, and pleasure boats passed them skimming the surface of the misty harbor. Roberto was in the middle of one of his New York boyhood stories when all three noticed a man several benches in front of them taking their picture. They were but a minute or two from docking, but Harry had a feeling that he had seen the fellow before.

"Let's find out who he is," he told his younger colleagues.

As they rose from their wood bench, the photographer began running toward the stairs and the lower deck. Roberto, a sprinter in high school, took off. The man was quick, but out of shape and no match for the trim athletic New Yorker, who tackled him at the bottom of the stairs, pinning the heavier man face down on the deck. Harry caught up, wrested the camera away, slipped the film into his pocket, and placed the camera back near its owner. Ellen arrived a second later, as Harry and Roberto sat their captive against the rail.

"Why were you taking our picture? And why did you run?" Harry asked in Cantonese.

"It is no sin to take pictures in Hong Kong, but it is often unwise to wait for potential assailants," the pale heavyset man replied. He had on a well-pressed blue suit, white dress shirt, with French cuffs, and no tie. It was unusually formal clothing for this late hour on the ferry.

"I suppose we need to let you go, but ..." Harry thought better of saying anything else.

As they helped the man to his feet, he regained his composure, grasped the camera and stalked off the boat.

"Harry, why did we go to the trouble of chasing him down if we were to let him go? He'll just go to the police and file a complaint," asked Ellen.

"I don't think so. I doubt he relies on that version of authority. I think I know where I've seen our friend before," said Harry. "Let's get back to the hotel. We've got a dinner to enjoy."

While enjoying crab soup and honey duck in a small restaurant near the Tung Choi market in Mong Kok, Harry told his partners his suspicions.

"Our friend this evening was driving the Cressida that tailed Xi and me the other day after our tea meeting. Someone is looking for extraordinary information or for a way to spoil this deal. Maybe both. Who, I'm not sure, but the leading candidates aren't hard to guess."

"Tea? What tea? Where was this?" asked Roberto. Harry looked at him, but offered no explanation. "Okay, whatever," Roberto finally said.

"Yao Lanxin, the executive assistant?" asked Ellen.

"How about the old man himself, Xiaobin Li?" Harry said.

"Why would he scuttle it? He sought the merger, and will become a very wealthy stockholder?" Roberto leaned back in the rickety blue and red stool to sip his fragrant yellow tea.

"But SRI and its lady chief may be taxing his tolerance of the new China," Ellen said. "Possibly, but the Red Army had some female officers. Remember, few things are as they seem in China," sighed Harry. "Berto, see if you can get these negatives developed. Let's see what was so interesting to our friend."

They finished the meal while chatting about what they would like to transport back to Washington. It's like having the San Francisco Bay instead of the Potomac at the foot of Georgetown mused Ellen. Once outside, they walked through the market, which was just closing its clothing and utensil stalls for the evening. Sounds of rapid forceful Cantonese, boisterous laughter, and an occasional melody from a sidewalk radio filled the night. Smells of stale fish, over-ripe melons, and fragrant rice wine rose from the broken sidewalks. Men in tattered tee shirts collapsed their stalls and repacked unsold goods into cardboard boxes. No one else had on white-collar business attire, but no one paid the strollers any mind. Merchants actively gesticulated to their colleagues and hurried the remaining customers through their sales routines. The long entrepreneurial day in open air Hong Kong was winding down.

The long plane ride back to Washington on Sunday and early Monday provided a restful change of pace, as the consultants finished up reports, looked at movies, read paperbacks, and slept.

CHAPTER SEVEN

香港

"Hey, how was school, son?" Harry greeted Mark at the front door Monday afternoon.

"Not so good, Dad. I had a fight with Bobby Boyd," Mark said, avoiding his father's gaze. He dropped his book bag at the foot of the slowly spiraling oak staircase, turned to the living room, trudged a few paces and fell into the beige velvet-covered sofa. Harry followed quietly, took a seat on the sofa next to the boy, placed his glass of Cabernet on an end table and waited.

"Do you want to talk about it?"

"Not much to talk about. Bobby kept up his noise, and he pushed me. So, I punched him in the nose. He dropped like a bad prizefighter and started whimpering like a baby. Sorry…"

"Well, you know we don't fight to settle things, son. But he does seem to have been asking for it."

Father and son talked for an hour, went into the yard to throw a football, and had put the fighting incident behind them when they heard Mary calling from the screened in kitchen.

"Harry? Phone for you."

Morton tossed one more fifteen-yard pass to Mark, then turned and mounted the steps to the kitchen. He gave his wife a peck on the cheek and took the phone.

"Morton, what the hell's your boy doing bullying my Bobby?" shouted Robert Boyd into the phone.

"How you feeling, Robert? Your boy run into a little more than he could handle, did he?"

"This is not funny, Morton. Boy could have had a broken nose."

"Maybe Bobby will pick on somebody else to bully, next time."

"What do you mean? Your Mark picked a fight."

"I don't think so. Bobby has been bad-mouthing Mark all year. Check it out with the teachers. Kid's in the wrong school, Boyd. Needs to be someplace where there aren't so many different types of kids. Someplace he can be comfortable. Know what I mean, Boyd?" Harry said.

"You son of a bitch. What are you saying, Morton? That's my boy."

"Like father, like son. I can't draw you a map, Robert, but you might do your son a favor and let him develop his own prejudices." Harry hung up.

"Harry, what was that about?" Mary was standing in the door to the yard, hands on hips.

"Our old friend, Robert Boyd. His kid's been picking on Mark all year, as you know. Seems Mark finally hit him in the face, and the little bully went running to Daddy."

"That's terrible. Mark shouldn't be hitting people," Mary looked into the yard and started to call her son.

"I agree, but in this case, he may have been in the right," Harry offered without tone or emphasis in his voice.

"Harry, that male competitiveness and aggression…"

"I wish you would lay off that theme. We're not talking about going to war, here. This is simply boys growing up. Our boy needs to be able to defend himself, and the little Boyd kid needs to learn to respect people."

"You don't' need to raise your voice at me, Harry Morton. If you were around more, maybe our guidelines for Mark would be more in sync. The boy needs a father around."

"He seems to be doing just fine, baby. I can't believe we're arguing over this." Harry said, slamming his palm on the counter top. "You know, Mary, my job is in *international* consulting, which means I have to travel."

"I know, but you could be a lot more attentive to both of us when you are at home."

"Mom, Dad, don't fight. I'm sorry." Their son had entered the kitchen without them noticing.

"Son, it's okay," Harry responded, hoping he would pass through and let them talk the issue out.

"Mark, your father seems to approve of your fighting, but I don't and don't care to hear excuses about it."

The boy didn't look at either adult, walked through the kitchen to the family room, picked up a book, and headed up stairs to his room.

"That's nice, baby. Why do you have to paint me as the bad, unprincipled father?"

"I didn't, sweetheart; but if the shoe fits…"

Later that evening, after a fairly silent dinner, Harry called up his friend George Birch and arranged to meet at a nightclub, called *Faces*, a mile or so below Walter Reed Hospital. It had been a hangout for middle aged, middle class black professionals for years.

"Man, I know something's up. It's not like you to escape during the week," said George, as he eased into a stiff-backed walnut cane chair.

"Mary's getting on my nerves," Harry said after he'd ordered a Jack Daniels over ice. He told Birch the story about Mark, Bobby Boyd, and the rest.

"This is the first time in a long time I remember you and Mary having a fight. Come to think of it, yeah, I don't ever remember seeing you two argue for years," George sipped a beer and watched a young female lawyer they both knew switch her hips toward their table.

"That's just it; we usually quietly work out our differences. I don't know. This feels like more than an argument about Mark." Harry, intent on his drink, paused to actually taste his bourbon and was a little surprised to hear Janet Hall's husky voice.

"Boys' night out? I thought you two were very married," gin fizz in hand the medium brown skin, former DC teen socialite leaned against the back of an empty chair at their table, Harry was slow to react, still thinking about his home situation. George, much less attached to the subject being discussed, took in the whole curvaceous body. Though professionally dressed, Janet's frame forcefully tested the buttons holding together the panels of silk and wool.

"Well, well, well. I thought you had so much client paperwork that you never had time to network, Ms. Hall. And what about your marriage? How come you're out here sippin' and grinnin' on a school night?" George straightened up in his chair.

"George Birch, you are behind the times. Billy and I broke up a year and a half ago. Although that's really none of your business. And I'm now a partner, so I have plenty of help with the paperwork, as you call it. Hello, Harry. May I sit down? Or is this private?"

"Hey, Janet. It was private, but you're welcome to sit," Harry dove into the moment, engaged his male barroom demeanor, and half cracked a smile.

"Harry, don't see you about anymore," said Janet.

"I've been traveling a bit."

"I've been around and I haven't seen you, Janet," George cut in with a hand on hers. As he and Janet continued their flirtation, Harry's attention drifted back to Mark and Mary. He recalled wonderful Sunday afternoons, Mark on his shoulders, as they visited the newly arrived pandas at the National Zoo; picnicking on the sloping lawn of Wolf Trap Farm in Virginia, where they joined friends for pop concerts; dancing in the aisles at the very proper Kennedy Center to the farewell concert of the Four Tops and the Temptations. Those public times and the precious walks alone with Mary, as a young couple, along the wooded trails of Rock Creek Park beside Beech Road moved across his mind's eye. Where had it all gone?

"George, don't you want to make money, or do something meaningful?" Janet, allowing George to hold her free hand in a friendly way, chided the table's one attentive male. The question, one Harry had often thought of asking his much too contented friend, brought him back to the table's conversation.

"I can't be content drinking gin fizzes in uptown Chocolate City speakeasies. I want influence, to make lots of money, and to travel. I don't mind people knowing I'm ambitious. Hey, it works for the `pink toes.'" Janet sipped through a straw.

Pointing at the Carmen red crushed velvet wallpaper, she continued, "I can't stay behind. Look at this place. It's like that bar in that jazz flick, *Kansas City*. Here we are. Sitting in a bar filled with smoke, when everybody else in the country is giving up cigarettes. This loud soul music is bound to make half this crowd deaf before they turn sixty. Table after table of folks talkin' about nothin', makin' the most benign local political bullshit sound like acts of national security. Everybody's a power-broker."

"My, my. What's in your drink, darlin'? Did we have a tough day? The white boys in the firm too much to deal with, were they?" George roared with laughter, while Harry nodded, still pretending to be interested.

"You watch. I'm going to be doing deals in South Africa, trading in Nigeria, and I'll be opening up accounts in Cuba while you turkeys are sipping bourbon on Georgia Avenue. Harry, I know you could help a sister out, if you wanted to."

"Janet, sounds to me like you got things planned out nicely, without any help from any of us."

"Brothers," she grunted.

"You know why sisters are trying out the other side more, these days, don't you, fellas? Brothers don't want to take a serious sister seriously. You want someone to look good, talk right, and cover your back. Well, some of us need a more equal relationship than that. But I guess you boys can't handle that?"

Aretha finished singing "Baby, Baby, Sweet Baby" and started "Respect" over the speakers, and George sang along in perfect harmony. Both men smiled at Janet, who drank deeply, having momentarily relieved a well of pent up frustration.

"Well, have nice evening fellas," said Janet as she rose, pulled her skirt down, and moved off to another table.

"Why didn't you hit on her, Harry? She clearly was interested in you."

"I'm getting' too old, buddy. Besides, she's got a few things to work out. Issues."

"I'm not talkin' about marryin' her, just hittin' on the sistah."

"I'd best be getting back. Thanks for the drink, George."

"But, what about your situation? We didn't come up with any solution."

"I'm not sure there is one yet. Just talking about it helps. I'm cool for now. 'Night George."

Harry walked to the door, nodding at two or three patrons he knew. He was glad to be outside in the slightly humid night air and stood on the curb above the parking lot for several minutes before walking to his car. Janet Hall, she's got the right competitive spirit and wants to get beyond the sleepy parts of this town. Right spirit, he thought. Good luck to her.

Driving up Georgia Avenue with his windows wide open, Harry cleared his head of foxy single women, of man talk, and didn't think about work. He didn't even think about his son. As his gold Porsche sped through brick row house and stone façade mom and pop commercial strips, he wondered why he had gotten so annoyed at his wife. She gave him space to travel and pursue a career he almost didn't need. She did a great job of raising Mark, while she propelled herself up through the ranks at Brookings. She is still loving and attentive. What is not to like?

No answer came. An occasional car, a stray cat, and swaying poplar and tulip trees provided the only movement on an otherwise still blue-black evening. It was past midnight before he pulled into his driveway tucked away in the northern corner of the District.

"Are you still awake, baby?" Harry leaned over his slumbering wife. No answer.

After he undressed and climbed into bed, he gently put his arm around his wife.

"I'm sorry for earlier tonight, Mary."

She rolled over and half opened her eyes. "What's happening to you? You don't jump on me like that for nothing. What's bothering you, Harry Morton?"

"I don't know. Maybe it's Mark, or this current assignment. I really don't know."

"Maybe you feel guilty about not being here all that much." Mary turned over, a grimace on her face, and went back to sleep.

"Maybe." He thought about the last few days in D.C. and the last China trip. He reran events as if they were film clips in his mind. None of the scenes made him smile. Eventually, Harry allowed sleep to claim him.

At five the next morning, Harry rose, placed a pressed shirt and tie and blue suit in a suit bag, and dressed in his golf khakis and a teal blue golf shirt. On his way out of the bathroom, he opened Mark's bedroom door, crept to his son's bed, kissed his cheek, and made his way back out to the landing and down the winding front staircase. The morning outside the Morton's front porch was still, about 68 degrees and dry. Bending to pick up the morning paper, he smiled at the manicured and assiduously designed landscapes on his block. Pink and white Azaleas, cream leafed Magnolias and towering twenty-foot red and pink Crape Myrtles shaped the properties and defined the neighborhood.

"This too is part of who I am," he thought.

He stood erect, inhaled deeply and decided it was great golf weather. Harry scanned the paper on his way back inside. In the kitchen, he downed a glass of orange juice, chewed half a bagel, finished the headlines, grabbed his bag and headed for the car in the front driveway.

It only took him twenty minutes, driving on almost deserted streets, to reach suburban Maryland's exclusive Members' Country Club. Although not a member, Morton was a familiar figure in the clubhouse, since he was a frequent guest of Don Bartram and a few other business colleagues from client companies. He sat in one of the dining rooms reading the *Wall Street Journal,* sipping coffee, and waiting for Don and their six-fifteen tee time.

"I don't see how you can stand the travel, Morton. You could play two or three times a week, knock a few points off your game, and still make a nice living," drawled his boss as he approached his table at about ten minutes before six.

"Whose side are you on? And who would land all the big foreign merger deals?" Harry grinned and stood halfway up to shake Don's hand.

Harry had gained enormous respect for the game of golf since he'd started playing five years earlier. It was proving more difficult to master than any sport he had tried. He didn't talk much in clichés about its challenges except when on the course. He hit a solid, perfectly straight drive off the first tee, and after Bartram hit a similarly strong first shot the two colleagues climbed into their cart and headed down the fairway. For a little over an hour, they matched drives, fairway irons, lobs, chips and putts, both remaining at three over par.

"This is the seventh hole, and you haven't let up. I don't get it. I've been playing all my life. It's enough to drive one to distraction. Anyway, let's talk a little business. That should disrupt your game."

Bartram chuckled deeply. The dew had begun to dry, and the morning smells and sounds provided a pastoral backdrop for the best catch up talk the two had had in weeks. Harry refreshed Bartram's memory on the key elements of the SRI deal. "We only got a piece of this baby. Who's doing the financial stuff?" Don asked, while slowly lining up his tee shot.

"Camden & Lybrand, so that's not a hold-up," Harry responded referring to another leading accounting and consulting firm.

"I don't get it. This ain't that complex a deal. Two willing parties, right? Both are Chinese for Christ's sake. I know. Different political systems." Don focused on his shot, took a measured back swing, and hooked his shot 190 yards down the fairway into a grove of 50-foot pine trees.

"Shit. Look at that, will you. Best concentrate on this for a minute."

"That looks like a fine shot to me." Morton didn't even try to keep a straight face.

"Look, Don. You know all kinds of things happen as principals get close to money time."

Harry decided to use his more reliable 3-wood, rather than risk the trees with his driver. He deliberately turned his shoulders further back as he torqued his body, and then uncorked a powerful swing. "Ping." The sound of the ball on the face of the club indicated solid contact, and Harry's left arm had remained stiff and straight. The ball sailed high in the morning sky, escaping the treetops. It climbed smoothly and disappeared down the middle of the canal of blue sky above the middle of the fairway.

"Well, I'll be..." Don remained speechless in admiration for at least fifteen seconds. Or so it seemed to both men.

"I think I got most of that ball. Know what I mean, Don?" Harry shoved his club back in his bag as a gunslinger reholsters his smoking pistol. "Let's go find your ball."

"You know, Harry, it's not smart to embarrass your boss."

"Embarrass? Let me get this straight. One great... I will admit it was great. But, one great shot not even half way through a round embarrasses you? I don't think so. If I really did, Don, I truly apologize."

"You might have a point there, partner. Anyway, why can't this deal finish up on the next trip?"

"It can, if everybody acts in their best economic interest. But I sense it's going to get nasty first. Ol' General Xiaobin Li has at least one more battle in him, and I think he feels he can milk more out of this deal. You also have to factor in that Xi comes from a successful commercial, big time business background. She and many others in Hong Kong are having to suspend old stereotypes about assumed unsophisticated, country bumpkins from the southern part of the mainland. There's quite a bit of testing and feeling out the other side going on."

"At some point, he's got to believe SRI will walk away. He can't be so Communist that he doesn't get how merger economics work."

"Hell, look at all the US companies that don't understand how mergers work."

"Good point. Well, okay, I guess you've thought this out."

"Thank you, Don. I try my best."

The cart pulled along the woods, circled through some underbrush, and Don found his ball. He fell behind Harry on the seventh, eight, and ninth holes. Don chatted off and on, but Harry was fairly quiet for most of the middle holes.

"You awright, Harry?"

"Yeah, fine. Why?"

"You jess seem quiet." Don stared at his companion in the seat next to him as they pulled up to the twelfth tee. "You're not really worried about this job, are you?"

"No, but I don't have the end-game strategy clear yet, and I'm a little tired. Catching up on the jobs I've turned over to staff for awhile."

"Is that it? Everything okay with Mary?"

"Damn, baby. When did you turn into a mother hen? Everything's fine. I suggest you figure out how you're going to pick up four strokes. This match won't look good on your resume." He changed the subject. Don felt he had expressed his concerns. He felt that if something was wrong, Harry would fix it, now that he knew it was showing. They resumed a more jocular and friendly banter for the final six holes, as Harry's lead slipped to three shots.

"Thanks, old man; I enjoyed that," Harry extended his hand after one of the club's assistants cleaned his clubs and put his bag in the trunk of his car.

Don handed the teenager a ten-dollar bill and closed his trunk as Harry shut his door.

"See you back at the office?" Harry asked.

"I'm not going straight in. Oh, I almost forgot. While you all were away, Peter Burke detected an attempted break into our financial database. Guess where the hacker was traced to?" Don's sun-dried creases and red skin stretched tightly around his thin lips. He looked uncharacteristically intent.

"Guangzhou, China."

"You got it. How'd you guess?"

Harry turned off his engine and told Don about the car following him, the man on the ferry, and his theory about Xiaobin's looking for a way to discredit the deal.

"Harry, be careful. You're not James Bond, and these guys may not play by the same rules we do."

"The rules may be different. This is not, however, Russia or Sicily."

"Be careful, anyway. Keep me posted," Don reached in Harry's car and patted him on the shoulder. Harry drove off, leaving the older man walking slowly to his car.

As Harry's car reached the George Washington Parkway exit on the Beltway, the phone rang. He let it ring a couple of times as he checked his rear-view mirror to ensure that he could safely merge onto the Parkway towards downtown Washington.

"Hello."

"Harry? This is Peter."

"Hey, Burke. How's it going? What's up?"

"We have a phone message from the Camden guy on the SRI deal. You met him on the last trip, apparently. "

"Oh, yeah. Bob something."

"Bob Jenkins. Anyway, he wants to set up a call for later today."

"In an hour would be fine. I should be in the office in thirty minutes." Harry pressed the "end" button on the built in cell phone. He then pushed the "on" button to his radio to get a few minutes of Wynton Kelly, playing piano solos on a taped concert Harry had started several days ago. Harry relaxed as the green hilly shores of the Potomac passed in the distance to his left and on the other side the high wooded banks of McLean, Virginia sheltered the road from any remnant of even low density urban development. Harry's multi-million dollar life again felt as if it were on comfortable cruise control, as he sped towards his office.

"Afternoon, Mr. Morton. Your wife called about ten minutes ago. You must have turned your cell phone off," said Hazel Marsh.

"How are you, Hazel? Any other messages?"

"Nothing that won't wait. She sounded hassled."

Harry dropped his briefcase inside the door on one of the matching blue-green upholstered chairs beside his mahogany desk.

He picked up the sheath of prints Roberto had left on his desk. They revealed nothing remarkable or noteworthy—various angles of the three consultants sitting and chatting on the ferry.

Sinking into his swivel chair, he hit the hands-free button and the two-digit code on his speed dial to get his wife's direct line.

"Hello. Harry, is it you?"

"Yeah, baby. Is there something the matter?"

"No. I just have to go to Chicago to work with my research team on some data we just got in. I've arranged for a neighbor to drop Mark off after school sports. Can you get home early and handle him for a couple of days?"

"Sure, but you know I go to Hong Kong again at the end of the week."

"I'm very well aware of your schedule, Harry. I just need a little consideration here. Can you---"

"No, problem dear. I hope your trip is fruitful." Harry started to hang up.

"You know, Harry, you might occasionally show some interest in my work. This labor study could prove extremely useful to the federal government."

"I'm sorry, Mary. I do care about your work. Let's talk when you return."

"Yeah, fine."

Her hostile tone stunned Morton. For a man with exceptional powers of observation and renowned ability to 'read' people, he often had surprising difficulty anticipating when Mary was feeling beleaguered.

"Mark will be home at six thirty. Please be there. Thank you, Harry."

"Have a good trip." Harry realized the line was dead. He sat leaning back in his chair, feet up on the desk, looking at impressive glass and steel structures across K Street. The irony didn't escape him. Harry sat high atop a prestigious professional perch along Washington's fabled canyon of lobbying and consulting power based, in no small part, on his well-honed bargaining skills. Yet, negotiating a simple exchange with his wife sometimes was as challenging as piloting a bark-covered canoe down the Grand Canyon. What is going on with her this time? He wondered.

The decision to stay in business had been made jointly, and Mary had certainly never complained about the lifestyle his success had made possible. You make choices and live the best you can with the consequences. That's a credo Harry had thought that he and Mary shared.

He sank deep into his memory; back to when his mother was still alive. At one point, Harry had felt no stronger urge than to pursue local and state politics in Pennsylvania. Public service seemed the ideal way for him to be fulfilled. Family had all been so proud during his term as a Philadelphia city councilman. But that term left him tired, frustrated, and even disgusted with headline seeking colleagues, incompetent bureaucrats, and the seemingly unending "process" involved in getting anything accomplished. He had been successful in achieving significant fund increases for low-income housing, and steering large sums into job training programs. He rationalized his leaving public service and starting Team Management by suggesting that he could leverage more community improvements and employment by making minority companies more successful. That path, however, proved difficult, as well.

One Sunday morning, about two years after starting TMA, his family doctor approached him after church.

"Harry. Everything all right? You look like you carryin' the weight of the world on your shoulders."

"Hi, Doc. Everything is fine. How is Mrs. Bravely today?"

"Come on son. I've known you since you were a little boy. I remember you trying to act like those big old hypodermic needles didn't hurt. Fine is not the way you appear to me."

"Well, you remember I started this company a couple of years ago. After I left the Council."

"Yes, and I hear you doin' great," said the silver haired physician with a proud grin.

"This last quarter I brought in some more demanding contracts and four of the five guys that started the firm with me haven't been able to deliver the new level of quality."

"So you had to let some folks go. That's business."

"Yeah, but they were all brothers, and for the first time, I've hired white partners."

"What's the deal, son? "

"I was hoping to keep my firm a minority practice. But, the young black MBAs around here are at such a premium, they don't want to risk working for a black firm. It's not what I counted on. Doc, you've been able to serve North Philadelphia your whole career. And you haven't done so badly."

"Harry, from what I hear down at the white business clubs, you have a chance to really get big. You've had a nice colored clientele and helped a bunch of businesses. You have to decide if you want to play in the big leagues. If you do, you aren't always going to be able to be a race man."

"You know Doc; I never thought I'd seriously take advice from a Republican. A colored one at that."

"Think about it. You'll take some grief from your boys, but never forget that our community in Philadelphia too often resembles crabs in a barrel. One of us begins to do well and climb up, and the rest try to pull him down. I say, go for it. Besides, I know how you were raised. You won't forget where you're from."

"There's Mom; she's ready to go."

"Lena, how are you this morning? Spirit catch you up?"

"James, you talking nonsense into Harry's head? You two been chatting too long for it to be about the Lord or the weather."

"You are sharp as usual, and looking fine, too," James Bravely leaned over a gave Lena Morton a friendly kiss on the cheek.

"See you next week, James," said Lena grabbing hold of her son's arm and steering him towards the parking lot.

"Doc, thank you," said Harry over his shoulder as he walked his sixty-year-old mother to his car.

"Harry, I can tell you're worried about letting those boys go."

"Mom, I've moved on. It was---"

"Let me give you one piece of advice that I hope you're old enough to take, even from your mother. You've formed your beliefs and values and they're very sound. They're Christian. Don't worry about being approved. Do what's right and it will always pay off in the end. People will respect you. That's going to be more important than being liked. Some things are constant. Be true to your principles, Harry."

Morton didn't say anything, but he reached across the steering wheel and squeezed his mother's hand.

That was over fifteen years ago. And fewer and fewer clients were minority companies now. Maybe I should have stuck it out. I might be representing Pennsylvania in the House or Senate by now. But how content would I be? Now, at least I choose who I work for, Morton thought.

"Be truthful, Harry. How much real choice do you really have in life?" he smiled, because he knew the question came from his mother.

A beep from his computer drew Harry out of his reverie. The e-mail message was some pro-forma meeting reminder from the managing partner. Harry opened up his search engine and pulled up several Far East newspapers. Headlines about the markets in Tokyo, Singapore and Hong Kong indicated that trading was down and investors were still worried about the downward decline of the Japanese economy. He picked up the phone.

"Peter, what's your assessment of the recent Hong Kong market activity's impact on our little deal?" Harry was once again fully engaged in work. The amber tint of late afternoon bathed one wall. The beautiful sparkles leaping from picture frame to window and back were not even a minor distraction to Morton as he focused on a merger halfway around the world.

"I don't see any real impact. These are private companies with solid ratios and big bank accounts. We're fine."

"By the way, Bartram mentioned that you detected some cyber snooping last week," Harry paused to let Peter Burke shift gears.

"Yeah, I traced the offender to southern China. They didn't get past the second layer of security, however."

"I'll bet it's our friend Xiaobin Li. South China is looking for a way to squeeze or squelch this deal. I'm not sure which. Anyway, keep me posted."

"I don't get it. From the reports, this deal's got merger magic written all over it. The purchase premium is on the money; company sizes are compatible; there's no real competition with internal lines of business; and the business cultures aren't too dissimilar. What's Xiaobin not like, making too much money as he retires?"

"It is hard to figure, but the answer's got to do with old-fashion male pride, I think. Anyway, thanks for your help; pal. Talk to you later." Harry hung up his line and looked up at his old chestnut burl wall clock. Six o'clock.

"Hazel, I have to get home for Mark. See you in the morning."

"Tell that little angel I said hi and would love to see him sometime."

"Will do."

Mark Morton was throwing a football up in the air, running under, and catching it, all the while presenting commentary to no one in particular on his spectacular play, as he darted here and there across the lawn. He paused only momentarily as his father pulled into their driveway.

"Morton fades to pass, looks off the Cincinnati Bengal cornerback to the right, pumps and reloads. He ducks the charge of a burly middle linebacker, steps into the pocket and fires deep to Morton. He dives, arms extended, and pulls the spiral into his chest with his extra-large hands. Touchdown Redskins. Touchdown Redskins." Little Mark rolled in delight in the low-cropped grass.

"Quite a grab. How about you go out and I'll throw you some?" Harry tossed his jacket on the lawn and rolled up his sleeves.

Forty minutes later, the sun began to set and the two Mortons headed inside to wash up and inspect the kitchen for dinner.

"You know, Mark, I'm so happy with our backyard team's performance that I'll take you guys out to have pizza. You beat up on those Bengals pretty bad. What do you say?"

"We accept. `Tiger! Tiger! Burning bright in the forests of the night.'"

"Is that Edgar Allen Poe?"

"Nah, that's William Blake," Mark beamed.

"Blake? That's pretty advanced for your age, isn't it?"

"Well, I don't pick 'em. I study what Ms. Evans assigns, Dad."

Minutes later, as they fastened the car seat belts around their waists, Harry turned to Mark.

"How is school these days?"

"I think it's fine, but Mom wants me to do better. And you will too when you see my grades."

"What about you, son? What do you think? Are you satisfied?"

"I guess not. I probably don't study hard enough in between tests."

"How about your classmates? Any more problems with Bobby Byrd?"

"Not since I clubbed him."

A Ray Charles CD filtered through the cushioned interior as Harry's Porsche cruised over East-West Highway north of the District to Georgia Avenue and their local pizza parlor. Within minutes, Harry and Mark exchanged the leather bucket seats of Harry's car for the hard plastic backs in a noisy Pizza Hut.

"Daddy, get this one. Who said, `The only thing we have fear is fear itself?'

"Boy, wipe the cheese off of your chin. Let's see, must have been Deacon Jones from the 1950's Los Angeles Rams."

"A football player? No, Dad. This was a president of the United States."

"Let's see. President Clinton's famous line when confiding in his golf buddy, Vernon Jordan?"

"No, Daddy. Get serious; this is a history question."

"How about Franklin Roosevelt, when committing the U.S. to enter the Second World War?"

Harry widened his eyes in mock amazement. Mark put down his pizza and stared at his father. "You knew all along, didn't you?"

"I might have heard that one before." Harry reached over and patted the boy on his shoulder.

On Wednesday, Harry finished up details of likely satisfactory deal scenarios, had Peter Burke set a meeting in New York with the Camden and Lybrand financial team working for SRI, and he and his young team outlined five different options to gradually retire the CEO of a purchased company. At seven 'clock, he called home, got the housekeeper who had agreed to stay late, and learned that Mark had eaten, done homework, and was reading in bed.

"Put him on a second, would you Mrs. Brown?"

"Hello, Mark. How was the day?"

"Mine was okay, Daddy. When are you coming home?"

"I'll be home in an hour, but you should get your sleep. How about Friday night we go to a movie? It's the last night before Mommy gets back."

"Cool. See you in the morning."

Harry hung up and dialed his friend George Birch. "Hello, George. How you doing? What's up, tonight?"

"How am I doin'? Man, you can't be callin' me at home on a weeknight. I might be out with you. Know what I mean?"

"Yeah man. I'm sorry. Just felt like a drink. But you're right. How is Mabel, anyway?"

"Fine."

"Tell her hi. I'll catch you another time."

"Good idea, Harry. Chill man. Mary's back on the weekend, right?"

"Yeah. Saturday. You going to the Board of Trade dinner?"

"Not last time I checked. Too stiff for me. And I'm still waiting for my first piece of business to come out of one of those affairs."

"Okay. Catch you later."

Harry hung up and walked down the office corridor to the pantry/lunch room. There, he found Roberto Higgins sipping coffee and looking at the news on CNN. Harry filled his cup and turned to head back to his office.

"Look at that. Boy, your home town is tense tonight," Roberto said while his eyes were glued to the TV. Harry saw a picture of students filling Philadelphia's Market Street near the University of Pennsylvania's Law School. The president of the University was on the steps of the law school, urging calm. The *Washington Post* had been carrying the story of African American students protesting lack of faculty representation and assorted other grievances. Harry had paid the articles little mind. But now the sights and sounds before him captured his full attention. He didn't respond to Roberto, but just stood staring at the TV console. What was before his eyes, however, was not what Roberto saw.

"My friends, this is not about self interest. This is not about center city. This, my colleagues, is about what's right. This tax bill is not about saving

Chestnut Hill pennies on an already healthy dollar; this is about equity for folks blocks from this building with nothing but a rundown rat hole for shelter. This is about why we ran, Republicans and Democrats, alike.

George, Brent, Willie, Dorothy, Marcia, have you all forgotten? This is not Harrisburg; this is Philadelphia. This is South Street, it's North Philly, it's Manayunk, it's the Northeast, and Germantown. People, hang with me on this one.

I know who paid for my campaign. I know who paid for yours. I'm not stupid, but where are your guts? Where's your courage?"

Harry's chest pushed forward and upward as if he were delivering a Puccini aria. His arms moved in circle, and then pointed, alternately grasping the left and right side of his podium. With each athletic jab of the air, pointing to the gallery, to the dais around him, or to the imagined constituency chanting on the steps of City Hall, council members flinched or lowered eyes. His voice wavered in rhythm with the poetic ebb and flow of his prose. His rich baritone bounced off chamber walls, rippled the still air holding up the ornately carved ceiling, and pierced the resistance of every city council member seated in the hall. Those in the chamber audience broke into a standing ovation, led by Harry's friend, Johnny Burns, who was then a Temple University campus radical.

It is still remembered by southern Pennsylvania political junkies as one of the decade's most moving speeches. Philadelphia's City Council that year, however, had a different calling than the one heralded by Harry Morton. It was not to be the year to feed the hungry and clothe the naked, but to protect the pre-election bankroll. Harry forced a roll-call vote. He lost the measure on campaign contribution reform by one vote.

115

"Harry, are you still watching this channel? There are better sports on NBC," asked Roberto only partially looking Harry's way.

"No, go ahead. I'm not really watching, Roberto."

CHAPTER EIGHT

香港

"Heng, thank you, I'll get home on my own. Good night." Wong Xi dismissed her chauffeur after he stopped in front of the Sheraton Hong Kong, across Nathan Road from the Peninsula Hotel. She had spent the afternoon at SRI factories in the New Territories, reviewing manufacturing procedures. She was now meeting Margaret Schultz, a friend who was a deputy at the Asia Development Bank in Manila. Schultz was in town for a conference. She had been a Harvard Business School classmate.

"Do you fully get this case?" Xi whispered to the attractive Indian-looking woman seated next to her in a small lecture hall.

"Actually, I was hoping you or one of these American colleagues could explain the marketing assumptions built into this case. I don't get it either," said Margaret Schultz.

"I'm Xi, by the way."

"Margaret. A pleasure, Xi."

Hours later, at a coffee shop off-campus, the two were still talking. "It's amazing how these Yanks class a whole continent of numerous races and scores of nationalities as 'Asians'," Margaret said.

"Well, they're the next empire," Xi smiled.

"I don't think even the British were this arrogant."

"Might I ask you a more personal question, Margaret?"

"Fire away."

"I noticed you don't sport a ring. Is that because…"

"I'm sure that my experience is not too dissimilar from yours. Indian, I'll even venture to say Asian men, well the ones I've been attracted to, don't fancy a lifetime with a wife who's as accomplished as they are. Am I wrong?"

"Unfortunately, I've noticed the same phenomenon. But, we're young, yet. And, after all, all Asians aren't alike." They laughed like elementary school girls.

For the next two years, the two women became close friends, and maintained at least periodic phone contact since graduation.

She was about ten minutes early. Inside the sumptuous lobby draped with priceless crystal chandeliers and lively teal and gold wallpaper, Xi looked for the rest room. The one she found was down a long shop-lined corridor, and as she opened the door she noted that the last two shops on each side of the corridor were the only ones already closed for the night. After freshening up, she exited the lavatory and checked her watch before heading for the bar on the other side of the lobby. She had five minutes, so she stopped to look at the ladies' fashions in one of the unlit shops.

Suddenly, she was pressed up against the shop window by a very muscular and wide male body. She could barely breathe, but she smelled the heavy garlic breath on her neck as the side of her face was pressed against a shop window.

"Ms. Wong, you close now. Deal will be fine. No more negotiations. If not, you will find out this is a man's game and will get hurt very badly." In the store window, she could see the reflection of a man with a brush cut and unusual scar across his nose. He appeared no more than two inches taller than Xi. Before she could register more details, he shoved her to the ground and left back down the darkened end of the hall.

She quickly got to her feet and thought of following the brute. No, that would be stupid, she realized. She retreated to the ladies' room to check for bruises. The wall mirror revealed a somewhat disheveled and shaking female executive. For a few seconds, fear clutched her throat; her eyes widened and her hands moistened. But fright gave way quickly to anger. She sipped a couple hands full of tap water and carefully washed her face. As she reapplied her make-up and straightened her dress, she tried to put the incident behind her. But as she again approached the lobby, she more carefully surveyed her surroundings, quietly uttering "Bloody bastard. I'll teach that old man to mess with me. I'll cut his balls off and he'll wish for the deal he once had," she thought.

"Hi, Xi. You look so intense. What did I do?" She was standing in front of a bar table near the lobby facing Margaret Schultz.

"Oh, Margaret. You don't know how wonderful it is to see you. Jolly good to see you." They embraced; Xi stepped back. "It's great to see you. I'll have to explain my look. Let's order a drink first." They sat down.

"It feels like it's been ten years. You're now running SRI. I'm now third in line at ADB. Who would have ever thought?" Margaret smiled broadly at her friend. She was a brunette of medium height, with chestnut eyes and an olive complexion whose ethnicity was hard to categorize. In fact, her father had been an Indian-born British civil servant and her mother was a Yorkshire lass of Welsh descent, who'd been a columnist for the *Times of London*. Dressed in a simple light gray suit with a peach silk blouse, she looked the part of the handful of new Asian super businesswoman. A generation ago, she might have aspired to be a TV beat reporter. Western males found her enchanting, but Indian, other South Asian, and Chinese men were wary. She possessed all of the beauty and even more of the natural smarts of her friend, Xi. One difference, however, was fundamental. While Xi was an East Asian who knew a great deal about the West, Margaret was thoroughly a Westerner who knew and loved Southeast Asia.

After the waiter carefully placed down a dry martini in front of Margaret and a B&B scotch in a tumbler of ice before Xi, the friends clinked glasses and drank moderate sips.

"Margaret, do you ever get tired of the climb? Tired of the total commitment?" Xi finally relaxed and smiled slightly at her friend.

"Climb? You've hit the summit. Last time I checked, there was only one other female Tai-Pan in Hong Kong." Margaret gazed seriously into Xi's eyes.

"Some summit. Last week, our guard caught a man trying to burglarize our office. My father is needling me about using Masterfield Consulting on a deal because the lead is an American black man. And, just now, some Hong Kong thug threatens me to get us to cave in on the same deal Masterfield's working on."

She then told her friend about the South China deal, and her suspicions about Xiaobin Li and his tactics. She took fifteen minutes, while Margaret listened intently.

"You remember that American song that we adopted as a theme song to toughen us up at school?" Margaret pushed the olive around with her index finger in the remainder of her drink, and then finished the gin and the olive.

"What? Oh, you mean James Brown's *It's a Man's World?*" She laughed for the first time that night, drawing polite attention from every male sitting at the bar.

"Seriously, I haven't run into physical threats yet, but…"

"My family and I will take care of Mr. Xiaobin's poor manners," Xi quickly snapped.

"Hold on. Didn't the *Wall Street Journal* do an article on this guy when Masterfield bought him out a couple of years ago?"

"Possibly." Xi said.

"Morton. Yes, Morton. Right. I remember. They compared his rise to Reginald Lewis at Beatrice a few years earlier. My advice is to keep him. My gut tells me he'll provide you with sound advice and probably will keep others off balance, just by being who he is. After all, based on that article, he didn't have too much easier a climb than we have to get to where he is. No; played right, he's an ally." Margaret said in monotone, with a laser-like concentration and reassuring confidence.

"Don't forget," said Xi, "I had family help in my climb. You did it all on your own."

"Sounds like your family can be a hindrance when it decides to be. No matter. This guy Morton will prove to be a weapon, I think. Just feminine business instinct." Margaret looked into her glass, smiled and added, "By the way, is the American attractive?"

"Not to your average Han or Brahmin. But, Margaret, to a liberated and worldly soul like you, he's gorgeous."

"To me? How about to my arranged marriage southern Chinese friend?"

"I'll have to admit that it's difficult not to fantasize about him," Xi smiled and took another sip. "But, this isn't London or Paris, Margaret. This is Hong Kong."

"Don't try to tell me with a straight face that affairs don't happen in Hong Kong."

Both women laughed and covered their mouths with their hands, as if they were hiding braces.

"Anyway, legend has it that one very successful, very tough Hong Kong Tai-Pan succeeded even after marrying an English woman," Margaret said.

"That's true, but Momma died early, so I think the Han here were more forgiving and made it possible for Father to rise in trade and banking. Besides, southern Chinese have complex feelings about the Brits. You know that, Margaret." Xi ran an index finger around the sweating tumbler of scotch, as she paused.

"Margaret, do you ever regret choosing the fast track path you're on?"

"Not really. I've led a pretty spiffy existence, I'd say."

"What about marriage? You turned that Yorkshire chap down. Do you ever think back on that?"

"No. Living the life of some wealthy family add-on would be terribly dull, I'm quite sure. No, if I get married, I'll have to be sure I can maintain the sort of freedom I now enjoy."

"It might be difficult to find an Indian man, or any Asian man for that matter who can bear up under such freedom."

"I'm not stuck on an Asian man. It would be preferable, yes. But, I think his personal qualities will be more important than his heritage."

"In some ways, for a split second here or there, I wonder what it would be like to be totally free," Xi mused.

"Neither of us is living the life of a kept woman. Neither have children, yet. Besides, who is ever totally free? Life offers us a series of choices and compromises, with no guarantees. One thing's for certain. Ain't no free lunch, as the Yanks say."

"You're right, of course. Anyway..." Xi finished her scotch.

"I do love seeing you. Let's get dinner and talk about you. Speaking of men, I want all of the latest." Xi paid the bill and the two ladies walked to the hotel dining room.

It was an elegant room, with walls of red velvet, deep brown oak floors polished cherry-wood dining chairs was only partially full, so Xi and Margaret were in the care of a waiter almost immediately. Margaret began to tell her friend of her most recent love interest. She had met a middle aged Delhi native at a banking conference in Singapore where he had been a panelist. She was unfolding a tale of coy courtship when their first course of bird's nest soup arrived.

"This is wonderful," said Xi between characteristically loud Chinese slurps.

"Margaret? Do you see that African couple at the table by the door?"

"Yes, handsome couple. They look Ethiopian," said Margaret barely turning from her soup.

"No, I mean, they were here before us and still haven't been served."

Xi caught the attention of their waiter and carefully asked, "Excuse me, but has that African couple ordered?"

"I believe so. They are insisting on waiting for their meal," whispered the waiter.

Xi's complexion reddened. "You make sure that they are served before anyone else gets another course, or I'm going to the manager. You understand me?"

The stunned waiter rocked back and hesitated, not sure what to do.

"Do you know who I am, Mr. Choi?" Xi strained slightly to read the gold nametag.

"Certainly. Ms. Wong is one of our most honored customers," recovered the waiter.

"Then, you had best treat that couple the same way and quickly." Xi's angry stare could have penetrated steel. The waiter quickly walked to the kitchen.

"What was that about?"

"Chinese prejudice; that's what it is about. The staff must feel that they can take their time with dark-skinned foreigners. It's rude, stupid, and uncalled for."

"Right, I understand your point. But why the big deal? That happens all the time."

"You're right, Margaret. And, occasionally, someone has to call them on it." Xi was somewhat surprised at herself, for she had never challenged public slights before. And, she momentarily reflected on her negative reaction to Morton embracing his 'radical looking' friend, Mr X. Was one situation representative of savvy business caution, and the other lack of common courtesy? She wasn't sure.

Xi was still analyzing her feelings, when she noted that the manager accompanied the food-bearing waiter to the Africans' table.

"Well, at least they know how to try to cover up and fake civility," said Xi while scissoring chopsticks. "I'm sorry. So, what happened after the conference, Margaret?"

"Well, Rajib is a forty year old unmarried economist from Delhi. He has somehow escaped the Indian caste consciousness. Probably because he was raised in Brazil, of all places. He loves to travel, speaks five languages, races bicycles, and is much more interesting than your average economist."

"Is this serious, Margaret?"

"We see each other about once a month. No, not serious. But, there's potential."

"Well, have you traveled together?"

"No, not exactly."

"Not exactly?"

"Right, well we've hung out a bit in London."

"Margaret, you're being awfully circumspect. This does seem deliciously serious."

"Don't worry, Xi. I'll let you know if we become serious." The two friends continued catching up and dreaming about the future deep into the evening.

Saturday night at the Washington Hilton, half the world away, the Mortons were attending the annual dinner of the regional chamber of commerce, known as the Greater Washington Board of Trade. Mary's recent labor studies were read and read about by a significant number of the regionally minded CEOs in the Washington area. She had recently spoken at a few national business conferences, so she was not an unknown figure at the dinner. Harry had been a past officer of the Board, so he greeted and was in turn greeted by scores of business people as if they were long lost friends.

"Mary, you look lovely, as usual. Why do I have to come to these dreadful events to see the most charming and interesting member of the Morton family?" Don Bartram planted a genteel southern kiss on Mary's cheek.

"Why, Don, you just don't get out enough. Is Dorothy with you?"

"She's in the crowd somewhere. Let's sit together at our table and catch up."

"Yes, let's." Mary smiled and moved off toward a bar. She never could truly warm to Harry's boss. She used to try to find a way to like him, for Harry's sake. But his pronounced drawl and reddish complexion and his wife's ultra blond look and exaggerated politeness were hard for her to get past. Mary's reaction bothered her, since she recognized that she was repressing the vision of some stereotypical mint julep swilling Faulkner era bigoted Southern plantation owner and wife. The feeling was similar to that she experienced when white colleagues were extolling the unquestioned magnificence of the film, "Gone with the Wind." The rational econometric Mary reminded her other self that she didn't know the Bartrams anywhere near well enough to assess their motives and prejudices. And, since being true friends with the Bartrams never had been a real requirement for Harry's success at Masterfield, she could easily handle being just socially friendly.

Harry was on his third glass of Chardonnay and at least his twentieth mini conversation before the dinner bell summoned guests downstairs to the ballroom. He was totally at home with the stand-up black tie chitchat, corporate gossip, client schmoozing and prospect networking. It was his element.

"How's it going, Grace?"

"Hey, congratulations on that fabulous fourth quarter, Mike."

"My man, Roger. Glad to see you made it, brother." Harry greeted a mutual friend of his and George Birch's, who had recently been promoted to senior vice president of the local office of one of the country's biggest real estate companies. All three men had long suspected that race was the reason Roger Green wasn't yet regional vice president.

"*Ni hao*. Looking forward to the Chinese New Year at the restaurant, Lee. I have an opportunity that might interest you in Hong Kong." Harry turned to buttonhole the Taiwanese owner of a chain of area restaurants, and a golfing pal.

He had befriended many; he knew databases full of tidbits; he had attended bar mitzvahs, christenings, weddings, funerals, and ceremonies of all sorts. He knew who was comfortable with what sort of banter. Those whose glances might suggest displeasure at his access and facility, who might be jealous, or resentful of this very rich and attractive black man in a predominantly white venue, he noted and often dismissed. This was his movie, and he and Mary clearly had starring roles.

"Fancy meeting you at this impressive table, Mrs. Morton."

"Hello, sweetheart. Your lips must be chapped from so much ass-kissing," Mary whispered as her husband pulled his seat to the table.

Harry felt his hands relax slightly, for the speeches at the podium had begun and attention around the table was on the salad or directed towards the stage. He was out of limelight for now.

"You know, this really ends up being work," he said.

"But you're so good at it," she responded.

"So are you, my dear."

He hadn't always felt comfortable in such settings. Years ago, he had felt rebuffed, insulted, even angered at the coolness with which he had often been greeted by the white moguls of the region. He couldn't tell whether he had changed, whether they had, or both. Slowly, it had seemed he gained the confidence of one CEO after another. As Team Management became successful, prejudice dissipated, or so it seemed in retrospect. As he scanned the darkened room, Harry noted with satisfaction that African Americans could be spotted in every quadrant. Things had changed. The hard stares were now so infrequent that Harry rarely thought of the bigotry he'd experienced early on in his Washington life. He knew, however, that he was not the only actor in this movie. Human emotions permitted no one to achieve success without being detested by someone. Just as there were clients and colleagues, there were surely enemies in the room. Harry was well versed in the stories of black business successes in the seventies that had seen clients mysteriously dry up as they reached the zenith of their industries, ready to eclipse white male competitors. He didn't dwell on it; his discipline forbade it. Harry knew, however, that success in people businesses could collapse like the turn of a lover's favor.

Harry also fully recognized that vicious jealousy and retribution was not reserved for folks of color. The Heatherton Group was the top management-coaching firm in the area for five years. Barbara Heatherton, an attractive white Californian was becoming a regional celebrity for her ability to help politicians polish their TV skills. Her client list was exploding and she attracted the brightest young staff from around the country with apparent effortlessness. Three years ago, however, her business began to mysteriously dry up. She was unable to attract new clients and very successful regulars began canceling. Within six months of her downturn, Heatherton was out of business. By the time she closed her doors the mystery had been solved. Prior to several key congressional discussions, a seventy-year-old conservative politician, who happened to be the head of the House Appropriations Committee couldn't get a Heatherton appointment when he wanted it.

During dinner, Harry and Mary chatted with guests of the firm at their table. Mary paid studied attention to the social chatter of Dorothy Bartram, while keeping a check on any substantive economic or political conversation around the table she was tempted to pursue. Before dessert and the featured speaker, they politely excused themselves, shook a few hands at other tables, and went quietly to a side door. Outside the ballroom, they briskly walked to the front door and Harry paid while an attendant fetched the Porsche.

"You know what I sometimes love about numbers, honey?" Mary asked as the little sports car quickly negotiated the curves of DC's in-town wooded park, Rock Creek.

"No, baby. What?" Harry reached over and squeezed his wife's knee.

"They're truthful, they're binary, and they operate by rules that are predictable and knowable."

"Why Mary. Are you saying that people are not predictable?"

"Interactions are just so exaggerated. It's as if these people feel that some overt display of affection really has meaning."

"Well, it's better than an overt display of hostility."

"Harry, you understand exactly what I'm saying."

"It's just folks having a good time. This need for showy social interaction is why business success can never be reduced purely to numbers, or to interaction over a computer screen."

"It's obnoxious. But, anyway thank you for leaving early."

They drove north silently for a few minutes.

"Sometimes, I wonder if you can ever get back to your core self. The Harry Morton with whom I fell so deeply in love all of those years ago. Is he still in there inside, baby?"

Harry tightened his grip on the steering wheel and just drove for several minutes.

"I think he's still here. Yes, I think so." Harry projected several screens in front of his mind's eye.

Almost simultaneously, he saw his brother Pierce staring at him across a tennis net, challenging a call Harry had just made.

His father put an arm around Harry's shoulder and asked if he thought he would soon tire of playing games and whether he might settle down and study soon.

His mother was seated in front of him in her big high-backed paisley chair, asking if he'd read some poem by Elizabeth Barrett Browning, if he'd let it sink in, or if he'd really absorbed it.

Without realizing it, Harry reached up to his cheeks and brushed away his tears. He felt embraced, connected, and yet very much alone.

"What are you thinking about?" Mary was staring at the slow tears brimming over her husband's eyelids.

"I miss my people, my family, those early days, those innocent and easy times. I sometimes imagine that I can open the front door and they'll all be sitting there in the living room. You never get used to the concept of death, do you? You know, no matter what words you use to describe what happens, where they go, how they're with God, or whatever; they never quite satisfy. I know I'm lucky to have you and Mark, but…"

"I know, dear. I know." Mary thought how much she loved this man when he was genuinely reflective. Yet, in the pit of her stomach she sensed that she would never fully decipher him.

As he opened their front door, Harry whispered, 'It's so strange that I can scan a room of foreigners, listen to their conversation, watch their gestures, catch the smallest crow's foot movement beside an eye and intuit what is happening. Yet, if I hold a mirror up to myself that same intuition often fails. Funny huh?"

"I love you, Harry Morton." Mary stood on her toes and kissed him.

CHAPTER NINE

香港

Almost a week later, Xi placed the *South China Morning Post* on her glass coffee table, stood and walked over to her top-floor, glassed-in view of Victoria harbor. She smiled slightly, for buried on page four of the paper was a brief article about a Hong Kong thug who'd been found floating near the World Com Centre pier off Kowloon. There was no indication of cause of death, but police had easily identified the victim, who apparently had an extensive criminal vitae. She had refused her father's offer of further security, but had accepted his handling the threat from the Xiaobin camp. She, her father, and husband felt that she should press for completion of the deal as quickly as possible. It was clear to them and her most trusted internal advisor, Ho Duang, that Mr. Xiaobin must be given a fair settlement, but that he must have nothing to do with the resulting company.

"You understand, Mr. Xiaobin, that I am no longer able to offer you a substantial position in the merged company. I will, however, increase your personal portion of the new stock." Xiaobin Li had nodded his acceptance to the only business content of a half hour tea with Xi at a restaurant near Admiralty Centre. They had also agreed to meet with their teams after the Saturday races at the Royal Hong Kong Jockey Club. All other exchanges during the conversation had been about food, weather, or the opera.

Xi had had calls placed to her financial, legal, and corporate advisors to meet Friday and be prepared for extensive final negotiations following the races. Prior to flying over for the weekend meetings, Harry, Peter Burke, and Ellen Kwan had read the e-mails and faxed memos from SRI with excruciating care to try and decipher unwritten meaning. The urgency of closing the deal was palpable, as was the notion of finding a satisfactory buy-out for Xiaobin Li. The reason for the urgency was not clear. On the flight, they crammed in news clips and journal articles, but nothing in the international press or in the feedback from sources in Hong Kong or Southern China provided any clue as to why the deal should require immediate closing.

While Friday's briefings at the SRI office were helpful in laying out closing options and clarifying roles for each of the advisors, no light was shed on the underlying urgency.

As Harry and his team prepared to leave the office, Ying Yi, Xi's young and aggressive administrative assistant asked Harry if he could meet with Xi in a few minutes prior to going off to dinner.

"Ellen, Peter, I'll meet you back at the hotel," Harry bade his crew goodbye as they took the elevator down from the SRI corporate suite.

Ying Yi led the way down a long corridor, whose left wall was ten-foot high plate glass that offered a panoramic view of the harbor. Ms. Ying stopped three quarters of the way, turned to face him and gestured that he was to continue down the hall to the well-furnished entrance to the executive suite.

"I think Ms. Wong is already in her office. Please, tell the guard she's expecting you. I look forward to seeing you tomorrow."

"The pleasure will be mine, Ms.Ying," said Harry as he shook the assistant's hand.

The guard in front of Xi's office barely looked at him as he waved Harry through the ante room and on into Xi's office.

"Thank you, Mr. Morton – Harry - for coming."

"No problem. Things seem to be in order for tomorrow, Xi." he took the comfortable leather seat across the coffee table from his client.

"Could I offer you a spot of tea, or a coffee?"

"No thank you. I'm fine."

"Right. Well, do you think things are fine on the deal?"

"Well, we've just gotten back and caught up. The only puzzle I see now is why you seem in a hurry to settle." Harry was distracted slightly from holding Xi's gaze by a reflection in the picture glass behind her. He thought he saw the reflection of an arm raise itself quickly and point towards them. In one quick motion, Harry turned to glimpse the open door reflected in the window and instinctively pulled her to the carpet with his right arm. A vase on the desk that had been behind Harry's head seconds before shattered as a small caliber bullet ripped through it and lodged in the heavy plate glass. Xi and Harry heard steps racing down the corridor towards the elevator before they moved.

"Are you okay?" Harry asked.

"I'll be fine in a minute. What about you?" Xi wobbled as she rose, gripping her chair.

"I'm fine." Harry got to his feet hesitantly, the impact of what had just happened still not fully registering. He walked to the ante-room and out into the corridor beyond the guard desk.

"He must have had the elevator propped. I should have asked you about your guard when I came in."

"What do you mean?"

"Whoever shot at you was wearing your guard's uniform. I sensed something when I came in but assumed the fellow at the desk was from another shift than the one covering when I first came up."

"Harry, you probably saved my life. Thank you. But that shot was meant for you, I'm quite sure."

Harry straightened.

"What happened? I heard some commotion. Where's Han, the guard?" Ying Yi ran into the room.

"We're not sure about Han, but someone dressed like him tried to kill one of us. Call the police." Harry gave orders, assuming command.

"Harry, this is Hong Kong," Xi tried to take control.

"Yes, and this time the authorities should be called."

"Okay, Yi. Please, call the police," Xi acceded.

"I'm a bit shaken. Still. Would you join me in a stiff drink as soon as we straighten up here?" Xi leaned on his arm and turned back to the office.

Harry nodded acceptance and continued surveying the office. He noticed that part of the panel to the left of the guard's station seemed to be sticking out from the wall and the carpet in front of that part of the wall was stained and wet.

"Xi, is that a closet door?" he asked.

"Yes. Why? Oh, no."

"I think we may have found Mr. Han." He walked to the hidden Han, a knife sticking in his throat. He was clothed in boxer shorts and another man's blue suit was thrown over much of his body.

Two hours later, after the Hong Kong police had left the crime scene having asked the bevy of predictable questions, Xi dismissed her assistant and asked Harry if he'd stay for a moment. Harry had worked out his fear and tension from the attack in dealing with the police. He felt strangely relaxed and in command. It was as if the incident were part of some frightening adventure. But an adventure nonetheless.

"I'm sorry for being, what do you say? A *woos*. But, I should have told you before. This is the second attack, or attempted attack. I may have underestimated Xiaobin Li's emotions about this deal. And, I just met with the S.O.B. to reassure him about any doubts he might have."

"Second attack?" Why didn't you tell me? That's the great hurry to close the deal now, isn't it?"

"Yes. Harry, I can't stay here now. Would you mind if I gave you a ride to your hotel? I need to get some air."

"Sure. I've sure had enough of this building for one day."

As they finished straightening up the room, Harry asked, "Why jeopardize the deal? What's Xiaobin got to gain?"

"Perhaps, desperate plans were put in place a long time ago, or…oh, I don't know, exactly."

"You've got pretty good security, here. I'm curious how he got in."

"Harry, I appreciate your analysis, but I can't function, now."

"Sorry. Let's go. This can wait, or your staff will get it."

In the limousine on the way back to Kowloon, Xi told Harry about the attack at the Sheraton. She also told him enough of what followed that he easily understood the fate of the thug. He thought that it didn't make sense that Xiaobin would try to kill Xi so soon after the thug incident, unless the attack had been previously planned and attempts to change instructions has gotten fouled up. No. More than likely, this attack had nothing to do with her partner/adversary.

"So, you think the ex-general is merely escalating the war?" he asked.

"Yes. But I now question the wisdom of retaliation. At least while the deal is still alive."

"Is it alive? What happened to the obligatory return of fire?"

"Perhaps, the tactics of your civil rights movement have merit in Asia. After all, King was a student of Gandhi."

"Right. Where did this philosophical, non-violent thought come from, Xi?"

"Oh, civil disobedience can be quite hard-nosed. It just needs to be economically or politically punishing. And the leader has to have iron-clad faith." Xi said without iron-clad conviction.

"I don't know many business people, men or women, who would be that tough. Well, we're approaching the ferry. Would you still like to come over and have that drink?"

Xi hesitated, looked at her driver in his rear-view mirror, and then asked the driver to take them to Staunton's in SoHo instead of to the Peninsula Hotel.

"Yes, I think I would like that."

The bar was almost empty as both Xi and Harry ordered scotch on the rocks. They toasted to luck and to life.

"You know, I don't really know how you came to Hong Kong, Xi," Harry said above the rim of his glass.

"I was actually born in Shanghai. My mother was a British correspondent when she and my father fell in love in the mid -1950s. All I remember about her is that she was very loving and very pretty. When I was three, she caught yellow fever and died."

"I'm very sorry."

"Thank you, but I've been very lucky. Father was terribly distraught and decided to leave the mainland. He later told me that he just needed to start again and felt that the Communist revolution was likely to strip him of his entrepreneurial opportunities. So, in 1960 we packed up, he closed down his businesses and came to Hong Kong. My aunt Li raised me from the time I was five until I went to Britain to university."

"So, you don't really remember much about your mother?"

"It's odd actually, but I began to wonder more intently about her and imagine what she would have been like after I went abroad. Oxford was my first time in a Western, Caucasian-dominated society. I'd see lovely ladies on the road and imagine them to be my mom. I wish I had known her longer. On the other hand, had she lived and had I been constantly identified as a Eurasian child, life may have been a great deal more difficult."

"Your father is quite a remarkable man. It must not have been easy to have a European bride back then. Even in Shanghai."

"He'll tell you that anything that makes you stand out as an individual in Chinese culture makes life more difficult. But, he has always felt that he was destined to be different. To be different and to excel."

"Well, he has certainly excelled. And his daughter hasn't done badly, herself."

Harry raised his second scotch in a toast.

"Do you want another?"

"I'll just have a glass of tea, thank you."

For the first time in their acquaintanceship masks stayed pulled down and they continued to talk casually and comfortably about each one's upbringing. They noted a common love of and respect for family. Similarly, each had a drive to achieve instilled by their parents that set them apart from many friends. Without detailing the important anecdotes or chronicling the hallmark events, they could see clearly that their tolerance, even interest in foreign cultures also placed distance between them and their "natural" peer group. An hour and a half passed quickly in Staunton's.

"I am so much more relaxed. Thank you, Harry. Maybe if we act as though none of this shooting business has happened, this deal can be put to bed tomorrow. Then, I'll think about how to deal with Mr. Xiaobin Li," said Xi as she stood to leave the bar.

"Maybe after tomorrow, Mr. Xiaobin will be happy enough that you won't have to ever think about him. I must say, however, that I'm not convinced this is his doing."

"That would be a great deal to wish for. Good night, Harry." She extended a firm hand. Harry thought about kissing her on the cheek, but merely smiled and took her hand. He walked her out to Staunton St., which was now lively with club goers, late shoppers, and the hip young adults of Hong Kong. Her driver stood waiting.

"Can we offer you a ride?"

"I think I'll wander around SoHo a bit, thanks. Until tomorrow, Xi."

He walked over the pedestrian escalators going from Central up to the "mid-levels" apartments, on the way up to Victoria Peak. He took the tram down to Central and walked to the Star Ferry. The office building lights faded into the background of the island's hills and framed the street-level color of neon signs, bustling entertainment, food, and urban sounds where the cultures of the world come out to play. The night air was extraordinarily refreshing and Harry allowed himself to marvel at his fortune in being able to inhale nighttime Hong Kong. Not bad work, he thought.

The hustle and bustle of life on the Kowloon side of Hong Kong begins at dawn. Morning scenery includes street-sweeping merchants whisking off the wet sidewalks; men in shorts and tee-shirts squatting on their haunches reading the morning paper; women hanging novellas and journals on the sides of stores like news racks for street libraries; wrinkled women with cigarettes on their bottom lips, carrying rattan baskets full of vegetables; straw-hatted farmers with long bamboo poles across their backs laden with baskets of pig, goat, chicken, even dog parts; and an occasional red double-decker transit bus. Harry absorbed it all as he jogged along the streets and alleys, but he was concentrating on the day's approaching meeting.

While jogging, he thought about the mounting pressure from the SRI side to close this deal. He knew enough, however, not to attempt to force an early conclusion. He had been consultant on enough Chinese deals to remain comfortable with a fairly high level of ambiguity. And he thought the revelations shared last night by Xi, save for the attack itself, were best kept secret for the time being.

As he returned to the hotel, Harry passed a shop window whose mannequins sported gray suits, black shirts and pink ties. "Just like the Jersey Mafia back in the day," he thought. His knees locked and Harry almost fell over in coming to a dead stop.

Triads. Of course, the young Chinese Mafioso. Many Hong Kong business dealings in trade attracted the 'protection' of the territory's increasingly violent gangs. Any misread by an unsophisticated triad leader might cause him to send a 'signal.' Maybe Xi hadn't been the target. Maybe the guard was simply in the wrong place and the next bullet had been meant for Harry. A signal to Xi. Harry was uncomfortable with his speculation, but had no better theory to explain the incident.

He briefed Ellen and Peter at breakfast at the hotel, so that each had time to absorb the seriousness of the proceedings. By the time they exited the elevator to the private boxes atop the racetrack

Late Saturday morning, he felt they were as prepared as possible. His younger colleagues, however, immediately headed for the elegantly clad waiter balancing a tray of champagne glasses. Harry remained 100% sober.

The lobby outside the actual boxes was crowded with elegantly coiffed Chinese and British women and casually suited men from the "soon-to-be-former" colony. One of the first people Harry recognized was a stern-faced Xiaobin Li.

"How nice to see you, Mr. Morton. But, I would have more expected to see you at a baseball game," Mr. Xiaobin offered an exaggerated grin.

"A pleasure to see you, Mr. Xiaobin," said Harry, firmly gripping the general's hand.

"I'll admit that I'm more used to the people's track at Happy Valley. But, we have horse racing in our country, and I'm sure you'd be entertained by the number of people who can afford to attend. Perhaps you are surprised today, because gambling is not as addictive nor compulsive to Americans as it appears to be for *you Chinese*," Harry delivered his retort with a pleasant "gotcha" smile. But as he stared unflinchingly in Xiaobin Li's face, Harry could feel the heat of resentment rising slowly up his belly to his chest.

"That was just a lucky tackle, niggah. You're not smart enough to anticipate our plays, are you?" the Chinese looking fullback for the other high school team had said as he pushed Harry's shoulder pads into the mud beneath the pile of bodies at the fifty yard line. The big, mean kid, David Lee, had missed

his block on Harry, and Central High School's all-city linebacker had dropped West Catholic's star halfback for a two-yard loss.

On fourth down, two plays later, the big fullback took the hand-off and was rumbling around his left end, protected by a big tackle, as he motored toward Central's forty-yard line and a crucial first down. Harry, playing outside right linebacker, sidestepped the blocker and almost knocked the fullback's head through the back of his helmet with the thrust of his right shoulder. When Lee's head hit a hardened spot on the November turf, Harry drove his upper body down on the opponent's helmet. As he heard a groan beneath him, Harry spat into the space between Lee's facemask and chin strap, "Smart enough for your tired yellow ass, chink?"

David Lee's body went limp, the ball fell from his grasp, and Harry rolled on top of the fumbled football.

The cheers, tuba, and bugle on the public school side were thunderous, for Harry's tackle had stopped what was to prove the last and the best drive of the Catholic League's champions that day in 1961's city championship game. But as Harry rose to leave the field, he noticed that Lee lay still stretched out on the turf. Harry's extra jolt after Lee was down had injured the fullback's neck and he lay motionless as West Catholic's doctor rushed onto the field. Harry, still intensely angered and exhilarated all at once, joined his teammates on the sidelines, accepting pats on the butt and "at-a-boys" as he headed for the bench.

"That will teach that slant-eyed mother..." Harry's friend and the team's defensive halfback George Birch growled at Harry.

Ethnic slurs were as commonplace as Philadelphia gang rivalries in the early '60's. While Chinese and Chinese-Americans were a tiny part of the school population, their small numbers didn't shield them from the taunts of blacks,

Italians, or the Irish. Neither George nor Harry actually knew any Asians, nor had they any real intense feelings when not fighting or playing sports.

After five minutes, Harry's adrenaline and his bravado subsided. David Lee continued to lie motionless. After another few minutes, Harry, consumed with fear and guilt, was back on the field standing in the clump of players watching as Lee was carried from the field on a stretcher, moving ever so slightly. David Lee suffered a concussion and severely strained neck.

Harry had to mention the play when telling his brother, mother and father about the city championship that night. Harry's father listened closely and with pride as he asked his son to describe the key plays of the game. He lost his smile, and put down his chicken breast, however, when he asked his son if the play that knocked out David Lee had been clean. Harry first said that there had been no penalty, in half justification.

"Son, I asked you if it was a clean play? Don't play games with me."

"Probably not."

"Probably?"

"No, sir. I went overboard."

The next day, John Morton called the hospital and found that the young Lee was awake and going to be fine. He then told Harry to put on clean slacks and a jacket, because they were going to take the trolley car ride to the hospital to apologize to the youth. The sixteen year-old Harry knew better than to argue.

"You let a little ignorant word like `niggah' hurt you, son? You think it's all right to trash other people the way we get trashed by some of these whites around here, just because he's Chinese? Is that the way we raised you, boy?"

The human rights lesson on that trolley ride seemed endless to Harry. He would rather face any gang in the city than deal with one of his father's moral *lectures. There was no yelling or screaming, just the deliberate, all-encompassing, penetrating delivery of God's truth two feet from his face. The cold walk from the trolley car stop to the hospital did nothing to blunt John Morton's slow burn. They stopped at the front desk, got directions and took the three flights of stairs to the room David Lee was sharing with two white men asleep in various leg and arm casts.*

Harry was relieved to see that Lee was moving in bed and touched that he was genuinely appreciative of the visit. No one else had visited him, not even team members. The big kid's eyes watered as Harry apologized. They talked about the season. They talked about the chance both hoped they would have of going to college. Based on the lack of references in David's chatter, Harry guessed that David Lee had few friends, certainly not many of his white teammates. Over the course of an hour, Harry sensed that he could have a new friend for life, if he wanted. John Morton sat in an uncomfortable metal chair for a while. Then he went off to get coffee and left the two boys alone with the snoring roommates. What for Harry began as an anxious visit gave way to relief, and then to enjoyment. He even thanked his father for making him do "the right thing" on the way home.

Harry's attention returned to the hallway in the Hong Kong racetrack and he was able to calmly carry on a respectable surface conversation with Xiaobin. Both men continued with idle chitchat until they had an opportunity to politely dismiss each other.

"Unless I'm way off, our friend was making a racial dig, not just a cultural one," Ellen said as she raised a glass of champagne to her mouth, while standing slightly behind Harry.

"You're not off. Maybe, he's sore because his goon missed last night." Harry turned to the box and the race, but still simmering over the slight by Xiaobin. He allowed his head to turn slowly and take in the entire box of white and brownish-yellow complexions. Uncharacteristically, he felt slightly out of place. Then he steeled his focus. Xiaobin had obviously intended to make him feel uncomfortable. Back home, as a boy, he might have gotten skittish, allowing that twinge of inferiority to creep into his consciousness, but not a grown Harry Morton, not in Asia. He buried the discomfort beneath layers of self-confidence.

A tall Caucasian eased into the seat next to Harry. "I don't believe we've met, old boy. I'm Rip Drake, from---"

"From the Bank of England, advising South China on the SRI merger." Harry, smile in place, extended his hand to the tanned, blond, investment banker.

"Very good, old chap. I see you're as thorough as your excellent reputation suggests."

"And, I believe the complement is equally applicable to you, Mr. Drake."

"Oh, come now. Call me Rip, please. I'm not much on formality when not addressing royalty," Drake grinned a genuine, gin-soaked smile.

"I understand our clients are anxious to close and move on. Have you also just returned to Hong Kong?" Harry asked benignly, knowing the answer.

"Right. At least you get to work with the most gorgeous CEO in Hong Kong, while we…well, Mr. Xiaobin Li pays well." Another smile. Harry wanted to like this crafty golden Brit, but it would take awhile to distinguish friendliness from inappropriate familiarity, from strategy, from racism. Why racism? Harry realized that Xiaobin's approach still had an unsettling and uncharacteristic lingering effect. Perhaps it was the shooting. Maybe the assailant was instructed to miss. After all, Harry was no James Bond, so a trained killer should have been able to hit one or both of them last night. Now, racism? Harry just hadn't been prepared for a racist dig; so now he was a bit more cautious. And despite his years of practice confronting countless slights and his layers of impressive self-confidence he could not simply enjoy the horses. In any event, he would have to focus on his surroundings and go over the pending meeting while in the boxes.

"He's an Oxford version of a Columbia-trained MBA, and he practiced at KPMG before going to the Bank of England. Smooth," Peter was quietly saying to Harry as they sat in the front row of the box, leaning over the rail.

"Smooth is right. Keep an eye on Rip, Peter. He's your assignment," Harry was now actually enjoying a Chinese beer and focused on the fifth race. More importantly, he was back in control of every level of his being. In between races, he'd had even able to sneak up on Xiaobin Li and offer him a tip on the fifth race. So expertly, and in such perfect Guangzhou dialect that Xiaobin nodded thankfully (as if to an aide) and didn't realize who had offered the advice until Harry had almost returned to his seat two rows in front.

As the horse Harry had studied won by two lengths, Harry turned, and a less stern, almost appreciative Xiaobin Li gave him an appropriate nod of thanks. Harry nodded slightly and was returning his attention to the preliminary activity for the sixth race when he caught a glimpse of Wong Xi, Ho Duan, and one of their Hong Kong attorneys entering a private suite across the lobby from their box.

On instinct, Harry knew he should check with his client one more time prior to the initial meeting after the races. He excused himself from Ellen, Peter, and others in the box and headed first for the men's room. He entered, washed his hands in the obsidian basin, allowed the attendant to dry his hands, accepted a breath mint, tipped the grateful custodian and exited. The horses were being called to the gate, and Harry saw that all attention was on the track, so he approached the private suite. The heavy oak door swung open easily, but before Harry could complete his second step, an unusually tall Cantonese man dressed in the garnet and gray colors of the racetrack approached him. Harry quickly told him who he was and that he had business with his host, Ms. Wong Xi. The doorman asked that Harry wait in one of the gold-embroidered chairs by the entrance.

The vestibule was not large, and he could peer into the main room of the suite. There were three game tables set up, all occupied with mahjong players noisily drinking and busily smoking. Several men looked up, but paid no attention to the tall dark foreigner in the doorway. Harry sat down and picked up a British racing magazine. While glancing through the magazine, he wondered if there was more to the deal and the dangerous events surrounding it that he didn't, but should know. Why he was not invited to this pre-meeting? He thought again about the possibility of triad involvement.

You're being paranoid, he told himself. There's nothing strange about not involving any particular merger and acquisition (M&A) consultant in a given planning meeting.

Harry momentarily convinced himself to relax. He occasionally looked up at the TV monitor whenever the announcer became particularly excited while calling the race. Before the horses could round the backstretch of the mile and a quarter track, the doorman had returned and was motioning Harry to follow him. A few mahjong players acknowledged his passing, but by and large, Harry was recognized as any other non-Chinese rich foreigner entering the inner sanctum of the East's privileged class.

"Please, Mr. Morton," the doorman held the teak door to a brightly painted inner room of the suite.

Ho and Xi were seated around an oblong mahogany table set for four with small plates of some sort of dumplings and a pitcher of half-drunken iced tea.

"Harry, this is good timing. Miles Fung went out to join the other lawyers in the box. I think we're pretty well set for the meeting," Xi was smiling, relaxed and very confident.

"Well, I'm glad that things are lined up. I think these should prove interesting sessions." Harry pulled up to the table in the ornate high backed chair that had clearly not yet been occupied.

"You and Ms. Kwan, actually all of your team, were a big help last night at the prep session," Ho Duan noted, showing no indication that he was aware of what followed the session.

"Harry, you should try the shark fin dumplings. They are quite exceptional here." Xi looked as if she were surveying the room and seeing the paintings set against soft emerald-colored wallpaper for the first time.

"It would be very helpful if you gave us an analysis of how far down we would have to go in South China's organization to be sure that the remaining employees will be able to transfer loyalty to the new entity after the merge." She touched Harry's arm in making the request.

"We can do that easily in the next few days. I think we have a good feel for the management. Of course, I can usually be of more assistance if I know the full detail behind the surface negotiation." Harry held his client's gaze for several seconds.

"Old Chinese proverb states: `Bee without knowledge of danger will not sting,'" Ho said.

"True, but drone without accurate map of hive cannot protect queen." Harry's response brought grins to everyone's face. Xi lifted her glass in a silent toast.

Turning squarely to face her consultant, she reiterated the description of the first attack and her family's decision to pay Xiaobin Li off, finish the deal, and get him out of the picture. She skipped any detail about the retaliation against Xiaobin's thug or much reference to the apparent link with the previous night's attempt. Harry knew he was to act as if this was the first he had heard of the first incident.

"How do you know Xiaobin won't collect his fee and then have some high government official scuttle your end of the deal, or at least make it prohibitively expensive to register all final documents?"

"Good question and appropriately cynical, but all documents will be registered before he is paid in full, and this is still British Hong Kong, so Mr. Xiaobin doesn't have quite the reach he will have after 1997. All the same, we're being extra careful."

"In addition, we think he has clear notion that this Hong Kong Wong knows old customs and can play by old rules, if necessary." Ho knew by the glare in Xi's eyes that he had said too much. Harry quickly realized that Ho had been referring to what must have happened to Xi's attacker, but he remained silent and reached for one of the dumplings with his chopsticks.

"Umm, they are excellent," Morton graciously changed the topic. "Well, I'll see you later. Your background information is safe." "That was, of course, assumed." Xi unfolded, stood, and placed her arm through Harry's as she escorted him to the door. "Perhaps, we'll soon be able to toast to a larger SRI, and celebrate in Western style. We'll see you in a bit, Harry."

There were only two active game tables when Harry walked back out of the suite, but he barely noticed, since he was primarily focused elsewhere. He was more convinced now that there was quite a bit he did not know about the South China deal and about his client.

He settled back into his box seat at the end of the eighth race, giving Ellen and Peter enough of the background to satisfy their curiosity without the definitive details.

"Okay, why don't we skip the last race, go for a walk, and go over our options for tonight?" Harry suggested to his young colleagues.

"Good. This afternoon sun is brutal, today. And, I've seen enough of horses and listened to enough 'Old Boy' and 'Sterling Chap' chatter to last for awhile." Peter sprang from his seat and led the threesome to the elevator. They got off at the mid-level concourse and walked to the outer ring. They rested by an exit whose concrete pillars were spaced wide enough to offer a wonderful view of lush green hillsides offering partial glimpses of colorful roves and balconies on 20th century mansions.

"We're on the organization structure committee. SRI will offer South China one or two insignificant positions, but neither Xiaobin, Yao, nor Yi will get anything worthwhile. The new company is to be *SRI prime*. Personnel analysis and initial team building we did is almost for naught. We have to figure out whom to offer a slot below the top management level to allow South China to save some face," Harry said.

"Harry, how about V.P. for New Markets?" Peter offered.

"That's good. I like that. What do you think, Ellen?" Harry turned towards the concourse as club members and guests walked by towards the exit gate.

"Well, we could design a Deputy CFO slot, which has little more than title."

"Good. See, my sense is that the Guangzhou crew knows that the best they get now is cash. I'm just not quite sure why they don't bag this deal and look for another buyer." Harry openly wondered.

"My guess is, looking at the kind of deals in this marketplace; there may not be another opportunity this lucrative for a long while. They are already the largest dry goods outfit in the southern part of China. I think it's SRI or nothing for longer than a bunch of sixty-year olds want to wait," Peter said.

"Ellen, I have a feeling that SRI may be dealing with more than one interested party in this deal. When you get a chance, see if you can find any triad connection," Harry asked in a flat monotone. "Triad? These parties are tough, but they seem totally above board to me," she said with a start.

"All the more reason to check. Remember, many a foreigner has jumped at a false illusion to his own peril in China. We may be making some naïve assumptions."

"Thank you both. Let's go have this first session. I don't know about you two, but I'm ready to be treated to some exquisite imported Nanjing cuisine." Harry had already taken a long stride towards the exit that would allow them access to club level elevators. The late afternoon meeting and evening banquet were to be held on the top level, above their box seats.

Reaching the small foyer of the club level, Ellen and Peter entered a decorative splendor approached only by the lobby of the Peninsula Hotel.

"Wow, this is like a miniature Kennedy Center or Carnegie Hall. The drapes, vases, oils..." Ellen's mouth hung open.

"This is what I'd call a `club.' And you seem to be popular, Harry." Peter noticed the stares Morton drew in this rarified setting. Harry felt a bit strange. Not uncomfortable, but not fully in control and definitely on display.

"This is not the Board of Trade annual dinner," he muttered, basically to himself.

"Well, let me open my mouth to a stranger or two, so they can get over me *not* being British or Australian," Peter laughed and cheerfully headed for a tray of hors d'ouevres.

"Here comes my favorite CFO, Yi Li," Ellen warned Harry, as her body stiffened slightly.

"Miss Kwan, were our most mediocre Chinese races of some entertainment for you?" Yi's face did not betray the intensity of his sarcasm.

"But Hong Kong races are of world class fame. And well deserved. Yes, I thoroughly enjoyed the afternoon, thank you." Ellen smiled with girlish enthusiasm.

After a small chat with Harry, Yi excused himself and sought Peter.

"Well, the mainland folks still love Koreans," Ellen's quiet sarcasm could only be heard by Harry.

"That's what that was about? I have a funny feeling our colleagues think they can gain some sort of advantage by their equivalent of 'playing the race card.' Ignore the comments, as you did." Harry confidently advised his protégé. Strangely, Ellen's encounter had relaxed him and given him back the full focus Xiaobin had been able to pierce earlier.

The American team located their SRI counterparts, chatted about the races, and soon moved towards the meeting rooms set up for the various work groups: debt finance, equity, public relations and marketing, organizational structure and legal.

"This seems like a lot of ceremony and expense when most of the decisions in this deal are done," commented Peter Burke as they passed the debt finance crowd and headed down a hall to mostly observe the discussion on structure orchestrated by Ho Duan. Wong Xi was starting the critical equity session across the table from Xiaobin Li as the Americans passed.

"You can tell we're approaching the end of a deal," Harry noted as he and his colleagues took their seats among the fifteen participants assembled around a circular table.

"How so?" asked Peter.

"Tea, salted plums, dried vegetables. The bare minimum for food. You saw how Duan took our position suggestions a few minutes ago with barely a grunt. This will be relatively short, if not sweet."

"Comrades, I hope that you all enjoyed the races. We were pleased to see a few surprise winners. Perhaps all of the colts did not understand their roles for today." Ho Duan opened the session, and the table shook from the laughter of those assembled. Roberto Higgins would have been impressed.

Ho Duan took half an hour to lay out the basic proposed structure for the new organization, including the two positions Ellen and Peter had devised a mere few minutes prior to the meeting.

"Mr. Ho, you have been gracious in hosting this day. We have enjoyed your company and that of Mr. Morton and his colleagues. Do not insult us, however, with this shell of an organization. Your proposal offers Southern China no positions of power in the new organization," Yao Lanxin said while smiling directly at Ho Duan.

Ho wanted to ask Yao if he had been informed or if he had merely forgotten about the consequences South China now had to absorb due to their stupid aggressive threats. He resisted, however.

"It has been our pleasure to entertain our honored cousins from Guangzhou, and I can assure you that no slight was intended by our proposal," Ho Duan responded.

"Given the capitalization and the responsibilities in the revised business prospectus, the structure seems fair," Harry chimed in. He noticed that Ho Duan stared straight ahead, a signal that Harry may have inserted himself too early in the discussion.

"Is SRI now letting foreigners speak for them on major decisions? " Yao asked, maintaining his eye contact with Mr. Ho only.

Harry winced. He noticed the ochre pallor of Mr. Yao under the dim light and found himself flashing on old Charlie Chan movies and the buck-toothed Hollywood caricature of the stereotypical "Chinaman" of the fifties. He frowned at his own bigotry and then refocused on the bargaining table, and the tactics being employed.

Ho was speaking, "Quite frankly, we thought it obvious that your firm no longer desired traditional partnership when Xi was approached." Having now referred to the threats Xi had gotten, Ho tapped his finger on the table, a signal for Harry to return to the structural issue. However, as he began to restate the positions, Harry was cut off again by Yao Lanxin.

"In the West, it may be appropriate for consultants to present major positions, but in China---"

"Perhaps my cousin has not kept up with the times, for it is common in MODERN Asian business dealings to allow consultants to speak on behalf of the firms. Particularly when the consultants are as distinguished and accomplished as Mr. Morton," Ho firmly interrupted. He continued as his South China counterpart reddened, recognizing his major miscalculation. "Perhaps South China wishes to find a negotiator more comfortable with modern business."

"Of course, we shall follow procedures as you wish," said Yao.

Harry proceeded without further interruption. South China agreed to consider the organization proposed and the group broke for dinner. As Harry and Yao shook hands before leaving the room, the American revealed no hint of the fiery anger that burned inside. Recalling David Lee, he convinced himself that slights were not personal, merely part of "the game," and turned to the other negotiators. He appeared to all in the room the picture of composure, as if the intensity of the last couple of hours' negotiations had never materialized. He was in control.

Prior to dinner, the SRI team huddled. Things were proceeding apace except for South China's new insistence, in the financial group negotiations, that another five million dollars be added to the price. It was not a great sum, except when added to previous concessions. The number was now significant; because it could mean that SRI might have to absorb loses for six months after the merger. It was a deal-breaker. All SRI consultants advised the financial team to toe the line. Financial negotiations, which SRI had thought all but settled prior to the day, made no headway. The parties concluded all other aspects of the deal by dinner and agreed to reconvene the financial negotiations at one on Wednesday afternoon, leaving a few days to rest and regroup.

The SRI team was chauffeured back to their offices. As they passed brightly lit docks along the harbor, Harry pointed out the loading process for mammoth commercial vessels. Peter and Ellen both lowered their windows to get better views of the activity. The warm night air was pungent with ginger, as baskets of the spice were loaded onto lorries. Some sections of the docks revealed bolts of brilliant silk, or boxes of fresh cut tea, or pallets piled high with camphor-wood furniture bound for the foyers and dining rooms of the nouveau riche.

"We're passing by twentieth century Hong Kong. What you see over on Kowloon- cell phones at every ear, fax machines in every merchant's stall, Rolls-Royces as common as Toyotas- that's the dawn of 21st century Hong Kong and southern China," Harry commented. The trip to the office provided a time traveler's transition from the Jockey Club's Qing Dynasty opulence to the simple, spare, Scandinavian modern interior of SRI's suite.

"It's as if Yi Li suddenly has all of our numbers. The meeting was uncanny. He continued to negotiate just outside of our threshold," an annoyed Wong Xi sputtered, seated at her coffee table later that evening.

Ellen couldn't focus on the deal. "This is eerie; sitting in this office, one day after the killing. It's hard not to think about the guard, the shooting. I'm sorry. Have the police found anything?"

"No, my little sister. And they probably won't find anything useful," said an avuncular Ho Duan.

"Could that be possible?" asked Harry, holding a scotch.

"Could what be possible?" Ho Duan responded.

"Is it possible that they've acquired your confidential financials?" Harry set down his glass and dropped his head into cupped hands in an effort to ward off late night weariness.

Xi's head shook in emphatic rejection of the notion.

"Think about what's happened. Someone knows Xi is going to have a drink at the Sheraton. Somebody anticipates our meeting last night in this office. And Li's team gets right to the edge of the deal of a lifetime and plays greedy hardball with the `right' numbers. Bogart would say 'That's a lot of coincidences,'" said Harry, his mind now racing over possibilities.

"You're right. But, that's pure Hollywood." Xi smiled at her associates for the first time in what seemed like days. "Final agreements are not easily cemented in China."

"Then what's a more logical theory?" Harry pursued his point.

"Burke, you were in the debt finance meeting. What do you think?"

"I think we need to sleep on this whole thing, boss."

"Smart man," agreed Ho Duan.

"Okay, let's head across the water." Harry rose and the team said good night.

"Harry, please let Wu Heng give you a ride. He has to go through the tunnel, anyway," offered Xi.

"If you drop us at the ferry that would be fine. The night air will do us good, Heng," Harry said as the whole party headed for the elevator.

After midnight, far across Victoria Harbor at the office of South China's lawyer, Yi Li held out a glass of spicy Hong Kong rice liquor in a toast to a grinning Xiaobin Li.

"I believe our part Western flower is beginning to wilt under the intensity of the Chinese sun."

"My good comrade I believe we see a marvelous conclusion to this amusing game." The older man returned the toast.

"Of course, it is you, Wang Ren that we all must toast. Your information is impeccable." Xiaobin Li had turned to address the casually clad thirty-something Cantonese employee, whose face bore only a slight resemblance to that of his first cousin, Wong Xi. The old army general didn't yet fully trust that Wang Ren was a mature and trustworthy confidant. The young man lacked Army-honed discipline and was too eager, thought Xiaobin. He winced as the informant absorbed the attention, smiled at each company officer, and bowed an inappropriately long time.

Meanwhile, at the Peninsula, Harry reclined on his bed. "How's Mark doing, baby?" Harry spoke slowly and carefully into the phone.

"We're all doing fine. When are you coming home?" Mary Morton asked her husband, as she looked out of her office window onto a bright Massachusetts Avenue in downtown Washington. "Harry, I thought you said you were about finished with this deal."

Harry wasn't so tired that he didn't recognize and resent his wife's annoyance. He wondered how much detail to give her. "We all thought it would be over by now. The other side is much more clever and persistent than we'd imagined. I still think I'll be on a flight by Thursday or Friday. I'm sorry, baby."

"Harry…? Never mind."

"What? What is it?"

"Nothing. Just hurry back, please. Bye- bye."

"Goodnight, baby."

He placed the receiver in its cradle and closed his eyes. Mark popped into his head, smiling and saying, "I'm so glad you're back, Daddy. Let me tell you what's happened at school."

Harry drifted off to sleep.

"Did you hear that noise, Mary?" Harry whispered to his wife. Mary Morton's breathing remained steady and her sleep deep.

He reached over and gently shook her shoulder. She mumbled half consciously, "What is it, darling?"

"Do you hear that rumbling or growling out front?"

"No, dear, but you can check it out if you'd feel better."

Harry sat listening, and for a few moments only heard the rustling of maple leaves in the backyard, outside the bedroom's partially opened window. He knew, however, that he had heard something else.

"I'll be right back," he said, stepping out of bed and into his robe and slippers.

Downstairs, he spied through the peephole in the solid oak front door. He saw nothing out of place on the brightly lit front porch. As he continued to stare, however, he heard the growling sound again. He grabbed a sturdy umbrella from the vestibule stand, turned the lock and slowly opened the door. As soon as the door cracked open, the noise stopped.

He stepped onto the porch, pulling the door closed behind him. The night air was mild for a Washington summer's evening, yet he felt a chill traverse his spine. Harry looked carefully at the details on the porch and in the yard as he stepped away from the door. Three foot Chinese porcelain Foo Dogs sat quietly on each side of the door; brightly colored pansies in wooden flower boxes that bracketed the porch seemed partially alert in the early morning stillness; and the azalea bushes adorning the garden path down to the front steps moved only slightly in almost imperceptible breezes. The motion detector lights on each corner of the Victorian were off, so nothing had recently moved around the side of the house.

Standing in the middle of the garden path in his robe, with an umbrella in his right hand, he felt a little foolish. Harry smiled and relaxed.

He turned to retrace his steps back to the house and the night changed. A fierce, wild cadence of growls came from two animals crouching on the front porch. The three foot high Foo Dogs were now larger beasts which looked like a mutant lion-pit bull combination. They were no longer porcelain, but pulsating flesh and bones. As long as he stood still, however, the animals remained on the porch and only moved their ferocious jaws. He took a couple of steps, pointing the umbrella like a sword. The animals began to descend the porch, heads pointed in different directions. "They're going to try to surround me," he thought.

He stopped moving and they stopped. His mind raced and he realized that the animals were acting like the mythological Chinese door gods that are painted on Hong Kong houses to protect the inhabitants from evil ghosts. "They are protecting Mary and Mark," he thought. "But why from me?"

He hoped he could wake his wife, son, or neighbors, but so far the only living creatures taking note of his presence were the animals. Minutes passed while he thought. Then, he decided to go on the attack himself, hoping to attract human attention. He stood erect; pumping up his muscular frame, then crouched, took a deep breath, let out a loud yell, and charged. The animal to his right sprang at him as he reached the first step of the porch, but Harry's umbrella caught the massive head with a vicious swipe, and it fell whimpering to the ground.

"Fool," he spat, plunging the umbrella into the animal's neck. Within seconds, he was again mounting the steps. As he landed on the top step and reached for the door, he heard a deafening roar, felt steamy dog's breath on his neck, and turned left into the cavernous mouth of the second animal.

167

"No," he yelled and sat up in bed. His body was soaked with sweat, but Harry was happy to have escaped his dream. He looked around the bedroom. He was not at home in Washington, but still in his Hong Kong hotel room.

"Don't try to figure it out now. Sleep," he mumbled to himself as he dozed back off.

CHAPTER TEN

香港

The phone rang at 7:30AM. Harry rolled over and noticed that he still had on his white shirt from Saturday's meeting.

"Hue," he muttered the Chinese greeting.

"Morning Mr. Morton. Do you have afternoon plans?"

"Xi? Is that you? What are you doing calling? What time is it?" He opened his eyes just wide enough to see the digital numbers on the alarm clock.

"Well, I was just wondering if you would mind accompanying me on a little light shopping errand to Stanley. It's a small village..."

"I know what Stanley is." Harry wondered about the invitation.

"Harry, are you still there?"

"Sure. I'd enjoy that. But, don't you have family obligations?" Harry asked.

"My husband has deserted me for a business trip. I have a serious shopping itch."

"Okay. I just wanted to be sure. Great. So, where and when should I meet you?"

"I'll be by at about ten thirty, okay?"

"Fine, I'll be in the lobby. Better yet, why not have your driver drop you and I'll drive. I've rented a car, but haven't had a chance to feel the road since I've been here. Is 10:30 still good?"

"You're on."

He got out of bed and laid a newly laundered mint-colored short-sleeve shirt and a pair of navy linen slacks on the bureau. He then pulled on his running shorts and an old University of

170

Pennsylvania tee shirt and laced up a well-worn pair of Adidas running shoes. For about thirty minutes he jogged leisurely up Canton Road, across Jordan Road, around the Kowloon Cricket Club, and back down Nathan Road to the hotel. Eyes wide open; he occasionally looked over his shoulder to see if he was followed. Before returning to the hotel, he stood for several minutes and merely looked out at the harbor.

He wanted to believe that the difficulties South China seemed to present the deal were ultimately nothing out of the ordinary. But, he knew that was a wish. The shooting attempt was an extraordinary event for this moderate level of a deal. He was convinced, however, that he would soon be back in Washington perusing e-mails, catching up with colleagues, and selecting his next interesting assignment.

Mr. Ding was not on the door when Harry reentered the hotel, so he proceeded to the elevator and headed to his room. As he dressed after a long shower, he noticed that the shirt he had laid out on a pair of pants was turned with the collar touching the bottom of the trouser cuffs. He never arranged his shirt and pants that way. By habit, Harry always laid the shirt collar over the pant belt. He checked his wallet, lying on the bedside table. Nothing was missing. The jackets, slacks, and suits in the closet, however, had clearly been moved. Someone had searched his room while he was running. They had not been looking for money. He checked his briefcase and turned on his laptop. Papers had been moved, but nothing had been taken. He could find nothing out of order with the computer.

He finished dressing, and decided not to mention the event to Xi, nor to his own staff. He would wait to see if any party tipped its hand with information that could only have been obtained by rifling his papers, e-mail, or the few memos he kept stored on his hard drive.

As they drove over hillside roads and around sharp two-lane bends, Harry and Xi reflected on the magic of the lush green rock once thought hospitable only to pirates.

"All right, without thinking, tell me, what's your favorite city?" he asked her as he looked out at azure harbor.

She didn't respond, but inhaled the floral fragrances of hillside vegetation. Smiling as she pushed back in her seat, she said "Next to this? Paris."

"I'll buy that."

"And what about you, Mr. Morton? What's your favorite?"

"Right here because of the complexity and the contrasts. It's Confucian, yet Christian, Buddhist, Muslim, and atheist simultaneously. It harbors the fabulously rich and the terribly poor. It's the confluence of east and west, north and south. Americans tend to lump Eastern people as Asians, but Hong Kong sparkles with Malays, Indians, Vietnamese, Japanese, Koreans, Aussies, Brits and, of course Chinese. You can listen to canto-rock music or discordant (to me) Chinese Opera. You can slurp noodles or scoop rice. Over there, you see the horizon has elegant estates and rooftop slums. Soon, it will be capitalist and communist. And it all works. What more could you want for a short vacation?"

"You are quite observant, Mr. Morton," Xi said, smiling.

"Ah, we're pulling into Stanley," he said, recognizing a beach just outside the village.

"Right. A few minutes straight on, there's a gravel lot. Do you know it? If you park there, we can walk down through the shopping streets."

He parked the rental car under one of the few shade trees on the lot's perimeter and they walked toward a small side street.

"Why don't you start looking on the main street, I mean lane, or path, or whatever? I need to pick up a couple of tee shirts for my boy right here. I'll catch up," Harry said, standing in front of one of the first stores near the parking lot and across the street from sunlit outdoor stalls.

"Right. I'll stay in the shops on the left." She waved, more like a schoolgirl excited to be in a department store than one of the East's most powerful women off to do some boutique shopping.

Harry spent about ten minutes negotiating his purchases, and then exited the tee shirt shop, walked down the path to the village's main thoroughfare. He strolled along the main lane lined with awnings overhanging the narrow sidewalks. Every variety of shop spilled out onto the sidewalk, as well as the occasional refreshment alcove to assuage the thirst of the weary shopper, or shopper's companion. Stanley's busy early 20th century feel, street design, mix of merchandise, colors and sounds offered visitors a leisurely alternative to Hong Kong's glassy modern central shopping district.

Although Harry sauntered at a leisurely pace, he soon caught sight of Xi no more than fifteen yards in front of him. He stopped to admire her in a way he would never permit himself to do while "on business."

"Go ahead, Xi. Where'd you get those moves?" He stood watching her full western hips sway to the hip-hop beat filling the air in front of a Malaysian clothing store. Hardly anyone else on the crowded street paid any attention to the American English being spoken above the din of Cantonese, Mandarin, Hindi, Australian English, and other tourist languages spoken.

Xi turned and smiled at him. The sun caught a glint off the frame of her jet-black sunglasses. Dressed in western jeans, sandals, and a loose purple cotton sweater, she was not recognizable as one of the island's most photographed executives. She could smile and relax.

"Do you realize that it's been years since I came over here to shop?" she shouted over her shoulder.

"How long has it been since you've swayed like that?" he asked, grinning.

"Are you making fun of my non-Chinese hips? I'm sure these come directly from my mother."

"She must have been quite a lady. You know, I don't believe I've seen you smile this much, since I have met you," continued Harry as he reached forward and gave Xi's slender left hand a squeeze.

"I almost forgot how wonderful it is to be anonymous, to blend in with the crowd. No one knows you, and no one cares. It's liberating."

He almost agreed, but he was still conscious of anybody who looked like they might be paying too much attention. Only when the deal was finished did he think he would fully relax. Hotel room break-ins, shootings, ubiquitous photographers were almost enough to make Harry buy a supply of Rolaids. No matter how he decided to deal with the tension, his experience warned that Xiaobin Li and his minions were not to be trusted. Corralling his impulse to tell Xi about the hotel room break-in, Harry willed himself to relax more. He wanted to fully enjoy the outing. He took a deep breath, but as he and Xi looked in the window of a South Asian women's clothing shop, he felt eyes on the back of his neck.

"Harry, I simply have to go in here," she said with excitement, stepping into a small shop with dresses hanging from a suspended wire; sweaters piled neatly on counters against two walls; and shawls, wraps and other silk items draped over stained wicker furniture in the middle. The aisles were filled with the light vapor of sandalwood incense. She was swallowed into this ten by thirty foot world of colors and materials.

Before following, Harry turned. He still felt someone watching them. He could see two teen-age girls staring and giggling in front of the store across the lane. He smiled at them, turned to enter the store, and thought to himself, *some of us cannot fully blend in."*

Before he could get through the door, the two girls had crossed the path and one was meekly addressing him, "Excuse me, but are you Bryant Grumble, of American news TV?"

Harry turned quickly, aggressively. When he saw their starstruck gazes, he calmed and smiled.

"No, I'm not Mr. Gumble. He's very short. But thank you for asking," he smiled.

The girls giggled, said "Sorry," and ambled back across the street.

"You handled that very nicely. I couldn't tell what you were going to say from your first expression," Xi said, putting her arm through Harry's and guiding him to a rack of flowing silk dresses.

Harry looked at the silks, but his attention was primarily on his gorgeous escort.

"You should try on that aqua piece with the orange fish. I think you'd look nice in it."

"What a perfect idea, Mr. Morton. Would you hold this?" She handed him her bag as the shop salesperson asked her if she needed the dressing room.

"Your lady very pretty," said the saleswoman, a dark brown, slimly built Filipina.

"Why, thank you, but she's just a friend."

"You like to sit? I can bring chair." She appeared overtly flirtatious.

"I think I'll stand and continue looking around. Thank you." The shop's lack of ventilation made it hot and close. He wiped sweat from his brow as he surveyed a rack of dresses he'd already seen.

"Okay, maybe I'll sit a moment."

The clerk almost knocked him over trying to shove a chair under him.

Harry smiled and her eyes and mouth opened in further delight. The dressing closet curtain opened and Xi stepped back out.

"Man, I'm glad this deal is almost over," Harry said with a wide grin.

"You don't like it?"

"It's a knockout. I don't think I could concentrate easily on business if you walked around dressed like that too often."

"I'll take it, please. And wrap it up with one of those green silk scarves, please," Xi spoke quickly in Cantonese.

"Sorry?"

"Try English, Xi. She's Filipina," offered Harry.

"Oh, I beg your pardon." She repeated her request.

Outside, she repositioned her sunglasses. "I'm usually sensitive to accents and ethnicity. That's embarrassing." She looked down an alley at another store.

After another forty-five minutes of shopping, Harry had bought some more tee shirts for Mark and a blouse for Mary. Xi had purchased a pair of casual shoes, and they had covered most of the main shopping street.

"Man, I could use a drink. How about you, Ms. CEO? I know a great bar in Aberdeen. You game?"

She stared at him for several seconds impassively, and he couldn't see through her glasses to gauge her expression.

"We have a little cottage above Repulse Bay that's stocked, and I could fix you an early light Cantonese dinner. After all, you have allowed me to have such a wonderful afternoon."

A drop of sweat forming on Harry's back became a stream running down his spine to his belt. *Can I really do this?* He wondered. *What about Mary? Then again, it's just a dinner. Will it make me feel differently about Xi, the deal? Be a man; it's a fling. That's what George would say. You're in your fifties, for God's sake. What's the big deal?*

"Lead on Ms. Wong."

Forty minutes later, Xi stood on a mountainside balcony that was shaded by hanging, crimson `bleeding hearts,' through whose leaves they could view the horizon over a deep blue South China Sea. The late afternoon sun intensified the tones of the floral rainbow on the hillsides visible to the right and left.

"This is the best scotch I've had in years. First the shopping, this phenomenal setting, your taste in scotch, cooking. You are quite an unfolding mystery, Ms. Wong," He lifted his glass in a toast.

She returned the toast standing too close for Harry not to feel her warmth. He kissed her softly on her parted lips. She put an arm around his neck and kissed him again, emitting a moan. Both were quickly excited by the touch of a prospective lover who was considerably younger and more muscular than their spouses.

Harry easily lifted her in his arms and carried her into the bedroom. Her cotton sweater ruffled her silky hair as he lifted it above her head. Harry stared at the hardening olive-colored nipples as his tongue slowly stroked her breasts. He inhaled deeply her sandalwood scent. They explored each other like adolescents experiencing new and novel pleasures. Xi's hips began to grind against Harry's pelvis well before he reached down to pull off her scant panties. She stroked his erection with a gentleness that teased every vein. They made love on the sheets, under the sheets, and even on the pillows; sometimes instructing, other times exploring, but constantly pleasing until they drifted off into exhausted sleep.

Xi woke first, showered, slipped into a pink silk robe and began retrieving cold delicacies from the refrigerator.

"What a day. You're quite a lover, Xi," said Harry as he arose and headed for the bathroom.

"I left a towel for you on the hook behind the door," she said, pouring herself a glass of wine.

Darkness had descended when they sat down to a light dinner of cold Cantonese meats, fish and dumplings.

"Xi, let me ask you a business question." Harry's skin still tingled from his cool shower as he leaned against the rail of her balcony, sipping a cool Australian chardonnay. "Who has access to your private calendar?"

"Must we return so soon to business, Harry?" she asked while nibbling and kissing his ear.

"I know. I don't want to be a killjoy, but let's trace out one thing." His expression was serious, with no hint of the enjoyment he'd experienced.

"You think we're being watched?" The warmth left her face.

"Well, that's possible, but I'm thinking about the encounter I had after we had that lunch months ago. Your close call in the hotel hallway. And Yi Li's improbable grasp of our numbers."

She stared into the night.

"The only one is Yi, my assistant Ying Yi. But, I can't imagine any scenario…Well, if her family were threatened. That's about the only situation…"

"There may be some other motive. Let's list them: jealousy, revenge, a life threat, love---"

"Love? How could that be involved? Wait, wait. It's remote."

"What?"

"Last year, Yi had a crush on my devilish cousin, Wang Ren."

"Devilish? How?"

"Well, my husband took pity on him and asked me to give him a job. Ren had been bounced out of several firms for immature behavior, doing stupid things. He just never stays serious enough to focus on work. He once changed the voice message on an office's phone system so that callers thought they had reached a massage parlor, instead of a financial institution. He was fired. Anyway, we still gave him a shot, but had to gracefully have him leave after nine months."

"Gracefully?"

"Yes, I arranged for him to be offered a sales job with a travel agency. I then made it clear to him that it was an offer he should accept."

"And he went willingly?"

"Oh, yes. He knew that it was the best way to save face for all of us."

"Where is he now, still with the travel firm?"

"I really don't know. I must admit that I haven't thought about him. But he did spend a little time with Yi before he left. She was rather smitten, I think."

"Xi, can you track him down? I have a feeling your cousin is very much still involved with SRI."

CHAPTER ELEVEN

香港

"It's been a most unexpected and lovely evening, Max," Mary Morton said as she lightly returned the kiss of her old friend.

"This is just the second time I've seen you in fifteen years, and I feel like the time when we were all together back in Philadelphia was yesterday. You're just as fascinating and as gorgeous..."

"Okay, Max. I really have to go in and relieve the baby sitter."

"Is it all right if I call you when I come back to the States?"

Max Dupree slowly released his grasp of Mary's waist.

"You know, Max. I have a family. And---"

"And I envy Harry and your son. My intentions are above board, Mary. I'd just like to see you again. Old friends," Max said.

Mary thought for a very quiet minute.

"If you like. Goodnight," Mary had to avert her eyes from his stare.

She closed the door behind her, but leaned against it with the back of her shoulders, smiling up at the cathedral ceiling. After she heard the taxi pull off, she took a deep breath.

The sitter came down the stairs, reported that Mark had gone to bed two hours ago. Mary thanked and paid her, and watched the teenager walk down the block and across the street to her house. She carried her briefcase from the hall to the first floor study, emptied its papers on the desk and sat for a moment. She had cleared her mind of early evening events when the phone rang.

"Mary? It's Mabel. Listen, George and I have tickets to the Redskins game on Sunday and thought you and Mark might want to go."

"Oh, Mabel, that's nice of you to think of us, but---"

"Good. We'll pick you up at ten-thirty. A little outdoor yelling will do you good, and you know Mark will love it." Mabel knew she wouldn't get strong resistance.

"Okay. Yeah, that would be nice. Well, good---"

"Wait a minute, girl friend. So, how's the job? What's happening in life? Tell me something."

"The job's fine. Nothing else." Mary sighed slightly. "Oh, you remember Max Dupree from Philadelphia?"

"Remember? Girl, I'm not that old, nor that married. Of course I remember that fine, fine brother. Didn't he move to Europe, though?"

"Yes. Well, he's in town and we had dinner tonight. Nothing but two old friends, but I---"

"But you found yourself wondering what it would be like. Well, good for you." Mabel Birch almost sounded indignant.

"It's nothing like that. It just felt good to talk to a friend like that and not feel any pressure to get home, to get to a meeting, to go to a school event for my baby. I don't know. It was comfortable."

"Yeah, I'll tell you what would be comfortable with Monsieur Max Dupree."

"No, seriously, I just---"

"I *am* serious. You can't tell me that you only enjoyed talking to the brother."

No one spoke for a long minute.

"He is still fine. I admit that," Mary finally said.

"We'll talk at the game. Sweet dreams, girlfriend."

"Goodnight, Mabel, and thanks for the tickets."

Mary decided not to read any economics papers and went upstairs to run a warm bubble bath. She just wanted to soak and be with her thoughts. Mark had recently reached some accommodation with the Byrd boy, Bobby. So he was much more productive at school, and Mary had had one less worry for the last few days. The soft water relaxed her. The heat and mild fragrance of the bubble bath soothed her. Mary didn't think about her up-coming labor economics conference. She wasn't thinking about her sleeping son, or her distant husband. She imagined scenes of London, and thought about seeing Max Dupree again.

CHAPTER TWELVE

香港

"Harry, sorry to call so early. I've been able to track down Wang Ren. You're right. He has been working for South China. If you don't mind, I'd like to get your team and Duan together away from the office to figure this out." Wong Xi spoke quietly but firmly into the phone.

"How about a business suite at the Hyatt Regency here on Nathan Road?"

"Good. What about ten o'clock?"

"Perfect. We can set it up."

Xi didn't tell Harry about some of the other complications that were adding stress to the situation. Ho Duan had received an envelope with indiscernible photo negatives and a note promising "interesting" shots of the SRI CEO later. She had also developed a slight rash on her arm that her husband had noted before she administered a cream that dried it up. She knew the deal and the affair were now increasing her anxiety and hoped that her husband didn't notice her extra stress.

Harry called Ellen and Peter to explain the change in plans and to get them thinking about ways to use the "mole" against Xiaobin Li and crew.

Harry, Ellen, Peter, Xi, and Ho Duan sat in a tenth floor lounge looking out towards Lantau Island, the construction site for a new ultra modern international airport.

"It must be Yi. She has access, motive, and means to feed your cousin information. All we have to do is give her false information that sounds palpable and see how it comes up in this week's negotiations." said Peter.

"I have difficulty believing she'd purposely harm anyone," said Xi.

"This is probably her first love. Come on, folks. Don't tell me you haven't seen young love or infatuation play on somebody's immature insecurities," Peter added.

"Like you're so mature. How would you know?" chided Ellen.

"I certainly see your theoretical point, but I simply don't see Yi as this naïve, insecure young woman," Xi insisted.

"May I ask how often she goes out?" Peter inquired.

"Probably not much. But look at her job. She has major responsibility for someone her age. Not many young women get the opportunities she's got," Xi calmly responded.

"Right. But, professional maturity or not, she's still a young woman." Peter said.

Xi stared at the young consultant but didn't respond.

"It can't hurt to try. If we're wrong about her, then South China operates on whatever information they now have. No harm done." Peter moved to a small end table in a corner of the room, as if to avoid Xi's gaze.

"Whatever the story we feed her had best be very credible. No point in placing her in any more jeopardy than necessary. These are not neophytes we're dealing with, Peter. South China is quite talented, sophisticated and deadly." Ho Duan stood as he lectured.

Walking around the seated group, from different vantage points in the room, Harry absorbed the ideas and arguments but said little.

"Peter, what if we tied the information to some apparent deal- making data?" Ellen rose to the edge of her seat.

"For example?"

"Well, suppose we let Yi know that the current price was a deal breaker, but that we would take four million less, and---"

"What's so astounding about that? That---"

"Hold on," Ellen went on. "We also let her know that we want them focused on cash, because we don't want to give up stock in this deal. That way, they are bound to insist that they take some substantial portion in equity."

"So?" both Peter and Ho Duan questioned her.

"Well, remember the stock that's remaining in the original SRI? That still exists, but has less than a third the value of the current merged company. Few people know about the difference. Am I right, Mr. Ho?"

"I believe you are. Nobody at South China would fall for that ploy. Their lawyers or accountants would spot the old shares instantly. Anyway, how did you know about that stock?"

"With all due respect, I do know how to research companies. Do you think the ploy will work?"

"Not really. However, it may be worth a try. They can only question the value and insist on other payment, if they recognize the play," Ho Duan said, only partially convinced.

"If they do know about the value of the old stock, we just give them cash, and the deal still works at the slightly reduced price." Ellen stared at the stunned and skeptical team.

"Ellen, finances aren't your area; how did you even know to investigate SRI stock?" Harry said.

"Let's say, the advantages of a Western West Coast education." Ellen smiled.

Deep in the arms of a framed Ming Dynasty look-alike chair Xi remained erect and in thought. She was looking directly at Ellen. She didn't blink, turn, nor move even the smallest muscle on her face. Harry couldn't even tell if she was breathing or not.

"Honorable Chairman, what do you think?" Ho, who had also noted her apparent trance, addressed Xi. But Xi continued staring at Ellen. Peter started to rise from his seat to walk over to Xi's chair, but Ho placed a firm hand on his arm.

"For a Westerner, it is usually sufficient for a proposition to be logically sound. For a Chinese it is not sufficient that a proposition be logically correct, but it must be at the same time in accord with human nature. In fact to be 'in accord with human nature,' to be *chinch'ing* ...is a greater consideration than that of logic." Xi paused. "Is that part of your understanding, Ellen?"

Ellen Kwan placed both her hands on her lap, looked about the room, and took a deep breath. She wasn't sure if she had inadvertently crossed some line of business ethics, but it was clear that Xi was challenging her. Clearly, Xi thought her proposal too pragmatic and, somehow, deficient for a Chinese negotiation. She was equally clear that Xi had quoted some scholar and was testing Ellen's knowledge as well as her understanding. She didn't know the source of the quote.

"I think I understand the distinction you are drawing, but my philosophical education is inadequate. I must apologize."

"It's Lin Yutang, from *My Country and My People*." Xi did not elaborate, which Harry and Ellen knew was out of respect for their presumed knowledge of Chinese philosophic thought. She permitted them all to save face.

"That is not to say, of course, that the approach will not work. It must be perceived as respectful and legitimate, and in harmony with this closing stage of the deal, or Xiaobin Li will dismiss the proposal."

Harry picked up a magnificent porcelain Fu Dog, carefully turned it in his hands so that he could feel the smooth blue enamel of the decorative dragon popping out in relief on the cylindrical surface. The morning sunlight lay on the porcelain background in such a way as to raise the dragon further out from the surface. Harry knew that Xi would examine and judge the cultural sensitivity of his business acumen based on his response and implied advice. She was not the chairman of SRI because of her looks, nor because she had a Harvard MBA. His brilliant but young colleague had raised the question of closure capability. Harry had to answer. He thought for a moment about the strength and beauty of the palm-sized statue.

"In two ways, I am reminded of the wisdom of an earlier scholar. First, Ellen's recommendation holds water. One of Xiaobin

Li's driving forces is greed, so he may find the offer acceptable, since he has no reason to suspect differentiated values. While Ellen presents a definitively Western argument, an earlier Chinese thinker offers support for her conclusion: *The Master recognized four prohibitions: Do not be swayed by personal opinion; recognize no inescapable necessity; do not be stubborn; do not be self-centered.*" Harry paused for a moment.

"I must admit, however, that the proposal bears further scrutiny, because it must not only feel right; it must be right. It must in the full spectrum of this deal be fair. The philosopher also said, '*To eat only vegetables without meat, to drink only water, to have only one's bent arm as a pillow: there can be joy in such a life. But to become rich and honored through injustices: for me such joy may be compared to an evanescent cloud*'."

"Confucius. A wise thinker, indeed," said Xi with a small but perceptible smile. "Then, let's try to make this work. If we can't make it feel right, or if we really end up jamming this bastard, we'll take another approach. I'd like to provide our mole some information tomorrow." She rose from her chair.

Almost eight hours later, at a window seat on the second floor of Hong Kong Island's Café Deco Bar and Grill Restaurant, Harry sat facing Johnny X. Both men were picking through the flaky, white, succulent meat of a Garoupa fish cooked in ginger and rice wine.

"I almost went for the cobra chow mien to stretch myself," Harry laughed.

"That's another amazing thing about folks on this island," said Johnny. "They take deadly snakes like cobra and krait and skin, cook, and dress them to produce the tastiest meat. These are delicacies of some of the world's most awesome chefs, but you'll also get this stuff offered in homes. Man, you got to give it to the Cantonese. They know how to present food and how to reach your culinary pleasure spot."

"So, tell me, Johnny, how come you never left the *movement* and went into business like so many brothers?"

X placed his chopsticks in their pillow-shaped pottery holders, looked around the noisy, bustling room, and sighed.

"I suppose it was a combination of real commitment and luck of the draw. You know, I've had opportunities, particularly in West Africa. But they never felt quite legitimate. You know, `Introduce me to so and so, and you'll make a few thousand.' 'Tell Mr. Jones I need this and that, and there will be a fat fee for you.' It never seemed like I would really be working and it always seemed like no one who didn't already have plenty of money would benefit. So much of what I got exposed to seemed sleazy and wrong-headed." He took a sip of plum wine and picked up his chopsticks.

"Besides, being a consultant and lecturer for the 'cause' ain't been a bad life."

"I suppose. But, on the other hand, you could have made honest money, like when we hit the `80's you could have gotten into exports or banking."

"Brother man, it's not in me. I don't have the desire and certainly not the passion."

"What about marriage, then? How come you never tied the knot?"

"I was married for a hot minute. Ex-pat sister who was living in Paris and working for the Mitterrand government in the 80's. Sweet lady. I guess I was too into my causes, the road, and my freedom. Sheila started talking family, and I started finding reasons to stay out of France. We lasted eighteen months."

"Sorry," said Harry.

"Hey. Nothin' for you to be sorry about. I made my choice. We all live with our choices. Know what I mean, man? It's the brothers without real choices that I fight for. You know, the left fork and the right fork in the road lead to the same dead end. That's who I cry for. No, I can't complain about my choices, Harry."

For several minutes, both men ate their meals, enjoyed their wine, and looked out over the hills of Hong Kong and the red, green and yellow lights across the harbor. They both deeply appreciated the silence.

"What about you, Harry? Why didn't you stick with politics?"

"I don't know. Probably for similar reasons. Didn't have the heart for the constant spotlight. It looked like the national level rough and tumble left so many players without principles. Also, Mary really didn't want to be part of a political marriage."

"So, you just let it go? Just like that?"

"I might have wondered early-on what I was giving up, but I love the adventure and challenge of business. Truth be told, I often miss feeling like I'm really contributing to something. Back then I felt that local politics gave me a chance to make a difference for some folks who needed a hand."

"The early fights, the movement and all that made it possible for us to have careers like the white boys." X said.

"No matter what happened in my life, I was blessed to be born to my parents. Blessed to be in that family. You got to give back somehow. Helping some execs in some top tier company figure out how to make more wealth that won't get shared with more than a handful of folks may contribute to the economy, but it's not fulfilling. It's not what my momma and dad would have felt counted enough. I know it's not---"

"It's not feeding the poor, educating the ignorant, and empowering the disenfranchised. Right?" Johnny smiled at his friend over a newly filled glass of wine.

"You know, I don't think I've found the reward you have. I'm not complaining, but I haven't gotten the satisfaction of doing something real."

"What happened, man? You were on track at the Council and even in the early years with TMA," Johnny's eyes softened.

"Man, I wish I knew. I suppose, I wanted to see how well I could do in the corporate world, how far I could go against the big white boys."

"That's that old Morton competitiveness. I can dig it."

"Yeah. It's funny, X. You know, I don't feel like I've sold out, but I know the power and influence I have is only marginally helping folks."

"You know you can change some of that, my brother."

"How's that?"

"I'm involved in what you would call 'legitimate projects' around the world that are feeding the hungry, clothing the naked, and all that shit. Pick your place. South Africa, Congo, Haiti, Philippines. You name it. They all need cash and know-how. "

"I don't know about sowing political instability. I---"

"I'm not talking about the revolutionary shit. I'm talkin' 'bout bread on the table, sanitation for villages, clean water, immunization for kids that otherwise don't have a prayer. This is legit stuff."

Harry ran his finger up the stem of his wine glass. He admired Xs sense of purpose and contentment with the life he lived. He wondered about his own life.

"Tell you what, Harry. I'll send you some material on these real live social investments. You judge."

"Fair enough," said Harry after another long pause. "Now, what you say we head over to Kowloon and have a nightcap at that restaurant in my hotel, the Felix? It's on me." Harry began to rise from the table.

"You're on, my brother."

Harry signed the credit card slip and X left Hong Kong dollars in the tray left by their waiter. Heads turned ever so slightly as the two striking black men, one in western pinstriped suit, and the other in a gold Ghanaian dashiki descended the stairs to the first floor of Deco. Two Asian businesswomen seated at a window table were winding up their dinner conversation. The woman with more

Chinese features was facing the stairs and happened to glance up as the two foreigners were heading for the door.

"What are you smiling about?" The Indian-looking woman with her back to the stairs turned as the two black men approached their table.

"Well, hello, Mr. Morton. What a pleasant surprise to see you here. Harry Morton, allow me to introduce you to my friend, Margaret Schultz."

"How do you do, Ms. Schultz? This is an old friend of mine, Johnny X."

"Mr. X." Both of the women smiled and shook hands all around.

"We're going over to *Felix's* for a drink. Care to join us?" Harry said, eyes on Xi's form-fitting robin's egg silk blouse and navy jacket.

"Thank you, but I'm running Margaret out to the airport on my way home."

"Well, nice to meet you ladies. Perhaps, some other time."

Johnny X bowed and both men left to catch the Peak Tram. On the street, X turned to Harry. "Homey, wasn't the Chinese looking babe the one you were having dinner with the last time I ran into you on the island?"

"X, there is nothing wrong with your memory. Right. Xi is the CEO of SRI.

"I'll tell you, either one of 'em could CEO my company. 'Fine' don't even come close to describing them. Know what I mean, bro?"

"Who you telling?"

On the way down the mountain and on the ferry to Kowloon, Harry told Johnny about the business aspects of the SRI deal.

Over a leisurely brandy, X told Harry about some of the harrowing experiences he had had in West Africa while advising two revolutionary movements. Finally, the friends rose to part.

"Stay in touch, and send me that material," Harry said as he escorted Johnny to the revolving door.

Harry had returned to his room, taken off his jacket, and had a fifteen minute call with Don Bartram when the phone beeped.

"Hold on Don, I've got another call."

"Look, we've pretty much finished. Let's talk in a couple of days," Don said.

"Okay, good to hear you and to get caught up."

"Bye, Harry. Call your wife. I saw her at the DC Chamber dinner. I'm sure she'd like to hear from you."

Harry wondered what Don's comment meant. It was a fleeting thought, however. He pressed the phone button to engage the other call.

"Harry, is that nightcap offer still open?"

"Xi, where are you?"

"I'm in the lobby. Not a place to leave a lady, do you think?"

"Come on up, but it's just me here."

"That's fine. Margaret has gone to the airport. See you in a minute."

She and Margaret had talked about her Saturday rendezvous on the ride to the airport.

"The more you tell me, the more crazy I really think this affair is. Attraction is one thing, but is it worth the risk?"

"Margaret, you yourself know how cosmopolitan Hong Kong has become."

"Yes, but it's still run by men. Most of them with traditional values. The gain is what? A bit more information on how Harry Morton thinks, how he reacts under different situations? But the risk is you being discredited. And you know how *South China has spies about.* You could lose the deal, your position, your father would croak, even Bao. It would be devastating. Not worth it, really."

"You're the only person I can count on for support and look---"

"Xi---"

"Margaret, I know. I have to break it off, soon. You're right, but he makes me realize how much I must have repressed for so long. But, you're right. I know."

"Xi. I'm with you on the attraction, on the unfairness of the roles still abroad in our countries, BUT there's too much to lose, in your case. Dear heart, think about---"

"It's so liberating to get outside our straightjackets for even an evening. Okay, okay. Snap out of it. Thank you." Xi lightly patted her own cheek.

He looked in his mini-bar to make sure there were some scotch bottles on hand, splashed water on his face, and flipped on the CNN news. A knock at the door ended his preparation.

"Hello, Mr. Morton," said Xi as she entered the suite. "Do you mind if I take my shoes off? I really don't know why we have acceded to the western style of high heels. They can kill your feet by the end of the day."

"Be my guest. Scotch?"

"No thanks. We need to do a lot of preparation, tomorrow. Besides, I think we need to discuss some issues. What we're risking, here."

"You don't mind if I have a drink for this discussion, do you?"

"Of course not." She watched Harry pour and wanted to relax. Feelings were a swirl.

"All right, what are the burning issues?"

"Our affair. It's too risky for me. I know I initiated it, and I love spending private time with you, but if we're discovered my career, my marriage, everything is gone in an instant."

"Xi, aren't you being a bit melodramatic? This isn't Beijing or Xian. It's British Hong Kong." Harry only pretended to look concerned.

"We're talking Chinese. Forget the British."

"You came up here to tell me this? Look, I have some trepidation, too. I have a family, and---"

"But, they're half way around the world. You're relatively safe."

"Fine. This should be something we both want. I'm not interested in forcing this thing." Harry squeezed her shoulder and offered his hand in a shake of friendship. Xi breathed out a tension-reducing sigh and slowly regained her composure.

"Shall we tie up some lose business ends?" he asked. "You sure you don't want a drink?"

She didn't answer for a moment. "Oh, why not?" Her expression was that of a business colleague relieved to be able to discuss a deal after a day of frustrating telephone tag. It was not that of an attractive woman interested in seducing her companion.

They sipped scotch and reviewed the possible ways to execute Ellen Kwan's plan. Harry introduced the triad subject and probed for any connection. Xi conceded the logic of such a proposition- a frustrated or angered mob partner. But, she ultimately rejected the thesis, without denying that the firm or the family had had dealings with triads on their own account. Harry wasn't convinced that she had carefully reexamined the potential, but it was clear that no obvious party came to mind.

After a third scotch, Harry smiled and said, "Lin Yutang, really. Hardly a well-known source of Chinese business philosophy."

"Yet, you know of him, Mr. Consultant."

"Only by coincidence. I probably read him in a Modern Asian Philosophy course in college."

"Nevertheless, you knew him and knew how to respond appropriately."

Xi held Harry's stare.

"How about if I turn off CNN?" he asked, moving to the TV without awaiting a response. He hit the off the TV button and flicked on the stereo, which he'd set to a new Hong Kong jazz station. A mellow Harry Connick Jr. ballad softly filled the room. Neither said anything as they held each others' glances. Perhaps they thought just this once more, but by whatever logic each pursued, they allowed the mood to change, tension to subside, and rationality to escape. The business partners placed their glasses on a coffee table and became lovers as they, embraced, kissed, and delicately undressed each other. Gone was the hesitance from earlier in the evening. He had convinced himself that the deal was not in jeopardy, nor at risk due to the affair. Harry had occasionally had affairs over the years, but never had he felt as involved as with Xi. Never had he had an affair with a current business associate; and never with a Chinese woman. *Which aspect of her novelty grabs me?* He asked himself. His drifting marriage couldn't implode any further, he rationalized. He had heard her worries and partially empathized with the level of her risk, but not enough. Harry's neck and stomach tightened, but the scotch helped him commit totally to the moment.

He felt that Xi was even more passionate than on their first encounter. She arched her hips, closed her eyes, and groaned quietly as he entered. Xi worried momentarily that the risk now w1ell exceeded any potential business reward, and that she had let her lust overwhelm her reason. Then, she stopped thinking. Both held their passion until their minds screamed for release, and collapsed in sweaty ecstasy after their lovemaking.

"In the old days, we'd both reach silently for a cigarette," he said, grinning into her deep hazel eyes.

"This is China. Feel free," she said rolling on top of and kissing him.

He continued to alternately brush her earlobe with his tongue and her aureole with his fingers. She lifted herself up, straddled his hips, bent backwards until her black hair almost touched his legs, and slowly moved her hips.

He held his smile as the explosion built in his groin. As she reached orgasm, Xi exclaimed, "Oh baby, oh baby, oh baby."

As they lay next to each other afterward, Harry, staring up at the ceiling, knit his eyebrows and asked, "Why did you say that?"

"Say what?"

"That 'Oh, Baby' business"

"I don't know. Expression of pleasure. Why? Am I supposed to censor my most private feelings with you?"

"It's just not that. Well, I don't know …"

"Not Chinese. Is that what you mean?"

"Well, yeah. Sort of."

"Surely, a man of your sophistication isn't presuming that women of specific ethnic groups make pillow talk a specific way when in the arms of their lovers?"

Harry felt sure he had crossed some line of sensitivity, but he didn't know what it was.

"No. It's silly. I'm sorry, really."

Xi propped herself on her elbows and looked over at Harry Morton.

"You wouldn't be thinking, perhaps, that American women have some claim on that phrase, would you?"

"No, of course not." He sensed that he had tapped some distant feeling. So he simply lay there with his arm around her.

"You know, sometimes the most hostility I felt at Harvard was not from prejudiced whites, where I had expected it. It was instead from black women."

"Were you dating a black guy?"

"No, I was just trying to be friendly and sit at a lunch table."

"At the 'black students' table?"

"I suppose, yes."

"Well, I'm surprised that you didn't study up on the rules of twentieth century American Apartheid."

"I was young and curious and wanted to meet all types of Americans."

"And, I'll bet the most forthcoming, other than Asian-Americans, were devout Christian whites."

"How did you know?"

"I grew up there and live there, remember?"

"I know about slavery, civil rights, and bigotry, but this was in the 1980's."

Harry rolled over onto his elbow and placed a few inches between them.

"Discrimination against us is alive and well. It's just not as overt."

"Why turn on a foreigner? Chinese didn't figure in American slavery. In fact, Chinese immigrants also received terrible treatment when they arrived."

"And, some still do. But the difference between being of slaves and having the majority think of you as such, and being despised because you are immigrants. Most immigrants to the US are ostracized when they first arrive. But white folks get over it, groups assimilate, make money, and, BOOM, they're hyphenated Americans. We're still 'niggers.'"

Xi sat up and pulled a pillow to her chest. "I still feel some people bring it on themselves. Why are women so much more hostile?"

"Come on, Xi. You're a trophy to a dude and a competitor to a woman. A woman who feels there are already too few educated, eligible middle-class brothers in the world. Let alone at Harvard."

"I still feel it's self-limiting…"

"I might agree with you. But let a black couple try to move into Chinatown, San Francisco. Or you come home from Harvard with an American boyfriend, a black one. How would your family have reacted?"

"That's different. You're practically an Asian scholar. You know how Chinese feel about foreigners of any race."

"How's it different? We're now twenty years after you were in school in the U.S. You know damn well how difficult the mainland, or even Hong Kong would make it on some African or African-American brother who married into the 'Middle Kingdom.' Impossible. Don't forget, I speak fluent Mandarin and Cantonese, and read body language quite well. Chinese families would disown any such offspring. Look at what happened to the kids of black American soldiers and Chinese Vietnamese women." His tone had turned to ice, and it was her turn to assess carefully how far to proceed.

He continued. "What about the silly fear northern Chinese women have of getting too much sun and turning dark like some Yunan minorities? Xi, my tribe is not the only one affected by generations of class and color conflicts. What you didn't like was that you were a princess in a strange environment, seeking interesting people, and got rebuffed. Not something you were used to."

"Harry, you know it's no picnic for female Eurasians in China either. Are you saying you think black women aren't hostile to outsiders? To certain black men, even?"

"Xi, where is this going? I've explained, and you know damned well, what's going on with some sisters in the US. Why are you trying to be dense? Let's look close to home. Nobody at SRI has been too open to Ellen Kwan, on my team."

"She's Ko…" she tried to stop herself.

"Say it. She's Korean. Actually, she's American. Her parents are Korean. So, how come she's treated with distant tolerance? On the other hand, folks around the office can't be kind enough to Peter. Is it because he looks British? Now, I would have thought you all had had enough of the British."

Neither was touching the other any longer. The anger in the room was palpable. The exchange seemed more than a lovers' quarrel to both of them. The jazz trumpet of Terence Blanchard playing riffs from an old Billie Holliday tune offered the only sound in the room. They were now both sitting against the headboard. They sat for a long time as if in deep meditation.

Xi masked her confusion. She had sought the relationship, without fully knowing what she would uncover that might assist her in the deal. She had felt she could escape detection by her colleagues and her husband. She had smothered her anxiety of being discovered in the joy of the encounter. That is until Margaret brought her up short and made her focus on the enormous risk of the relationship and the relatively low reward.

Finally, Harry spoke. "Look, we are not going to solve centuries' worth of psychological crap tonight, and we have a deal to finish this week. You may be right that this is not worth the tension, the angst, or the potential damage. Can we admit we don't know a great deal about each other? Even if we did, where can this go? Can we be courteous friends, for now?"

"Harry, I know it's silly. It's certainly not like a Tai-Pan. It may not even be Chinese. But, I want to know how you feel."

"About the world? The deal? The evening? What?"

"Don't be such a Western male. About me? How do you feel about me?"

"That is an out-of-character question."

"Maybe. This is an out-of-character situation. It's sublime and it's ridiculous, at the same time. But, will you answer?"

"You're my friend. I'm attracted to you and like making love to you. You're also a hard-nosed business woman capable of making as cold-blooded a decision as any man I've met. I feel that you are a special person. The rest is too complex to explore tonight."

She kissed him long on the lips and got up to shower and dress.

Later, as he lay in bed alone, he realized that he really didn't know how he felt. Xi had gotten deep into his being and released feelings and observations he had been subconsciously carrying about China and its mores. Until tonight, he had usually been able to call up the specific nuances about Chinese culture that he needed for deal-making in a dispassionate fashion. He had known that he'd absorbed much more about China than was required in casual conversation or in business negotiations. Xi had also forced him to defend behavior of blacks he himself had often rejected. He wondered what would happen if he really explored the deeper complexities and passions of his relationship with Xi as he drifted off to sleep.

"Captain Morton, with all due respect, you must certainly realize the problem your country faces," said Thieu Diem, a South Vietnamese military advisor on leave with Harry in Hong Kong during1969.

"You mean our unfamiliarity with the terrain?"

"Hardly. It's the spiritual and emotional confidence that the North Vietnamese feel about this war. For Americans, and to a lesser degree for the South, this is about strategic positioning, and economic and political imperatives. For the North, this is about their very being, the unification of one people. For them, there is no vision of loss. Do your military planners sitting comfortably back in Washington, D.C. understand that, Harry?"

Morton didn't even need to think about the question to respond.

"No, Diem, they don't."

Thieu picked up his glass of British Stout, held it for a few seconds before he took a sip.

"Harry, I sense you're more curious about the people of Asia than your average American medic or military officer. Why is that?"

"You have lovely women," Harry said, partially in jest.

"Thank you. But, there are gorgeous women all over the world. The short time I spent in your country before the war, I saw many beautiful women of all colors. It can't just be our women."

"Diem, I think it has to do with the depth of history that is manifest in so many ways in Asian societies with at least partially Chinese-based cultures. No offense to Vietnamese. There is a philosophical foundation that leads

individuals to subjugate ego to that of the group in a way that is not found in the West. Actually, it's similar to some areas of Africa."

"Well, my friend it is too bad that more of the non-medical officers don't understand and appreciate cultural differences more."

"Let's go find some real diversion from the killing we've got to return to," Harry said looking across the side walk café to three young Chinese women dressed in form-fitting chi paws.

Harry fell into a deeper sleep and submerged below recallable dreams until morning.

"Yi, what time is the South China meeting Wednesday?" Xi inquired of her assistant as she flipped through memos from each of the negotiation teams.

"It's ten o'clock, I believe.'

"Thank you. Would you get my father on the phone, please? He should have just returned from his morning exercises."

A half minute later, Yi buzzed her boss to let her know the line on which her father waited. She carefully pressed the same line herself. It was unusual for Xi not to dial her father herself, so Yi was curious about the call.

"How are you feeling today, Father?" Xi asked as outlined in their pre-arranged script.

"Not too bad, number one daughter. This old man still has a few wits about him."

"That's good, because I'd like to request some advice from those wits." Xi then summarized the strategy of getting South China to accept a cash price. Her father paused an appropriately long time and then agreed that it was worth a try, since SRI stock would surely later rise in value.

"Thank you for your advice. Sage as always. I shall see you for dinner Friday."

Ying Yi waited to be sure that Xi was on her next call before placing a quick call to Wang Ren to provide him with the latest deal information. "Be sure not to accept a majority of cash, insist on stock payment, because the value will soon climb."

"I've got it. Thanks. I can't wait until we next meet. Until this weekend, then."

She was so intent on passing on the information and getting off the phone that she did not notice the slight ticking noise, as her call was recorded.

Four days later, Harry Morton, Peter Burke, and Ellen Kwan bid goodbye to SRI management, shook hands with South China's executives, and boarded a plane for Tokyo and New York. South China had taken the gambit, required partial payment in stocks, accepted the subsidiary's stocks, and closed the deal. Final papers were to be signed in a week, but only formalities remained. The final negotiations had been somewhat of an anti-climax, with South China believing they had finally worn down SRI to get an outstanding price for their company. SRI was relieved that the actual value, though fair, was much more in their favor than South China realized. Harry and Xi exchanged a very business-like farewell handshake, but he held her glance and tried to guess her profound and more complex emotions.

He wanted to ask if this was it—is this the end? He was neither sad nor happy. He was simply looking forward to relaxing on the plane, with a chance to think through his balled up emotions.

Two days later, Ying Yi arrived home from work to find her belongings packed and an envelope containing a train ticket pinned to her suitcase. The ticket was for her home town in Sichuan Province, and an accompanying note informed her that she was never to return to Hong Kong. Further, she was not to advertise that she had worked at SRI. It also said that she would not reach Sichuan if she contacted South China. That night, her face drained of its color, Ying arrived at the station without having notified a soul of her departure, for she knew the note's instructions were to be strictly followed.

CHAPTER THIRTEEN

香港

"I don't know, man. Look Harry, I see things much more simply than you do." George Birch sipped his Crown Royal on the rocks. He looked across the bar table at his old friend.

"It feels to me like you've suppressed something for too long."

"I don't believe this shit. Not from you."

"Hear me out, Harry. What I mean is, it feels like the business you, that calculating Morton, has taken over way beyond the bounds of professional necessity."

Both men sat back in hard spindle-backed chairs, as Otis Redding's voice lifted over the smoke. He was singing, "I've got dreams to remember."

"You know your momma was one of the finest women I ever met. She challenged all us kids. She pushed us to learn, exposed us to white folks' music and art, tried to get us to read new stuff. She was strong and different…"

"What's Mom got to do---?"

"She was a pioneer, but you always knew she cared about us. To us, she was always Aunt Lena. She was very different, but unquestionably black."

"Is that what this is about? You think this business success, this Asia; this international thing has somehow robbed me of my 'blackness?'" Harry leaned hard against the table.

"It's like you don't feel the soul in life anymore. You don't even enjoy a good ball game anymore."

"George, I'm not in local DC. I don't work with the PEOPLE. I flip back and forth between dozens of subcultures weekly. It's complex, brother. Anyway, your view of my mom, flattering though it may be, represents the perspective of a kid looking up to some adult."

"Harry, you've been in international business for years. I've only sensed this change recently. I know you, man. This ain't some 'Wassup? Havin' a Bud' commercial. This is real, man."

"I don't know what it is, but you're right. Something is different. I gotta admit that it's taking a lot longer than normal to get back in sync with Mark," Harry said.

"What about Mary?" George was intent.

"I don't know, man. My travel, our two careers, Mark growing up. It's not as much fun anymore."

"I'm goin' to tell you like it is, homeboy. It doesn't feel like there is a relationship, when I see you two now."

Al Green softly mumbled and groaned the words to one of his ballads across the conversations in the bar. Both Harry and George looked around the crowd in *Faces* as if they expected to find a crony to pull them out of the depths of their conversation. No luck.

"Used to be that Mary and I could talk out our problems. Get to the bottom and things would clear up. We don't even really try now."

"We?"

"You're right. It's me. I guess I just try to avoid any confrontations with her."

After several long sips apiece, George said, "Hey, man. Let me give you a lift up the way. We'll talk later."

"George, despite what they say about you, you're okay." He placed his arm over the shorter man's shoulder.

"You're not too bad, either," George smiled up at his buddy. Neither said much on the drive up to the Maryland border. Harry couldn't stop thinking about his friend's observations, his tepid reception upon returning home from the latest Hong Kong trip, and some lingering questions about his affair.

Harry thanked George, shut the car door, and took long strides up the brick walk to his front porch. He could hear a soft Anita Baker ballad through his living room window as he stuck the key into the front door.

"Well, you're home early. How's George?" Mary looked up from her economics journal.

"He's fine. Fine." Harry sat next to his wife on the living room couch and tried to give her a peck on the cheek. She pulled away slightly.

"If you go up now, you might be able to say goodnight to Mark."

Harry tried to find some warmth in Mary's voice, but failed. He pushed off the back of the couch, stood up straight, and looked across the pale beige room at the Gauguin painting whose bottom was framed level with the teak fireplace mantel. That section of the room projected the essence of the 'South Pacific.' But, Harry's every fiber was tense and very much trapped in DC.

"I'll go up," he said flatly.

He pushed open the door to Mark's room.

"Hey, Dad. How was work? I'm glad you're back."

"So am I. How was your day, son?"

"School's good. I like my science class. We study bird habitats. That means homes. We learn their calls and even about their different feather colors for different seasons. It's cool. I even get along with Bobby Boyd, now." The boy's eyes sparkled with excitement. "But, when can we play football or go to a game? It's not the same with Mom."

"Well, your mother really loves to spend the time with you."

"I know, but she's not like a guy."

"What is it that you like about science, do you think?"

"Well, it's really about life and there are lots of mysteries that people have solved. Stuff like why birds fly south during the winter. You know, there's just a lot to learn that's interesting."

"It's great to be curious about life."

"But, what about a game?"

"Okay, I should be around for awhile now that the Hong Kong job is done." Harry leaned over and kissed his droopy-eyed son on the forehead.

"Good night, Mark."

"Night, Dad."

Harry retired to his second floor study but couldn't focus on the e-mail on his screen. Family pictures on two adjacent walls covered much of the wood-paneled room. He looked up at a photo of Mary leaning against a kikuyu tree in Maui thirteen years ago. She had a perfect hourglass figure and was teasingly showing cleavage as she pushed her bikinied chest into the camera. Harry smiled at the memory of the wonderful vacations they'd had early in their relationship. Next to that photo, Harry examined a color shot of the two of them at a Washington Chamber of Commerce dinner. They were dancing, looking into each other's eyes, and deep in love. Their love was still full of discovery then, he thought.

He drifted back to that week in June a quarter of a century ago when he returned to Philadelphia to attend his father's funeral and first met Mary. He had spent four long days with his mother, brother and friends grieving for John Morton. He'd had to take over arranging various affairs with the family lawyer. Then, he sat down in the tiny living-room of the row house in which he'd spent his childhood. Still choked up about the loss of his father, he forced himself to deal with the future.

"Mom, I'm not coming back to go to grad school. I'm going to be trained as a medic in Panama."

"Oh, for heaven's sake. They'll send you to Vietnam, Harry. What about your commitment to this family? Your father's not buried two days, and you're talking of going into harm's way. This war is bringing nothing but grief to the Vietnamese and to us. Let it be. It's their fight, if there has to be fighting. How about our needs here? Your father wouldn't like this, Harry," Lena Morton's eyes could have melted granite as she looked on her eldest son.

"I've got to go. I can't be a killer, but I can help the wounded. I can be a medic," he stated with growing conviction.

"You know deep down that this is an evil war. It's got nothing to do with what Nixon and that arrogant Kissinger says. It's wrong, period."

"Mom, I know how you feel, but I feel I have an obligation."

"Boy, you have an obligation all right, and that's to come home and work and help out for awhile." Lena Morton was close to tears, but she held them back. Even in her grief, she was tough to the core.

"Why not register as a conscientious objector and work in the U.S. for two years? I thought this Panama army stint was just for a year. Don't leave all of the family responsibility on your brother," Lena pleaded.

"Mom, I am registered as a C.O. That's how I get to be a medic."

"I hope I live to see the day when you lose some of that selfishness. It will keep you from doing great things in life. Learn to think of others before yourself, sometime. This is one time you don't have to wander off."

"Why do you have to always lay a guilt trip on me?" he asked, barely above a whisper.

"If you feel guilty, you should. You're a man now, Harry. Your selfish choices have real consequences for other people from here on out." She was no longer angry. She was preaching and teaching and hoping that her son would learn. "You know I'll always love you, no matter what you decide, but…"

"Mom, you know I'll always love you too." Harry couldn't say anymore, but he hugged his mother feeling more emotion than he could ever remember.

"Talk to your brother about this. If you go, you'll owe him a great debt."

"I will," he said through tears. "And, I will come back safely when this is over," he added still hugging her.

"Son, it will not be in your hands. But we'll all pray that you return safely."

With only a few days left before Harry had to return to the army in Panama, his brother, Pierce, suggested they go into 'Center City' for dinner and some music. Lena Morton encouraged her sons to go off and spend the time together. Pierce drove his little beat-up navy Alfa Romeo sports coupe through the rapid turns on the Wissahickon Drive, which wound its way along the Schuylkill River from Philadelphia's northwest suburban-like communities, past University of Pennsylvania boat houses and the Art Museum into the busy downtown.

"Harry, I never tire of this drive. Do they have gladiolas and rhododendrons in Panama with blues and purples like we do?"

"Pierce, I bet all I'll get to see is green jungle vine, green shrubs, and maybe green moss. There'll probably be no fragrance, other than G.I sweat."

After a moment's reflection, Harry again turned to his brother. "How do you think Mom is taking Daddy's death?"

Pierce thought for a moment. His older brother rarely asked his opinion on anything, so he just absorbed the moment, breathing in the floral early summer air as he drove into the twilight. Their normal lives were worlds apart, but at this moment were remembering a common past.

"Harry, you need to stop when you come to the net. You keep moving and that's why the ball keeps getting pushed over the baseline," Pierce's tone was calming.

"Thanks. I'll try again."

Harry's brother smoked a tennis shot deep into the corner. After Harry retrieved it, Pierce punched the next one short, just over the net, drawing his older brother in.

"Much better," grinned the stocky, but more athletic Morton.

"Thanks. You'll make a great teacher, one day. I appreciate the tips."

"I wish I could run down shots like that."

Harry admired his brother's patience. He displayed none of Harry's impatience, or critical tone, as he provided advice. Their friendship and respect grew as their separations, due to college, lengthened. Harry was now able to recognize and commend the artistic talent that his sibling possessed. By the time he was a college senior and Pierce was a junior, he began to look forward to their visits, and the sports or cultural activities they enjoyed together. He no longer felt a need to criticize Pierce's poor academic performance. Through Pierce, Harry began to understand the complexity and vast variety of human talent. He learned how singularly uninformative the word 'smart' is.

The two Mortons were rediscovering their childhood, thinking, sometimes sharing moments when the family, or simply the two of them had been together. During this week, however, they were getting to know each other for the first time as adults.

"She's not letting her grief out. It's like she is just trying to get through these first few days before she lets it sink in that he's really gone. That's the way she is."

"You know, it's funny. I realize that I never knew Daddy really. I mean he was always a father to me, I was a kid. I never got to know him once I was an adult."

"He was quiet, but always asked about you. 'Any letters from Panama?' he'd ask me. Always correcting Mom's English; and mine. When he wasn't fixing up around the house, he was always reading something. He loved Mom to death." Pierce began to cry quietly.

"Pierce, do you think I should come back?" He looked intently at his brother.

The younger Morton took his eyes off the road for an instant, as if to make sure it was his brother sitting in the seat next to him asking for advice.

"I would finish out your stint, but then it might be good if you came back to Philadelphia. I think Mom would like us both around for a bit. I can only hang around the house but so much anymore."

It was Harry's turn to stare. He realized how little he knew about the world of the handsome young man behind the steering wheel. He also began to appreciate how solid and dependable his kid brother was in their small family.

"Pierce, thanks for being a great son for both of them. And, thanks for being a great brother. I'm sorry that I'm not here for you during the rough periods. Yes, I'll come back when the stint's over. Thanks." Harry wiped the moisture from the corner of his eye.

Once in town, the two brothers enjoyed 'Shaft,' a black adventure movie starring Richard Roundtree and then drove to one of Pierce's favorite spots, a jazz club on the newly revitalized section of town called 'South Street.' He still took courses at the Philadelphia College of Art, although he had already begun working with a commercial graphics firm. Pierce had a wide network of student and young professional artist friends in Center City. The outgoing, garrulous, confident Pierce Morton that Harry observed in the yellow tint of early evening made him smile to himself. As a boy, Pierce had been frightfully shy and somewhat in Harry's shadow. He was now clearly comfortably engaged in a world of his peers.

'Jazz Alive' was a long rectangular lounge with a low stage halfway down the exposed brick wall, a bar at the far end, and tables seating five to six patrons scattered throughout. The long wall facing the stage was tastefully covered with black-and-whites of jazz greats: Miles, Trane, Dizzy, Bird, Monk, Lady Day.

"Nice, Pierce. Nice."

"Glad you like it. We can eat and chat for awhile before the show begins," Pierce said over his shoulder as he followed a waitress to a table close to the bar. Both men ordered scotch.

"How you doin,' Pierce?" A heavy-set dark skinned man had approached the table and gripped Pierce's hand in the soul shake.

"Jason, this is my brother, Harry."

"Hey, my pleasure, man. Sorry for both of you about the loss of Mr. John. He was a very well respected brother. He taught me and my brother in grade school. You didn't mess around in his class. He made you listen, but he also made stuff fun. Yeah, your father was all right."

After a few minutes of pleasantries, the man went back to his table.

"That's Jason Wheeler. He lives on the block in West Philly near old Pastor Wilson," Pierce said. "You remember he was the minister from Westside Baptist Church?"

"Remember? How could I forget that booming voice and that rocking rhythm?"

"*Brothas, sistahs, have you loved Jesus today? Have you cherished Jesus this mornin'? Have you gone that extra mile, that mile that paves your way to heaven? Have you turned that cheek, put out that hand? You know what I'm talkin' bout. Tell me you've been with Jesus and I'll sleep peacefully. Tell me you've walked a mile for the less fortunate and I'll rest my weary bones. Tell me you've looked at sin, touched sin, experienced sin, and then turned to Jesus. The Lord forgives, but you got to help.'*" Pierce was rocking back and forth, perfectly mimicking his old pastor. Harry could barely hold his laughter.

"You remember him? Well, that's now Reverend Jason Wheeler on Sundays. He's a trip."

The brothers downed their scotches as they trumped each other with memories of growing up. While digging into a fried chicken dinner, Harry noticed a honey colored woman occasionally staring at them from her perch on a bar stool.

"Am I blind, or is that a fox at the bar?" Harry put a hand on his brother's arm and nudged.

"We know you're blind, but that's Mary Stokes. And she is a fox, as well as a certified bitch."

"What do you mean?"

"She's very hard on brothers. I remember this one cat, ball player, she was dating at *Temple*. Broke it off when he asked for help on a history exam. Told him he was supposed to do his own studying. She's rough, boy."

"Well, that doesn't seem that bad, to me. She's got standards, I guess."

"Standards? She a royal you know what. Trying to get her to smile takes a major effort." Pierce shook his head. "She was an Art History major when I started at *Temple*. Then, she switched to Economics, transferred, and none of us saw her for a couple of years until she showed up at Head House Square selling some half-assed ceramics last summer. She's got to be a better economist than she is an artist. Anyway, nobody I know knows where she's in school. You need a blowtorch to melt that sister."

"So, you don't know her well enough to introduce us." Harry only partially listened to his brother, as he continued to gaze at the bar.

"Not really, but you were never shy, as I recall."

"Excuse me a second."

Harry stood up from the table, walked over to the bar, and stood next to Mary Stokes.

"Excuse me, but don't you sell pottery at Head House?"

Mary started to frown at the boldness of the stranger but was a bit taken back by his question.

"Why, yes, have you purchased from me?"

"No, but I would like to."

"You mean you've browsed and let a piece get away?"

"I have to admit that I've only passed by a couple of times." After a few more pleasantries, they introduced themselves and Harry said that he looked forward to coming by her stand when he came back to town later in the summer.

"Well, that was smooth," Pierce said when Harry returned to the table.

"Thanks to the background info on her selling at Head House."

Harry was able to extend his leave a few more days. He and Peirce saw Mary one more time when they had drinks after she tended her table at Head House.

Over the next year and a half, Mary learned to appreciate Pierce's artistic sensitivity and perspective, while maintaining a correspondence with his less artistic but more flamboyant brother. When she wasn't studying for her Ph.D., she spent afternoons with

Pierce at the Art Museum, going to movies, or hanging out with his crowd while listening to music.

When Harry returned from his army med stints in Panama and then Viet Nam, Mary was a friend of the family. She had let the Mortons in behind her haughty exterior, and they had provided her with a "home away from home." There was never an issue of jealousy, because it was clear that Mary saw Pierce as a companion and brother, while her true romantic fascination was with Harry. She also helped Lena Morton adjust to the loss of her husband and her concern for her enlisted son, by insisting that they go on shopping trips or simply on rides into the country. Later, Harry realized that Mary had truly become part of his small family while he was away.

The relationship with Pierce and Lena provided Mary with a non threatening way to relax and enjoy people who were fully outside of the world of her academic grind, yet stimulating and fun.

When Pierce prematurely died in a car accident a year after Harry returned to Philadelphia, Mary felt the loss almost as deeply as did Harry and Lena. The months following Pierce's death galvanized emotional patterns that would remain for decades. Harry became devoted to his mother and to insuring that she had physical, economic, and emotional security for the rest of her life. Lena's future daughter-in-law became a phone companion and a friend who could be counted upon for enduring support. Harry and Mary grew inseparable on weekends. Pierce's passing had created a void that their companionship and eventual love helped to fill. Harry often reflected with amazement on that period of his life as one of the most emotionally rich and rewarding in the midst of great sadness.

That was then. In the blink of his eye, Harry returned to 1996 and the desk chair in his den in Washington, D.C.

"I seal a major deal for the company, open up new market opportunities for Masterfield in Southeast Asia, yet return home and feel like a pariah. What the hell's happening?" Harry sighed to no one but the four walls of his study. His mind drifted off over many images, without focus.

"John Dunne was bullshitting. Man can indeed be an island." He stared at the oak bookshelves containing his father's collection of English literature. "Yeah, Daddy. Have I really made myself an island?" He turned off the light and went to bed.

A few days later, while finishing up reports on the SRI deal, Harry looked up from his office computer screen to see Don Bartram easing into the lounge chair next to his desk.

"I got to go to New York Friday, but I'm looking forward to you and Mary coming to the house for Saturday's party."

"That's kind, Don. But Mary is tied up with---"

"That's bullshit, Harry. I'm expecting you two. Donna hasn't seen either of you for months. It'll be fun. For a man who just scored big, you don't look like you're having much fun. Anyway, I hope things are fine at home. See you Saturday."

To Harry's surprise, Mary said that she'd like to go to the Bartrams for a dinner party.

"Besides, we can celebrate your being home for awhile after *living* in Hong Kong for the past half year."

"Thank you for understanding, Mary."

"Isn't that what wives are supposed to do, Harry? Understand?"

Morton just looked blankly at his wife, who smiled slightly and moved into their kitchen to place dinner dishes in the washer. "I'll go up and check on Mark," he said.

After listening to Mark's plans for a paper he had to write for the end of the week, Harry sat up on the end of the bed.

"We haven't been to the arboretum lately, have we?"

"I don't remember ever going with you, Dad. I went once on a school science project."

"How about we go Saturday morning before the suburbanites and tourists get there?"

"What do you do there? All I remember is trees"

"You'll see. There's a lot to see. I thought you liked science. That's nature."

Few cars were on the road going north on the Baltimore-Washington Parkway, as Harry turned the Porsche into the National Arboretum at 8 AM that Saturday morning. Mark was dozing in the seat next to him, subconsciously feeling more penalized than rewarded for the opportunity to arise early and go to some quiet outdoor place on a "sleep morning." Harry parked the car on a hill overlooking the 'Asia Collection.'

"Let's go down to this little section to the left. I want to show you something.'

"Dad, this is pretty, but---"

"Wait 'til we get down where those benches are, through the trees straight ahead."

They walked for several minutes in an open glen that seemed deep in woods and separated from the rest of the world. Alternating pink and white Cherry trees and clusters of white Pear trees framed the space, while hundreds of shades of green ferns covered the ground under the trees. When they reached an overlook cut into the sloping woods that offered a perch above the Anacostia River, Harry stopped.

"Wow, this is neat," Mark admitted. "I can imagine Cherokee scouts coming around that bend on canoes to sneak up on white settlers."

"Mark, at some point, we need to work on your history. Anyway, sit for a minute on this bench, look out over the river, and let your thoughts roam."

They sat in silence for five minutes.

"Right after your Uncle Pierce died, I had to come to D.C. on a business trip. One afternoon, I left my colleagues downtown and came up here to be with nature, with my memories, with his spirit, even with God. I did the same thing, when your grandmother died. Do you think that's strange?"

Mark didn't answer at first.

"You never talk about God, Daddy. You believe in Him?"

"Of course I do, son. Very much. I just don't go to church."

"Well, I can see why you'd come up here. It feels like just the birds and us. You know; nature. Yeah, I can see that."

Harry thought about lives he had shared, people and events that would always be part of him as he looked over the muddy flowing Anacostia River. He felt close to his distant past leaning back on the hard pine slatted bench. Much of what he pulled into his consciousness happened before Mark was born, and most of the memories of family occurred before he traveled so much. He wondered if it was the travel that had transformed him from the political being who thought about living out his days in one town: Philadelphia, Pennsylvania. Was it the travel or the death of his natural family?

"Dad, what can you do if you just study nature?"

"What do you mean?"

"I mean, do you just learn about animals?" Mark paused, more to think about his question than to hear an answer from his father. "I guess you can teach, huh?" Mark sounded a bit disappointed in his own conclusion.

"Teaching is one of the most important jobs you can have. Your grandparents were wonderful teachers."

"Yeah, I know, but nobody in school wants to be a teacher. I bet most of my teachers don't even really want to be teachers, do they?"

"Who told you that?"

"Some of the kids talk about it. Everybody with teacher parents, or uncles, or stuff lives in small houses, doesn't get to have nice vacations. It's definitely not cool to have to teach."

"Money isn't the only reason a person works, you know," Harry said, trying not to be annoyed.

"Besides, teaching's not the only thing you can do when you study nature. It depends on what part of nature you study. Plants, for example, make up a large portion of what humans beings eat, wear, and work with. Think of all of the vegetables we eat, the clothes we wear, medicines we take, or the things made of wood. They're all plant products whose use was figured out by a botanist or plant scientist of some sort."

"Yeah, but if we don't watch out, we'll use up all the forests. And doesn't that affect the weather?"

"That's right. So, there are many ways in which the study of plants can lead to a career: research, medicine, pharmaceuticals, new products, forestry, and on and on."

Father and son sat for a few more minutes and then Harry tapped Mark on the shoulder.

"How about we pick up some French bread, sandwich meat, and cheese and go eat brunch with Mom in the back yard?"

"I'll beat you back to the car," yelled Mark over his shoulder and took off up the grassy incline.

Later that evening, as they drove up the front drive to the Bartram's home in Bethesda, Mary smiled at her husband.

"That was sweet of you two to bring home that little picnic. I love it when we spend time together like that." She squeezed his hand after he released the steering wheel of the parked car.

"I really wish we could have more of those times. You know, I feel like Dad and I never had enough time together, and I sure don't want that to happen with Mark."

"That's nice to hear and you know who alone can make sure that doesn't happen, don't you?"

"How wonderful to see you, Mary." Donna Bartram greeted Mary with a big hug as they entered the rose-colored marble foyer, adorned with floor vases of pink Hydrangea..

"It's been too long, Donna. Since those few minutes at the Board of Trade dinner." Mary returned the salutation.

"Everyone is on the veranda, out back. Harry, I hope you won't mind, but I've invited some non-company people to keep the evening from being a total bore for spouses."

"Brilliant idea. It'll liven things up for all of us. The house looks spectacular, as always." Harry glanced at the vases of fresh flowers framing the huge living room sofa. They moved into the den and out onto the veranda- a flat area surrounded by blue and white three foot Hydrangeas and four foot pink Rhododendron. The shrubs formed a rectangle around the floor of brown and red ceramic Mexican tiles.

The party was in full swing. Liquor had lubricated all senses of humor, and guests were chatting and touching each other with the warmth of familiar colleagues and close friends. Harry and Mary moved among the crowd, locked arm and arm, for an hour before dinner. When the thirty or so guests were summoned onto the patio, two stone steps elevated from the veranda, they found four tables gaily set and name cards distributing the couples at separate tables. Harry was seated next to Harriet Jenks, a blond thirty-something girlfriend of Peter Burke. He found her very chatty, quite bright and Waspish, but ultimately young and uninformed. He spent much of the meal savoring quail and garlic-mashed potatoes, and sipping chilled chardonnay. Occasionally, he uttered "Oh, really," which was adequate to keep Harriet rolling. Finally, as the strawberry cheesecake arrived, Harry turned his full attention to Bob Harley, Don's stockbroker, who sat to his left.

Mary sat between Ellen Kwan and Roberto Higgins. Her dinner conversation was lively. She caught up on more than she ever wanted to know about Roberto's upbringing in "the city" and listened more astutely to Ellen's account of the last trip to Hong Kong. By the time her dessert arrived, Mary had explained her latest work on labor force participation and returned the conversation to Ellen's perceptions of SRI. For some reason, Mary sensed an unusual hesitance in Ellen while discussing the client. She assumed it was merely due to business confidences.

"It's unusual for a woman to lead such a large company in China, or Asia for that matter, isn't it?" Mary asked.

Ellen seemed to search for words before she responded. "Yes, it's more unusual than here or in Europe. I don't think it'll be too long, though, before more women rise to the top."

The two women didn't have time to continue their conversation, however, because Donna was calling people into the living room for coffee and brandy. Seated with Harry, back against the love seat, Mary quickly forgot the dinner conversation and was enveloped by the cleverness and good humor of the after-dinner story telling.

That evening, Mary and Harry made love with the enthusiasm of a newly reunited married couple. Each partner's alcohol did much of the work of arousing their passions. Afterwards, she remembered her conversation with Ellen Kwan about SRI's chief. In her European travels, Mary rarely encountered a female CEO. And, all of the Asian economists and business people she knew were men. Mary couldn't stop herself from wondering what she looked like. How had she become one of the few? Was she brilliant and cold? She decided not to ask her husband any of these questions.

CHAPTER FOURTEEN

香港

"Your daughter is an extraordinary young woman, Wong Shi. My compliments," said Xiaobin Li. He lifted a glass of ginger ale to toast his host at the lavish reception being thrown to celebrate the merged companies.

"You do me too much honor, Mr. Xiaobin. It is I who am in awe of your negotiating skill in the face of this young tiger." Mr. Wong cast a glance at his lovely daughter.

In the days since the end of the deal, it had become apparent to Wong Xi that her adversary knew full well the value of the stock he'd be getting. For whatever reason, Xiaobin was willing to accept the contract and move on. He and several of his top lieutenants appeared ready to retire and enjoy the fruits of their escapade into capitalism.

As she moved about the sparsely appointed living room of her father's house, Wong Xi seemed the picture of the modern Asian fashion model. Her blue, dragon-embroidered dress revealed enough of her figure to be complimentary, but not so much as to be improper. Her conversation, demeanor, and elegance seemed perfectly matched to the pale green floral patterned room and its party mood guests. While talking to a group of bankers, she peered over the shoulder of the very earnest Cantonese financier facing her and caught a glimpse of Rip Drake chatting with her friend Margaret Schultz. She had flown in, without Rajib, to help Xi celebrate. Xi had introduced her to Drake, who seemed quite taken by her.

Xi's husband, Bao Li joined her briefly with the Cantonese. They soon excused themselves to move to another group of guests.

"A pity the Americans couldn't be here. I would very much like to talk with this brilliant Mr. Morton. He seems to have made quite an impression on your colleagues."

Xi responded without changing her expression. "Yes, a pity. You recall that you found him quite interesting at the restaurant."

"Quite so," Bao said matter-of-factly. She planted a light kiss on his cheek, but filed away his expression of interest to recall and examine when she was alone.

While holding a glass of ginger ale, Xi moved in and out of the celebrating clusters scattered about the living room; Bao Li having remained with a group of his friends.

"It seems that modern women of Asia are attracted by the unique strangeness of foreigners," said Ho Duan as he cast a quick look from Xi to Margaret Schultz and Rip Drake.

"As my honorable colleague is well aware, the attraction of which you speak is neither new, nor limited to women," she responded with apparent detachment.

"Perhaps I'm just an old man, but it seems we lose so many of our brightest stars. We dilute our most promising strains," Ho continued.

"Well, in Margaret's case, the strain was diluted at birth. She's of mixed parentage. None of it is Chinese. If my honorable colleague were not intoxicated with good cheer, I'm sure he would have remembered that fact." Xi lost her smile.

"It still shows a lack of self-pride and cultural integrity," said Bao Li who had stepped into the small group.

"With all due respect to my elders, you both display an antiquated and surprisingly parochial view of 'culture.' If I'm not mistaken, my honorable husband had to adjust to the idea of a female CEO a mere seven years ago."

"I have no personal feeling, and am certainly not threatened by relationships between Chinese and foreigners. They just seem so unnecessary, given our numbers. But, of course there are marvelous exceptions." Bao added, smiling at his wife.

"Well, please excuse me. I believe there are guests to attend to." Xi politely bowed, turned, and walked across the beige-speckled marble floor to join her best friend.

"Xi, what a delightful surprise to meet Margaret. She attended Queens College only briefly after I had left Oxford, and knew several of my colleagues." Rip grinned rocking back on his heels.

"What do the Americans say about seven degrees of separation? Rip has been to my father's hometown in Punjab," Margaret seemed equally pleased with her new acquaintance.

As the trio chatted and sipped, Xi exchanged her ginger ale for Champagne. She momentarily lost track of the other guests. When she did look above her wineglass and glanced about the foyer, she saw her cousin. Wan Ren was greeting her father.

"He's got some nerve showing up here," she muttered to no one in particular.

"Excuse me chums; duty calls." Stepping away from Margaret and Rip, she moved towards the mini-family reunion in the foyer.

Even as she suppressed a distasteful acidic eruption in her throat, Xi reached over and pecked her cousin lightly on the cheek.

"How delightful to see you, my cousin." She feigned perfect joy as she straightened up and took a sip of her drink.

"The delight and pleasure is mine, cousin. And deepest congratulations on the successful merger."

She ached to take Ren aside and rip into his disloyal, despicable hide, despite her strong sense of propriety and of deference to her father. She was sure that her father had already sternly and severely addressed him for his selfish and stupid treachery that had almost cost her life. Had the assassin's bullet hit, Ren would be floating in Victoria Harbor right now. Once Ren's betrayal had been discovered, he would surely have been murdered along with Xiaobin Li and the rest of his corporate soldiers. By now, she was confident that her cousin had had to show appropriate apologies to the important men in the family and would be on his most deferential behavior for the foreseeable future. He would surely now know that South China could not shield him from family retribution.

"I hope my cousin can forgive my late arrival and will accept this small token of my congratulations upon her most masterful negotiation." Ren bowed and presented her with a simply wrapped square box, four inches on a side.

She took the package but didn't open it. "My cousin is too kind."

She said no more, no less than was required. Her stare, however, bore straight to the back of Ren's optic nerve. He felt a shiver of fear and could not return his cousin's glance. The stare lasted less than a second, but its effect on Ren was electric. He knew that he had brushed the tipping point of family tolerance, and that any further slip, no matter how slight, would provoke retribution more swift and severe than any triad could deliver.

Bao Li knew something had transpired, for he caught the greeting and gift exchange from fifteen feet away while partially engaged in conversation with South China's Yi Li and other mainland guests. Only Xi's father, standing in the foyer circle, saw and appreciated the full significance of the exchange.

"She's a master Tai-Pan. I can now relax. In both business and in family she has overcome her Western value dalliances. She has learned to instill the ultimate fear deeply shrouded in the actions of the most hospitable hostess," the proud father thought to himself.

Following a dinner of crispy Peking duck, pheasant eggs, steamed lotus and bok choy, spicy garlic-pepper noodles, and honey-sweet Mongolian beef, Xi sat back from the table and sipped fragrant Dragon's Well tea from Suzhou. She looked down the rows of mahogany-backed chairs at the quietly festive crowd. The large brush painting decorating the wall behind the far end of the dining room showed a solitary fishing boat adrift among the over-grown boulders that dot the waters of Guilin. None of the objects in the sparsely appointed room were distractions, but somehow framed the magnificent table setting.

Xi smiled to herself as she recalled her father arguing with the Thai decorator about which furniture, pictures, and chandelier would support the most perfect Chinese eating experience. Finally, Wong Shi recognized the "superiority" of the foreigner's taste and acceded. Even the off-white cream color of the walls perfectly set off the three large paintings of calligraphy poems. The fourth wall was a set of sliding glass doors opening onto a quiet rock garden and lily pond.

"Even our petty intolerances seem civilized at moments like these," she thought returning her attention to the table and the evening's conversation.

Later that evening, while reading a collection of the works of Lao Tze in bed, Bao Li suddenly looked over at his young wife and stared as if transfixed by a wispy apparition.

"Wong Xi, you have been a perfect partner. I am lucky that I met you after I had my children and could appreciate life with a modern Chinese woman."

"By modern, do you mean single minded, Li?" she smiled at her husband.

"I mean modern, bridging the gap from the China of emperors to that of a twentieth century world power. I mean a woman who somehow has absorbed the essence of our magnificent mainland culture, mastered the commercial ways of Hong Kong, and understands foreign Western thinking."

"It is I who am lucky to be the wife of the most complete man I've ever met."

They embraced and Bao Li felt aroused for the first time in many months. Their lovemaking was caring and fulfilling to both.

"What will SRI do, now that you have brought in a major supplier of material?" asked Bao.

"Well, we have to spend several months completing the design of new products to take advantage of our enhanced capability. Then we'll reassess the new European markets we've anticipated entering, establish contacts with buyers and outlets and implement our plan. And we must identify the nearest competition, discover their weaknesses, and exploit them. It is well thought-out, Li. Why do you ask?"

"I was just curious as to whether your use of Western consultants had influenced your direction. The plan still sounds solid, to me."

"As always, my husband, I welcome your consultation." Xi looked deeper into her husband's eyes, wondering what meaning his enquiries hid. She could find none.

"Good night, my little flower." He kissed her and turned on his side to sleep. Afterwards, they lay beside each other, eyes closed. Two bodies touching, yet independent. Only then did Xi think about Harry.

CHAPTER FIFTEEN

香港

Mark Morton looked over his shoulder as he walked from his schoolyard to the public library on Georgia Avenue, near the border with suburban Maryland. He wondered if the Asian-looking man in the tan Toyota had been following him. He dismissed the notion and entered the library to work on his homework.

It was near dark when he left the library to walk north several blocks to get the bus for home. He had forgotten the man until he saw the same tan car pass by him going the other direction on Georgia as he approached the bus stop. More conscious of his pursuer now, Mark watched out of the back of the bus for the short ride to his stop, and peered over his shoulder as he walked home through the streets of Potomac Village. He didn't see the car or the man again that night.

"It's so nice for all of us to be together at dinner. It feels like it's been such a long time." Harry said while drinking a glass of wine and grinning at his son and wife.

"Mark, are you okay, honey? You haven't said much tonight," Mary leaned over and touched her son's sleeve.

"I'm okay. It's just this weird thing happened on Georgia Avenue."

"Oh, really? What was that?"

"Well, I think I was followed by some Chinese man in a car," Mark sheepishly offered.

"What do you mean, you think? Did someone get out of a car?" Harry's voice was suddenly tight and tense.

"No. It's just when I walked into the library and then when I left, the same guy was in a car. I'm sure he followed me. Just like in the movies."

"It's probably nothing, son. But let me know if it happens again. Maybe one of us will pick you up next time you go to the library." Conversation soon moved on to school projects and national news.

Later that evening, when in their bedroom, Mary brought up the event again with Harry.

"Harry, I'm worried. Do you think this strange man has anything to do with your China business?"

"I highly doubt it. I just completed a business deal, not a job for the CIA. Besides, there are millions of Chinese around the world. We don't know for sure that this guy is Chinese, that he was following Mark, or much less that he's related to my business activities."

"I just don't want to dismiss this. I'm the one who---"

"Mary, I'm just as concerned about Mark's safety, so don't start with that."

"What should we do, then?"

"Well, for the next couple of days, I can pick him up if he has to go to the library, and let's see what happens. Okay?"

After a protracted, uneasy silence, Mary asked, "What kind of business deal is this? It's not something dangerous, is it?"

"Mary, you know I do M&A consulting. It's straightforward…"

"I know, but I guess we don't talk that much about work anymore. I mean, you're not doing something the CIA is involved in, are you?"

Harry laughed to release tension. "Baby, you've been reading too much John Grisham, or Le Carre, or somebody."

She looked at her husband, searching for truth. "Okay," she said finally.

"Goodnight, baby."

"Goodnight."

He hoped he had convinced her, but he wasn't convinced himself. He decided to contact SRI. Looking at his watch, he realized that the Hong Kong company's office would be opening in a few minutes. Waiting for her breathing to indicate that she had drifted into a deep sleep, he slipped out of bed. In his study, Harry dialed Wong Xi's direct line.

"*Hue*. Harry, what a pleasant surprise. To what do I owe the pleasure of this call?"

"I suppose I miss Hong Kong, as well the excitement of the deal."

"Is that all you miss, Harry?"

He laughed, but didn't answer. He asked about the final deal closing activities and the current state of affairs with the former South China crew. Nothing she said, however, gave him any indication that there would be reason for anyone to be stalking his son.

"Harry, why are you asking all of these questions? Is something wrong there?"

"I'm not sure." Harry hesitated for a moment and then decided to tell her about the man following Mark.

"That's terrible. Your family must be terribly anxious. Let me think. I really can't see why anyone connected with the deal here would be tracking you and bothering your son. Everything has been settled. If there were a problem, the likely targets would be my family, not yours."

"That's what I think. Okay. Sorry to bother you. Take care."

"It's no bother and please keep me apprised. If we have to do something here, let me know."

"Thanks, Xi. Bye."

Over the next week, Harry picked his son up when he normally would have traveled on public transportation. He thought he saw the tan car and Asian driver once, but he wasn't sure, because the vehicle he spotted was turning a corner. Mary and Mark's anxiety seemed to fade, but Harry remained tight inside for weeks. His brush with South China thugs was vivid in his memory. The incident also affected his concentration at work, although he told no one about the tracker.

Sitting inside a coffee shop whose front was open to 18th Street in Washington's Adams-Morgan section, Harry pulled up his office e-mail on his lap-top. There was a message from Don Bartram to see him about a deal with Sony in Tokyo. Harry dialed his office and got his assistant, Hazel Marsh.

"Morning, Hazel."

"Harry, you're not coming in today, right?" she sounded a bit anxious.

"Right. I'm at *Mario's* on 18th for a bite. Then, I'm meeting Roberto for a round of golf at one. By the way, did Don say anything about Tokyo?"

"He was just by here to see if you could chat."

"Patch me through, would you? You got anything?"

"No, all else is quiet. Here's Don. Bye."

"Harry, hit 'em straight today. Somebody has to hold up the older generation's integrity on the course. I sure couldn't while you were away."

"You know I'll do my best, but Roberto's tough. I got your e-mail. I thought the Sony deal was done. Last time I talked to Emory---"

"Well, we all thought it was done. Emory flew back over two days ago. He really thinks he needs a bit of help negotiating this thing back on track."

"Why me? I don't know this deal."

"Yeah, but you know Sony. And you're hot."

"I just promised Mary and Mark I'd be here for awhile. The last stretch was rough on them."

"Harry, take them with you. It's a couple of days; a week at most."

"Famous last words. No, the last thing Mary wants is a long trip to accompany me while I work. She's not that crazy about Asia to begin with."

"Meet them in Europe afterwards. You need a break anyway."

"Let me check. I'll call you later."

Harry hung up. He wasn't anxious to tell Mary he had another trip. No way would she believe it was for a brief period. She did love Europe, however. It was worth a shot. Harry started to dial her number, when a picture in the Metro section of the *Washington Post* caught his attention. "Suspected Child Molester Arrested." The story was about a man, suspected in three attacks on young boys, who had been caught through DNA tests. The picture was of an Asian man standing beside the car that Harry had seen the other day.

"Thank you, Jesus," Harry whispered to himself.

He dialed his wife.

"Mary, they caught the guy who followed Mark. Look on page two of 'Metro.'

"I know; I saw it this morning. You really think this is the person?"

"Positive, because the car also fits what I remember. Boy, Mark will be so relieved. You saw it and didn't call me?"

"No." Mary's voice was cold.

He thought for a few minutes but decided not to pursue it then. Instead, he launched into his other subject. "How would you like to spend a few days in London or Paris week after next?"

"Where are you going, Harry?"

"What do you mean?"

"I wasn't born yesterday. You just promised to stick around, and now you want us to meet in Europe? Where will you be coming from?"

"Don needs me to go to Tokyo for a few days."

Mary hissed. Then, to Harry's surprise she said she would meet him in Paris.

"Shall we take Mark? He'd like to see a foreign big city."

Again, Harry was surprised by his wife's answer.

"No. He needs to stay in school. I could have Poppa come east to stay. He'd love to see Mark." After a moment's pause, "That's not practical, I guess. Mark can stay with the Birches. Mabel is always asking to have him stay over."

"Sweetheart, this is unlike you."

"Why, because I want to enjoy life a bit too?"

After they hung up, Mary consulted a flyer from the *International Labor Economist*. She thought, "Why not?" She asked her assistant to see if she could arrange for her to get on a panel at the London conference. Calling back, she informed her boss of the panel topic, the flight from Paris to London, and the hotel. Mary, then, started to place a call to London, herself. She balked. I'll just take a chance, she decided. She took a deep breath, leaned back in her chair and couldn't fight back a wide smile.

CHAPTER SIXTEEN

香港

Harry got out of the taxi at the base of Montmartre and walked half a block to the Pension L'Oiseau Bleu, a three-story guesthouse in one of Paris's arts districts. He loved the gray stone exterior with stained oak gargoyles at the end of the drain bracketing each side of the roof.

"*Ca va, M. Morgan? Il y'a long temps,*" the matronly innkeeper greeted one of her favorite guests.

"*Madame Gorot, comment ca va?*" he responded, giving her a peck on both cheeks.

After a brief catch up conversation, she told him that his wife had arrived about an hour ago and was in their room, the suite at the top of the long third floor stairs. He carried his suitcase and briefcase up, but waited for a second before tapping on the door.

"*Oui? Qui est-ce?*" Mary asked from some distance beyond the solid living room door.

He thought for a about how to answer, set down his bag, and turned to pace. The door swung open before Harry could determine his response.

"You look gorgeous, babe," he said as he lifted his wife up by the waist and planted a long kiss.

"You look pretty nice yourself, Harry Morgan. Do you think it's the charm of Paris and the love that people claim permeates the atmosphere?" she enthusiastically returned her husband's kiss. "Close the door. I want to hear all about Tokyo while I take a bubble bath."

"By yourself?"

"No, silly. There's room in the tub for a tall slender husband."

They barely dried their hot wet bodies before they tumbled into bed and made long, lingering love.

"You know, sometimes I wonder about Don's sense of urgency. The advice I gave Emory Gans in Tokyo could have easily been given over the phone. One day reviewing documents, one day of meetings and one more day refining strategy…"

"Harry, you're the one who always says that face to face is important."

"It is, many times. Just not this time. Anyway, how's our son?"

"Sweetheart, he's fine. I think he was looking forward to having some time without either of us around," said Mary.

"Well, he'll soon be a teenager. You know about that independence gene that surfaces at twelve or thirteen."

"He's still a young boy, Harry. Mark is no teenager. Let's not rush him."

"Now, how's your work, baby?"

"Harry, I love my job, but it's a little tiring to do this labor market analysis and not have the ability to make things change for marginally trained folks. »

After a moment's pause, she added, "I suppose my job is fine."

"You could quit and work for a local job training program. How about working for the DC government?"

"You really want to depress me, don't you, sweetie?"

"No, that's where the rubber meets the road. That's where you could change policy and affect lives."

"Harry, I know myself well enough to know that the only life I would affect is my own. Negatively. You know I have a low tolerance for bureaucracy."

She looked away, deep in thought. Her hands rubbed his swollen biceps, taught from his regular workouts.

"I guess I sound indecisive. Labor market researchers often just celebrate the problems of the chronically unemployed. But, this is the field and subject matter that I enjoy pursuing. I'm really not bored."

They sat up in bed, listening to the occasional car horn or a passel of young Parisians chattering as they strolled only a few floors below, surrounded by mid-evening darkness. Finally, Mary spoke. "You know, you're sweet to ask about work, but could we maybe go out for a late snack? This is Paris, after all."

"Great idea."

The town worked its magic on Harry. Over the next three days, he enjoyed his wife's company at museums, jazz clubs, and theater; over sumptuous sauces and succulent wines; and arm and arm walking through history along some of France's most famous streetscapes. He almost never thought of Washington, save for two calls to Mark. He'd made one call to Tokyo, but Hong Kong had fallen completely from consciousness.

The days along the Seine had a different effect on Mary. Her step was not quite as peppy, her taste buds not so stimulated, nor did artists' colors seem as vivid as they did for Harry. Mary wasn't as fully present as they walked along the narrow alleys on the Left Bank or the grand boulevards of the old city. She relaxed and enjoyed the time, but she couldn't put her finger on what was missing.

"I can't remember when we've had such a good time. This has been wonderful," Harry smiled as he walked her through the airport to the plane for London.

"It has been a great change, sweetheart. Don't forget you have those thank-you gifts for George and Mabel. I'll be back in four days, and you have the number at the Chadwick Hotel?"

"Don't worry, baby. Just have a safe trip and a great conference." He kissed her and headed for his flight to Washington.

In London, early that afternoon, Mary picked up her conference materials, greeted American and European labor economist colleagues, and returned to her room for a brief nap. "Should I call?" She asked herself. "He's probably off somewhere in another part of the world."

She reached for her address book, found the number and dialed.

"Hello, is Mr. Dupree in, please?"

"Who shall I say is ringing?" responded a pleasant but very business-like voice.

"Dr. Morton." Mary wondered why she felt she had to be so formal.

"Mary? This is a pleasant surprise. Are you coming to London?"

"I'm already here, attending---"

"Oh, of course, the economists' conference at the university," Max cut her off. "When could I see you? How about a late dinner tonight? I could move some things around."

"That's sweet, Max. But, I just got in. Perhaps tomorrow would be possible."

"I'll pick you up at 7:30. Where shall I meet you?"

"Well," Mary hesitated. She wasn't comfortable having her colleagues see her with Max. Then, she thought: that's silly. But before she could respond, Max spoke again.

"How would it be if I meet you in your hotel lobby? I assume you're at the Chadwick, near the London School of Economics. We can take our pick of several lovely spots nearby."

"Good. I'll see you tomorrow night." She hung up and tried to nap for twenty minutes before walking the few blocks back to the conference.

The first day of the conference was fairly uneventful. The next day was loaded with meetings, papers, and side bar conversations. She was fully immersed and almost forgot about her dinner engagement.

"Oh, it's 6:30," she said suddenly looking up at a wall clock in the hotel bar. "Jeffrey, I have to go get ready for dinner with an old friend. See you in the morning."

Jeffery Short was a British labor economist with whom Mary was outlining a paper they were going to give at the spring meeting in six months.

"Okay, actually, I should be going myself. Until tomorrow, then."

Back at her hotel, she took the elevator to her seventeenth-floor room, took out a comfortable lavender suede suit and cream-colored silk blouse, stripped and climbed into the shower. Now, her every pore was awake as she smiled under the stream of hot water, thinking about her dinner date.

To her great relief, no one Mary knew from the conference was in the lobby when she spied Max coming through the revolving door. He approached her, grinning broadly, and gave her a friendly kiss on the cheek.

"Mary, you look marvelous."

"Why, thank you Max. You look wonderful yourself."

He took her by the elbow and guided her to the door.

"Do you know the Café de Luna? One of London's little-known, but fabulous Italian cafes. It's only fifteen minutes from here by taxi."

"That sounds perfect."

Deep into their second bottle of wine and a long conversation about their professional lives, Max suggested a nightcap at a jazz club five blocks back towards her hotel.

"Oh, Max, the direction is right, but I have a conference to attend in the morning."

"No paper to deliver, though, right?"

"No, but I do have a panel---"

"No buts. I know there's no way you'd take this trip and not be prepared, already. You'll love this place."

The fresh chilly air made her shiver as they walked through the moist fall evening. The lights, sounds and smells of London made Mary feel even more alive than she had in the restaurant. She felt totally comfortable with her arm hooked to that of her tall and handsome escort. The bounce she couldn't find in Paris was very much back in her step. They only stayed an hour at the club, and then caught a cab back to the hotel.

"Max, this has been a wonderful evening. I've learned more about international finance and the fun of non-theater night life in London than I ever thought existed."

Dupree pressed his legs hard against Mary's thighs and kissed her softly and deeply on the lips. She found her mouth and tongue actively seeking his.

"We really shouldn't be like a couple of teenagers by the lobby elevators," she said.

The elevator arrived and it seemed natural for Max to escort her back to the room. They didn't make another sound until Mary uttered a groan of pleasure as Max caressed her hardened bare nipples beneath the sheets. They made love until exhaustion claimed them and then they slept. Mary was sorry when they both realized it was five A.M., and Max took a shower, dressed and held her at arms' length to bid her goodbye.

"Mary, what's wrong? You seem withdrawn?" Max said.

"I'm sorry I'm leaving London so soon. That's all." Then she smiled.

"Right, Well, I'm flattered."

"I suppose I'm not ready to return to my life at home."

He put both arms around her and held her for a time, saying nothing. Then, he said, "Maybe you need to travel more to help you appreciate what you have in the U.S. A great child, exciting and prestigious think tank career, a social life that takes you to marvelous haunts like the National Gallery or the Phillips, embassies, swank receptions, and a time-tested successful marriage. Really, Mary- you're blessed."

"I know I am. In a sense, that's what is so disheartening. It all seems perfect on the surface. But I'm not so sure my marriage is standing the test of time. Why else would I be here?"

"If I might, let a long-time bachelor tell you that an affair can just as often strengthen one's marriage as tear it apart."

"You're sweet, Max. And I have loved spending this time with you."

"Next trip let me know earlier. London has a few more interesting sights you've probably never seen. I'd love to show her off to you."

"I will." She gave him one more long kiss, while wrapped in a towel. He looked into the hall and carefully closed the door behind him.

The last day of the conference, her panel presentation, and the long flight home were a blur. Several times on the plane, she giggled to herself and thought how silly it was to be acting like a college freshman after her first date. She also wondered what her attraction to Max meant for her relationship with Harry, but told herself it was just a diversion. It had been a freak occurrence that happened only because their stars were aligned that once. She tried to think about Mark, but Max Dupree kept slipping into her consciousness for much of the five plus hours back to the U.S.

Her plane arrived at Dulles Airport at 6 on a Friday night. As she waited for her luggage at the United Airlines carousel, she jumped in surprise when she heard Harry and Mark sing out in unison.

"Hi, Mom. Welcome home."

"Mark and Harry! What, what are you two doing here?"

"We thought it would be a nice surprise to meet you," Harry beamed.

"Yeah, Mommy. You really look surprised."

"Well, this is a nice treat, sweetheart."

Once in the car and heading towards Washington on the Dulles Access Road, Harry looked over, placed his right hand on his wife's leg and asked, "So, how was the conference?"

"Oh, very good. I had lots of good meetings and my panel went very well."

She hoped her husband would attribute her distant and confused tone to their surprise greeting. She felt totally disoriented

261

and realized that she had counted on the taxi ride home to compose herself and get back into her domestic environment.

"What have you been doing while Mommy and Daddy were away?"

"Well, Uncle George and Aunt Mabel were great. We went to a Redskins game and a movie."

"Did you do any school work?"

"Of course, Mom." The boy pulled himself up close to the front seat.

"I'm so glad to see both of you."

By the time they drove up to their house Mary had begun to tire, and she was not able to fully leave London behind her. She felt alternatively guilty about her affair and relieved to be home.

"You go on in and get comfortable, Mary. I'll bring the bags in." Harry uncharacteristically gave his wife a peck on the cheek. She gave a strained smile and climbed the front steps. When she opened the front door, the smell of boiled pork and cabbage greeted her nostrils. She went into the living room to sit and catch her breath when she heard some stirring in the kitchen.

"Mark? Is that you already in the kitchen? Who's cooking?"

"Surprise," said Mabel, bounding from the kitchen into the living room with a glass of Mary's favorite champagne.

"Oh, this is too much. You all---"

"Hush up, girl. It's not often that you have work abroad. Sit right there and relax."

After Mary settled in, the four adults and Mark had a slow Friday night dinner. The Birches filled her in on all of the fun they had had sitting their son. Mary managed to dredge up a few stories about the conference and a museum visit, but she mostly talked about her time with Harry in Paris.

"Girl, we'll let you get some rest. You look beat, but it's great to have you home. We'll talk," said Mabel as she and George went out the front door.

"Wow, that was wonderful, you two," Mary said hugging both Harry and Mark. "Little man, it's time for your bed. Actually, I'm not far behind. I'm tired."

"You two go on up. I'll clean up," Harry said.

Half an hour later, he sat with his feet over the side of a living room chair, listening to the late news and reflecting on the evening. He was happy to have Mary home, and thought maybe now, they might rekindle their relationship. Nothing, other than her exhaustion, had struck him as unusual about her homecoming, and he was glad that the Birches had come over so that he wasn't tempted to focus on their relationship and his sense of drifting.

In the week since he'd returned, Harry had tried to get back into several projects at work, but nothing held his interest. Finally, Don Bartram had suggested he take off a few weeks, since there was nothing urgent requiring his attention. Harry was still considering it. Maybe he'd play some late fall golf in West Virginia, spend time with Mark and Mary and piece his marriage back together.

The first time Harry and Mary found to talk was one Sunday brunch at the Rock Creek Deli just over the Maryland line, after Mark had gone off to visit a friend and watch football.

"Mary, I'm thinking about taking some time off."

"You do what you want to. I've never really been good at giving you advice that you value." She pushed back from the corner table. She was a bit surprised at her own disinterested tone.

"I'm serious. I think we need to find a way to get back in touch with each other."

"Well, isn't that nice that you've decided to be attentive again? Let's have the band strike up an encore."

"I don't get the hostility."

"I'm sorry. That was unfair. It's just that the contrast between being together abroad and life here in DC is so stark," she said.

"You sure you haven't changed, baby?"

"Maybe. On the other hand, maybe you should have learned to use some of your famed psychological analytic abilities on the home front, sweetie."

"What happened in London, Mary? We were fine after Paris."

She froze. She couldn't tell if he was fishing, had picked up some clue, or was truly reflecting his confusion. She said nothing, at first.

"Paris was wonderful, Harry. I love spending time together like that. I guess I'm tired of the normal routine here of you fitting Mark and me in when you can."

"Well, I feel like you're not willing to try."

"Maybe, I'm prejudging. Let's just drop it, for now. After you've chilled for a few days, played golf, taken care of Mark, and left work at the office, let's see how we feel."

He was dispirited, but at a profound level he knew Mary was right. No need to press her about London, now. Time was the only real healer.

On Monday, he left a message with Don that he was going to follow his advice for six weeks. He then sat in his study and made a list of all of the books he had stacked up unread and those off of the best-seller list that he'd noted over the past few years. Catching up on some current foreign policy essays, international thrillers, and biographies would be fun, he thought. He then made arrangements for a weekend golf trip later that fall. He also planned some weekend outings with Mark to see the ships in Annapolis, the aquarium in Baltimore, and the Skins play the Eagles up in Philadelphia. He bought theater tickets for that Friday, thinking it would be a great way to start reconnecting with Mary.

When he excitedly reported his new activities to Mary and Mark at the supper that he had prepared that evening, his son was ecstatic. His wife, however, said she had already made plans to go out with a couple of girlfriends on Friday. He forced a smile, but was hurt by her rebuff. Harry said he'd check with her beforehand next time. He realized he'd have to wait to schedule serious time with her.

CHAPTER SEVENTEEN

香港

That Saturday morning, Harry and Mark piled into the Porsche and drove up the interstate highway to Baltimore. They spent their first hour and a half out near Johns Hopkins University at the Baltimore Art Museum.

"Daddy?" Mark asked as they stood in front of an international glass exhibit. "How come we never go to museums, all of us together?"

"Well, son, I'm not sure I know the answer to that one. I was exposed to all sorts of art as a kid. Just like you. My brother Pierce- your uncle, - your mother and I used to go to museums and art shows in Philadelphia. I don't know why we, as a family, don't go. Let's try and do it soon, okay?"

Wandering further into the glass exhibit, Mark remarked, "In my school, art's a girls' thing."

"I'm surprised at you, son. I thought you already knew that there are very few things anymore that are solely for one gender. Actually, think of the most famous artists you can. I'll bet you come up with five men for every woman you can name."

Mark sat on a bench in the middle of the exhibit and thought silently.

"Well?"

"Yeah, I guess you're right. Sort of like cooks and chefs on T.V. They're mostly guys. But maybe that only proves that men get all the big jobs and fame."

"You might have something there. Anyway, I know that my appreciation grew after I met your mother and after I began to fully understand how good a painter your uncle was."

"I wish he hadn't died. It would be neat to have an uncle."

"I do too. He would have loved being a part of your growing up. You know, your uncle and grandmother would also have loved helping you with your music. And, your grandfather would have harmonized with you on his deep lower register bass for days. Any of them would have been a lot more fun to practice with than your mother is or I am."

The two Mortons passed much of the rest of the morning looking at modern oils, and then drove back downtown to the Inner Harbor. As they walked slowly towards the Aquarium, a chilly wind came off the water and rustled the loosely tied sails of a double-mast sailboat.

"Daddy, look at that guy on the boat. That's what I want to be, a sea captain. I want to sail the oceans and have adventures like you do."

"Like me? What do you mean, son? I don't sail and I sure don't have adventures at sea." "No, not like Captain Cook, or that guy in the book, *Kon Tiki*. I mean see other countries and meet different people."

"Well, that's part of what I do. But a lot of my work is done in the office downtown. When I'm abroad, I'm---"

"I know you make deals. Mr. Bartram, Peter, Roberto, Ellen and you. But it's with foreign people. It's cool."

"Well, maybe next weekend, we can go to Annapolis and see the tall ships. You can meet some real adventurers there." He was pleased that his son showed interest in what he did and had some abstract concept of what it involved. He hoped that this meant that the negative effect of his long absences was neither profound nor permanent.

After a two hour stroll through the underwater world of the aquarium, Harry and Mark bought hot dogs and sauerkraut with old fashion root beer at a street vendor stand. They ate their lunch on the waterfront in between constant conversation, made up mostly of Mark's questions about the sea creatures they had seen. The boy's interest lasted the entire fifty-minute ride back to Washington.

"Hello, my two explorers. How was Baltimore?" Mary greeted them as they entered the kitchen late in the afternoon.

"It was great once we got to the fish."

"Well, sweetheart, you can tell me all about it while Daddy goes to pick up things for dessert and tomorrow. Harry, I left a short list on the hall table. Would you mind going to the supermarket?" Mary looked at Harry without emotion in her eyes.

"No problem. I'll be right back."

Harry didn't notice any of the street furniture or buildings in the quarter mile drive to the *Giant* food store. He turned the car radio to the jazz station and tried to figure out what was wrong with his wife. Why did she seem so detached, so indifferent? At the store, he only needed a hand-held basket to carry the few items Mary needed from the vegetable, meat and dessert sections. While picking out frozen berries from the cooler, he heard a familiar voice behind him.

"Well, well, well, if it isn't Mr. Negro International. Been selling out any folks recently, Morton?"

Harry turned around and smiled at the grinning face of Robert Byrd.

"Why, hello, Robert. I see you got your list written out nice and neat. You aren't as dumb as everybody thinks you are."

Byrd's light complexion deepened in color.

"Look here, Morton. All right, I guess I asked for it. Anyway, it seems the boys are getting on better. That's what counts."

Harry stared at the man in front of him and started to turn back to the meat display. Then, purely on instinct, he extended his hand. A surprised Byrd reacted instinctively and grasped the other man's hand.

"Why don't we bury the hatchet, and at least be civil?" Harry offered.

"Okay," was all Byrd said. Both men looked at each other with less contempt. They felt a tolerable resolution had been reached. Harry finished his shopping and drove home.

The resolution of a tense situation or the righting of a wronged relationship usually relaxed Harry and restored his equilibrium. Not today.

I liked being with Mark today. I didn't love it. So, far, I've not found a really stimulating pastime. And Mary? Now that we're home, nothing seems to warm her. Harry didn't feel depressed. He was numb.

He placed the groceries on the kitchen counter and turned to put his coat in the front hall closet.

"Dinner's just about ready, you two. Oh, Harry, George wants you to give him a call after dinner. Something about cards tonight. Sweetheart, it's fine with me. Mark and I have a little studying to do." She handed him a salad bowl to place on the dining room table.

He waited until he had cleaned up dishes after a pleasant and uneventful diner, before he called George Birch.

"What's going on, George? Mary said something about cards."

"That's what I told her, but… Hey, man. Why don't you come on over in about a half hour? Some of the fellas are coming over to watch the fight and chew the fat."

"Thanks, but you know I'm not much of a fight fan," Harry said, thinking he'd start on some of his reading projects.

"Come on, now. It'll do you good to get out some." Harry knew that he had no other plans for the evening, so he gave in.

"Okay. I'll be over in a bit. Thanks."

Harry sat by the phone for a moment after he'd hung up. Normally, he wouldn't be tempted to spend time with George's 'boys.' They got boring. He thought they rarely talked about anything of substance, or tended to repeat the same old refrains about how screwed up the city government was, or how the "man" was preventing them from doing one thing or another, or embellished unnecessary details about recent sexual conquests. Only rarely did Harry find such evenings fun, unless there was some business reason for the event, but he didn't conduct business with any of George's pals. On occasion, it felt good to let the mind rest, relax and 'be in the moment' with some 'guys.' Tonight, he thought was one of those times.

He read some old management journals and skimmed a few chapter headings of two novels to see which one he wanted to actually read. It was almost ten when he checked his watch, left the study and told Mary that he was going over to George's for a short while.

The only sounds on the Birch's street were the occasional raucous laughter floating out of his English basement windows. Harry waited patiently on the steps until the door chime drew the attention of the revelers.

"Hey, man, George is on the phone. Grab a beer and come on in the den. Damn Lennox Lewis is taking the thing to the eleventh round. Hell of a fight." Demetrius Bradshaw, George's long-time friend and accountant, closed the front door behind Harry.

When he entered the den, Harry shook hands with Bob Dash, the Bell Atlantic phone executive who was a neighbor and ten-year friend of George's.

"How you doing, man? I hear you taking a break for a few months." Bob addressed Harry while the mute was depressed on the TV remote in between the eleventh and twelfth rounds.

"Yeah, it's the first real break I've had in ten years." Harry relaxed and sipped on an Amstel Light.

"Baby, with the cash you must have after selling the company, I'd be taking a permanent vacation," chortled Bradshaw.

"I thought about it, but I'd get bored and underfoot. If you know what I mean." Harry began to get into the chitchat rhythm of guy talk.

"And his old lady's foot is not one you want to fall under," added George as he entered the room, beer in hand. They all laughed. The fight only went two more rounds, with Lewis surprising champ Riddick Bowe with a devastating left hook to the chin. Bob Dash and Demetrius Bradshaw left soon after, but Harry stayed on to find out a little about what was going on in George's life.

"When are you going to leave the Chamber and make some money?" Harry chided his buddy.

"Man, I wager on the ponies; I bet on a ball game every now and then; I even chase a skirt on occasion. With my gig, I am risk adverse," George smiled as he leaned back in one of the deep cordovan red den chairs. "You forgetting when I had to rat out our director for dipping into the Chamber's reserve funds, after he wouldn't stop when I warned him? That was rough times." George's jaw tightened visibly.

"Five years ago? You bounded right back when they brought what's his name in."

"You know, man, it's so funny to live in this Beltway economy and in this city where policy people, politicians don't know squat about small business. They got no clue about how to get folks employed and how to get the motor running again. They all love to talk macroeconomic crap," George vented.

"Well, at least you don't have to take any more entrepreneurial risks. You're pretty set, aren't you?"

"I'm cool, but so many dudes aren't. Making big contributions to local pols, as if that's going to return them some business-saving quid pro quo." George took a sip and smiled.

"Yeah, I can now spend more time pretending I'm some young, rich brother."

"You mean the ladies?"

George merely winked.

"So, things have settled down with Mabel?" Harry asked.

"We seem to be cool, for the moment." George paused and looked hard at his friend.

"'Course I nearly lost it when I found out Mabel had had a weekend with that young brother from the Convention Center. I damn near killed her."

"That's understandable. Although there was a bit of double standard there, as I recall."

"Oh, so you're cool with Mary's London fling, I suppose?"

Harry looked at his friend as if he'd just been stunned by a left jab to the chin.

"What London fling? The conference? George, what are you talking about?"

"Oh, Lord. I thought you had to know."

"Know what, man?" Harry was strangling his beer bottle and leaning forward, his buttocks barely touching the chair beneath him. "George? Talk to me."

"Well, Mabel let slip a week ago that Mary had a one-nighter with some dude you all knew from Philly. Max, uh---"

"Max Dupree? Was it Max Dupree?"

"Yeah, that sounds like it."

"That sanctimonious bitch. That's some shit," Harry sputtered before George put up a hand on his friend's shoulder.

"We wouldn't happen to have a double standard here. Would we, my man?"

Harry glared at his best friend for what seemed to George Birch like an hour. Finally, he said, "You're right, George. I'm in no position to complain. However, now it fits."

"What does?"

"Mary's been distant for quite awhile. I thought it was my travel. I even thought she might have suspected something about Wong Xi in Hong Kong. But this explains it."

"It might be all of those things. She's very smart, as you know," George offered. "What you going to do?"

"Nothing I can do, right now. I don't know. I'm in no position to challenge her. Maybe I should move up one of those trips and just get away for a bit. Need to think. Get my life, my priorities straight. I don't know, man."

"Well, whatever you do, don't be hasty. And remember, I'm always here."

"Thanks, George. I appreciate that. As much as I think I can read people, I'm a disaster where it matters most."

"I wouldn't be so hard on yourself, man. After all, if this is the first time, think of how long she's been faithful. And, as far as I can tell, it was just a one-nighter."

"But, that might be more meaningful to her than some trysts I've had."

"Harry, don't over analyze the shit, man."

"You're right, George. I think I'll head home. I'm okay. It'll be fine," he said without strong conviction as he left his friend.

Harry wasn't sleepy when he returned to a darkened house. Both Mark and Mary had gone to bed. It was about one o'clock when Harry took a cup of green tea up to his study. He turned on the computer and went to his web browser, with no particular site in mind. He meandered through the web and almost absent-mindedly, he pulled down a site called *CEO Express*. He started to read headlines from various financial magazines.

"Damn, that sneaky bitch." He slapped the computer table, stinging his palm. For several minutes, he stared at the monitor without really seeing anything on the screen.

Eventually, wondering what was happening with the South China-SRI deal, he pulled down the *South China Post*. He read several back editions and found a few references to SRI and Xi, but nothing unusual, and nothing referring to the merger. Harry was about to switch to Japanese papers to check on the *Sony* deal he had consulted on recently when he caught glimpse of Xi in a style section photo.

She was accompanied by her husband at a reception at which she was honored as Hong Kong's 'businessman of the year.'

"Good for her. I guess everything worked out fine," he said to himself. He looked at her photo in a modestly cut black evening dress and smiled. She looked spectacular. Harry leaned back in his chair and recalled the last time they had made love.

Harry spent a few more minutes reading about the Sony deal and surfing the net before shutting down his PC. He looked around the den at the awards and photos with friends and family that, in many ways, chronicled his adult life. His eyes rested on a photo of Mary and he seated at a dinner table at a regional Board of Trade event at which he had been honored four years ago. They looked, and indeed were, extremely happy then. Harry clasped his hands behind his head and looked around the room at other pictures of his wife.

Fifteen minutes later, he extinguished the lights, walked down the hall to the master bedroom, undressed and slipped into bed next to Mary. He put his arm around her, but she turned away, half-conscious.

"Harry, I have to get up early tomorrow. Good night."

"Good night, love."

Morton lay awake feeling sad and betrayed, but not angry.

My feelings are too much on the surface. I need to get away for awhile, he concluded.

Late one morning later in the week, Harry answered the phone in an empty house.

"Morton, how's the sabbatical? Why aren't you someplace playing golf?" Don Bartram spoke into the phone with a chuckle.

"Well, if I was on a golf course in some far-off place, Don, you wouldn't be able to call me. What's up at the office?"

"Actually, it's sort of quiet and dull without you around, buddy." Don paused for a moment. "Harry, I want to bounce something off of you."

"Go ahead, Don. I got a few minutes."

Don Bartram thought his words through carefully before he continued.

"We have an odd but lucrative request that is somehow connected to you. Neither I nor your traveling companions can figure it out."

"Don, you might as well tell me straight up."

"Yesterday, I had lunch with some Brit from the Bank of England who's representing a Hong Kong company called China Towers Real Estate Development -CTRED. It seems this group wants to purchase a major piece of property off of New York Avenue for a high tech park. The bottom line is they want us to do title search, land assembly, and community reconnaissance."

"Not exactly our line of work," Harry interrupted.

"So I tell this guy that he needs to contact Gilbert & Jacobs, since they're the best real estate attorneys in town. He tells me his client doesn't want to use regular attorneys. They want to use us, he says. Further, they want to contract with you, Harry."

"Cute, but I'm unavailable."

"Yeah, I went through that."

"So, tell him you're sorry. What's the deal?"

"The deal is that he's prepared to give us a down payment of $8 million."

"He's crazy. That's easily a quarter of the value of the deal, of the land purchase."

"I know, but he's got good paper with him. All I need you to do is talk to this guy. Says he knows you."

"What's his name?" Then, before Don could answer, he continued, "It doesn't matter, Don. This is silly."

"It's Rip Drake."

Harry pulled the receiver away from his ear and stared into space, not focusing on anything in his home office.

"Okay, when do you want me to see him, Don?"

"Well, he's in New York today, but will be back here tomorrow. How about lunch? Just get a better handle on this. If it's fishy, we walk away."

"I'll see you tomorrow at Sam and Max's. If I'm late, order me a steak. At least I'll get a good meal out of this."

Harry played back his interaction with Drake at the racetrack in Hong Kong. He thought through the briefings Peter Burke had given him. Nothing strange stood out. This whole request, however, was too strange not to be connected in some way to the SRI deal. Wait and see, he told himself.

The next morning, he drove to the office at eleven to allow time to check his mail and walk over to the lunch appointment.

"Well, good to see you, old chum. Thank you for coming." Rip Drake got up off his bar stool and extended his hand.

"Rip, I wish I could say that it was good to see you. Frankly, however, I was enjoying not working. Don, how are you this fine afternoon?" Harry sat on a stool next to the two men.

"Let's go back to our table," said Bartram.

After the trio had settled into a leather-lined booth, they talked about the weather, the Hong Kong stock market, and the soccer World Cup returning to Europe in 1998. A waiter opened the glass doors to the main dining room, bringing in the buzz of conversation bouncing off the teak paneled restaurant walls.

"Wow, business has picked up in the last few minutes, eh, Richard?" Don addressed the waiter he'd known for twenty years.

"Yes, it has, Mr. Bartram. Mr. Morton, nice to see you, sir. May I tell you gentlemen about the specials?" Richard inquired. After listening to the juicy, high-priced and cholesterol-rich fare, the trio accepted menus and asked for another round of drinks, dismissing the waiter for a requisite ten minutes of uninterrupted table talk.

"Lovely, your American cuisine. I've quite had my fill of shrimp and fishtail soup, smoked eel, and chicken baked in mud-covered leaves," Rip quipped.

"Sounds awful," said Don.

"Actually," Harry interjected with British accent, "those are real delicacies."

"Whatever," Don snorted.

"*Kung hei fat choy,*" Rip said raising his glass in a toast.

"You realize that's a Happy New Year toast, old boy," Harry said.

"Absolutely. And here's hoping a new deal emerges today that defines the beginning of a bright new year," Rip joyfully said. The men clinked and sipped.

Harry turned to Drake.

"So, since when did you get into real estate?"

"Ever since my client made it worth my while."

"I see, and do I know your client, by chance?"

"You may, but they're not anyone I've run into before. They contacted us in London, asked for me specifically. We tried to put them in touch with a U.S. affiliate, but they insisted on me and offered too much to turn them down."

"And they really do want to buy this parcel? "

"That's what our research says."

"They have any other U.S. property?"

"No, but that's not strange. D.C. is hot now, and a lot of foreign companies are jumping into this marketplace."

"What do they own in Hong Kong?" Harry was enjoying the interrogatory.

"Excellent question." He pulled a manila folder from his brief and handed it to Harry.

"Impressive. Mostly in the New Territories, but some Kowloon and some Hong Kong Island," he said as he flipped through the pages of property holding descriptions.

"Okay, Rip. Even if the company is legitimate, why use Bank of England, Rip Drake and then Masterfield for a relatively straightforward purchase? "

"It is curious, but the purchase is not as straight forward as might appear from first glance," Don Bartram piped in.

"Oh?" Harry turned to his boss.

"It appears that there are some interesting liens on some of the parcels that will take some ingenuity to release. Several of the owners have long balked at selling, and it's clear that the D.C. government will need to be approached from several angles. It's not impossible, but there is a bit of digging and scheming to be done." Don leaned into the table and fixed his stare on Harry. He was sold and wanted this deal.

Harry thought for a moment. After years of a close business relationship and tension-filled negotiations, Don Bartram knew that Harry Morton could read thoughts as well as anyone he'd ever met. He'll let me do this, he thought.

"Suppose we do some due diligence and find this deal can be made? If we do, I'll want us to be able to give an interim report to your client, this CTRED. We'll want to do it face to face. And, it'll cost a second payment, let's say of $2 million. If the meeting goes fine, we'll complete the purchase for another $4 million at settlement."

"Not too greedy, are we, old chap?"

"Your clients obviously want this property, and for some undisclosed reason are willing to pay well above market. Take it or find someone else."

"Very good, Mr. Bartram. Might I report that Mr. Morton will be involved in any client contact?"

"You can count on it, mate." Don answered without taking his eyes off him.

"Let's eat. I'll check this afternoon and call you in the morning," said Drake.

After saying goodbye to Rip in front of the restaurant, Harry and Don waved off their limo and walked down 19th Street toward their K Street office.

"Don't worry, Harry, I've already got a team on his. Gilbert & Jacobs have compiled a lot of the property details. Roberto Higgins and a couple of our associates are checking out the politics. I'll just need you to fly to Hong Kong to handle the meeting with CTRED," Don confided.

"Don, doesn't this deal smell to you? There's no way this property is worth what they're willing to pay. Also, despite what our buddy Rip says, it's still bizarre that Bank of England or their client would need to go through us. It doesn't fit."

"The only sense I can make of it is when I reflect back to the late '80's. Remember the Japanese were bidding up the East Coast and particularly New York prices, based on major miscalculations about the anticipated rise in the market? These clients, whoever they are, expect big things in downtown."

"I don't buy it. What about us? What do we bring to the table?"

"That's easier for me. It's you, my friend. You are trusted and respected over there."

"But I don't know real estate and only a bird's ass about local politics."

"You know more than they do; it's your home territory; and you know how to dig. No, Harry, that part fits."

As the two men stood in front of their ten-story glass building workers from Washington's media and international financial firms passed briskly. Each struggled to find a comfortable middle ground, a way to placate each other.

"Tell you what, Don. I'll take a few days with Ellen Kwan doing some digging on this CTRED while the others are working on the D.C. end of the deal."

"That's fine. Remember, you only have to go on one trip, make one meeting, collect $2 million. It's a simple Hong Kong assignment. Then continue a nice swing of golf through Southeast Asia," Don was now smiling.

"Yeah, yeah. There's yet to be anything simple about any assignment in Hong Kong and the price you pay is always escalating. Tell Ellen I'll call later this afternoon. I'm going home."

After a thorough briefing over the phone, Ellen Kwan spent several days researching the transaction activity, tax filings, board members, and news stories on CTRED. Other than the fact that she couldn't find the name of most of the officers, certainly not the whole board, she saw nothing peculiar about the corporation. Withholding the identity of non-officers was not an unusual practice in Hong Kong, so neither Ellen nor Harry was concerned about the omissions. There were only a couple of recent stories about the corporation. But, in the very active and competitive Hong Kong market, modest sized companies rarely commanded news coverage. So, the relative obscurity meant nothing. Harry arranged to meet a CTRED representative in Hong Kong on Monday June 3.

He was straightforward in telling Mary why he had to go for another week's trip and, his wife reacted sarcastically.

"You could barely last a few weeks back here, could you?"

Harry experienced that slow burn that begins below the waist, traverses one's veins on through the stomach, warms the chest, and explodes in the skull. "You need to come off that high throne you like to sit on. I didn't say anything after you had your fling with homeboy Max Dupree. Pretending to be at some conference in London. You need to get your sweet ass off that chair, baby, and deal with you and me."

"What are you talking about? I don't know---"

"Let's not waste time, Mary. You've been sneakin' and creepin' and playin' the 'holier than thou' role one time too many." Harry stomped into the bedroom to pack his trip bag, but returned to the living room within minutes to confront a shaken Mary. "Let me make this clear. I'm going to take my son sailing this weekend and then I'm going to Hong Kong. You can do whatever you like."

He spent a long weekend with Mark on a sailboat out in the Chesapeake Bay. By the time he returned to DC to prepare for his trip, Harry had pushed his explosive confrontation into his subconscious. His goodbyes to family and the Birches were similar to the dozens of departures over the years, and he assured Mary and Mark that he'd return quickly and continue his sabbatical. In fact, he hoped the trip might afford him time to actually plan how he might spend some real retirement time.

CHAPTER EIGHTEEN

香港

"I'm surprised you're back so soon. It's good to hear your voice, Harry. Yes, let's have lunch. How about tomorrow?" Wong Xi said over the phone.

"That sounds good. Any place in particular you'd like to meet?".

"Why don't we meet at the Visage Free? It's---"

"It's a bar in SoHo, under the escalator. But, do they serve lunch?"

"Yes. They just started sushi and light sandwiches. It's quiet, and we can talk freely."

"Sounds perfect. How about 12:30?"

"That's good. Shall I meet you there? We shouldn't need reservations."

"See you then." He replaced the receiver.

Harry decided to try and gather more information on CTRED now that he was closer to better sources. He caught a taxi to the U.S. consulate and briskly climbed the stone steps to a Victorian building set back from its busy commercial street. As he reached into his suit jacket to pull out identification for the duty officer, he heard someone addressing him from across the large lobby.

"Harry Morton? Excuse me, but are you Harry Morton of Philadelphia?"

Harry turned to face a handsome, husky, six-foot tall Chinese man who, indeed, seemed to have an American accent similar to his own.

"Yes, I'm Harry Morton. You have me at a disadvantage. I don't believe…"

Harry stopped in mid sentence, for there was something about the carriage, the strong looking hands, and even the smile of the man before him that was vaguely familiar. He noticed that the man had waved off the duty officer. As both men extended their hands to shake, Harry remembered where they had met.

"You're not, can't be David Lee?"

"Very good. Right-o, as they say here. I just happened to be going back across the lobby to my office, when I thought I recognized the profile."

"Very good, yourself. But what are you doing in Hong Kong, in the consulate?" Harry relaxed and touched the elbow of his one-time adversary.

"It's a long story," he replied, looking at Harry as if he were some long lost friend. "Got time for tea? Maybe I can help you, and we could spend a minute catching up." He began guiding Harry toward a large sandalwood door at the rear of the lobby. Harry noticed that several consulate staff and the Marine guards followed the pair with their eyes as the two athletic men walked to the Deputy Chief of Mission's office.

"Can I offer you anything, Harry?"

"Seltzer with ice would be great."

"Coming straight away."

An attractive aide brought in a Schweppes Bitter Lemon for Lee and a sparkling water for Morton. The two men settled back into deep leather chairs.

"So let's start with the important data. Did you end up playing ball in college?" Harry smiled as he sipped his drink.

"No. You know I was never good enough. I ended up going to Villanova, like a good Catholic kid. But I did well enough with my courses to transfer to Haverford College. They'd been so bad in football that they had already dropped the sport in the mid sixties. What about you? Didn't I read that you played for Penn?"

"I got to play a little Ivy League ball. It was fun, but I got a banged up shoulder and decided to stop after three years."

"I'll never forget when you came to see me in the hospital after the city title game."

"My father wouldn't let me in the house if I didn't."

"Whatever the reason, it meant a great deal."

"Well, I did go overboard on the hit. So, what happened after college?"

"I got drafted and went to Nam. Like a lot of guys, that changed my life. Only for me, it was the first time I'd been in a piece of geography where I didn't look like a minority. I loved the few times I got leave to come to Hong Kong for R & R. I decided to go into the Foreign Service. So after discharge, I went to Georgetown and got a master in Government. My pop had a fit, since I'd been your stereotypically good Asian science and math student. He couldn't see why I'd waste my time with government. 'No money in that,' he'd say. Anyway, I eventually took the Foreign Service exam, had several posts in Africa and Asia, until I got the chance to come back to Hong Kong. You know, there's now lots of intrigue with all sides repositioning for the return to China in '97. One lesson from football has been reinforced for me here in Hong Kong. It's the recognition that while 'winning is important,' what really counts is an ability to appreciate the whole field, the true meaning and value of the contest and all of the games within the game. Life goes by so quickly, particularly if you're always focused on an end, a target. Anyway, I've loved it here. What about you, Harry? I figured you'd go into politics."

"I did. I held a seat on the city council, and enjoyed it for a while. But there's so much more to politics than speeches and good policy. I wasn't made to be a big city pol. Finding a professional life in Washington has been for me what coming to Hong Kong seems to have meant for you. For a black professional, it's pretty open. A hell of a lot different from when we were in high school." He described his business career and ended the story with a request for information on CTRED.

"We'll get you what we have, but it may not be much more than your assistant already dug up. I do know that you may have dodged a bullet with the SRI crowd. They play for keeps and are off-and-on under the watch of the Hong Kong special investigations unit."

"Well, my work with them is really over."

The men rose to leave. "Next time you're in town, bring your clubs," said David. "Your shoulder doesn't hurt a golf swing, does it?"

"No, no, I had surgery after college. My swing is fine. And I'll definitely take you up on that."

"If we find anything worthwhile, we'll send it over to your hotel." He escorted Harry all the way to the main door.

Both men left hoping they would be able to meet again.

Harry spent the afternoon at a university library reading two years' back issues of the real estate articles in the *Hong Kong Commercial Daily, Asia Times and Jang HK and South China Morning Post,* as well as a couple of Asian architectural journals to get a flavor of the type buildings currently being developed on the island. After a long work out in the hotel gym, he had dinner with an old college literature professor, now retired in Hong Kong.

Late the next morning, Harry took a taxi across the island to the SoHo area. He arrived at the restaurant first, found a table and ordered a pot of fragrant green tea. The décor was closer to that of a nicely appointed post-hippie club in Greenwich Village than to any venue in modern China, or England for that matter. He sipped his tea and wondered as to the origin of the owners. The clientele was mixed: some Australians and British business types and a few Chinese on break from nearby shops and offices. The only thing they all had in common was that they seemed to enjoy watching the street foot traffic while they slowly ate Western sandwiches, drank British black tea or Chinese green or white and listened to American jazz softly playing out of ceiling speakers. He relaxed and enjoyed his own people-watching though wondered why Xi had picked the *Visage Free*.

He caught sight of her crossing the street in front of the club. She looked as elegant as he had remembered. She was dressed in a lavender silk suit, her hair pulled back, and her identity, though not her beauty, obscured by black sunglasses.

He rose as she approached the table. "Madame CEO, you look as lovely as ever."

"You are too kind, Mr. Morton. It really is wonderful to see you. Is this place all right for you?" she inquired in rote fashion.

"Well, that depends," he said with a slight smile as he pushed her chair properly under her.

"Depends? Depends on what?"

"On what we discuss, of course. Xi, why don't you relax? You seem uptight."

"Well, I suppose. I mean, I just responded to your call instinctively, without thinking."

"And, for that I am grateful. Drink?"

Xi took off her glasses. "No, thank you. It's the middle of the day. Maybe I'll have tea. That looks good. "

"So, how are you? How's the merger?"

"I suppose we're working out the post-wedding legal details. Things have been a little stressed for the last few weeks. It's certainly different not having consultants around, but we're doing fine." She gently rubbed tired looking eyes, and thanked the waiter for the pot of oolong tea he placed on the table.

They talked about the Hong Kong business climate and about various deals that SRI was pursuing or contemplating. He also asked about her friend, Margaret Schultz, about Ho Duan and others on the staff, and about her husband and father.

"They're all splendid and will be glad to know that you remembered them. You may be interested to know that Margaret and that fellow Rip Drake are sort of seeing each other. It's causing a stir in some circles. I think they're a charming couple."

"Well, I bet they raise a few normally stiff eyebrows."

"Yes. This may be Hong Kong, but it's still very much China." Xi made no mention of her long conversation with her friend about the potential vexing consequences of Margaret choosing Rip over Rajib.

He decided not to mention anything about CTRED or his recent contact with Drake, so that his visit would appear solely to be for the purpose of maintaining contact. After a few moments of silence, Xi asked about Mark and the stalker. Harry recounted the story in a few short sentences, and then opened the subject of the impact that recent immigration from the Chinese country-side was having on metropolitan areas, like Hong Kong. They spent a pleasant hour discussing the perils and opportunities of urbanization before he pushed back his chair as if to rise. He hesitated for a moment.

"Xi, how about dinner tomorrow?"

The traces of facial lines smoothed out, and she turned away from him for a moment before responding. "I don't think that would be wise, Harry."

"Wise? I'm not talking about a marketing meeting. I'm suggesting we have some fun. You remember?"

"Harry, I know exactly what you mean. I'm at a critical juncture with the company. I can't risk any misunderstandings out there. I thought we both had agreed the last time that the risks were too severe."

"Are you telling me that you've rediscovered the sanctity of your marriage?"

Ignoring the question, she said, "You know, Harry, in some ways we're very much alike; and in others, we are so very different." Her eyes filled with compassion.

"So, tell me. How are we alike?"

"We're both bright in conventional Western ways, aren't we? We're pretty skilled at reading other cultures, and we're accomplished by any standards."

"Are we both so modest?" Harry tried not to smirk. "And how are we different—that is, in ways that aren't obvious?" Harry added.

"In my case, I have the need; call it greed if you like, to attain the pinnacle. I'm more possessed by the single-minded focus to obtain and use the maximum power I can. I've also learned to better evaluate risk, and to avoid the most unpredictable and uncontrollable situations. You, Harry, are not consumed with the same obsession. You're retired. In some sense, you're willing to assume personal risk, but want to avoid the corruption and contamination of power. I will now avoid personal risk, but will almost embrace the corruption of power. I accept that some corruption, even some death attends the maintenance of substantial power.

I'm not passing judgment, and I'm certainly not asserting moral worth, one way or the other. As brilliant as you are at reading others, I'm not sure you are as clear about yourself and your own conflicts. Or, maybe you traded the power game in when you sold to Masterfield. Me, I couldn't consult. I need to build, to expand and to control. Sounds awful, obviously. But I'm clear that's where I am in my life."

"Are you gloating, Xi?"

"No. And you know I'm not. I'm just remarking on how we're different. I need to be true to my goals and my purpose. In a quite significant way, you have helped me clarify that truth."

"I'm glad that you're clear. And I'm sure that this current complication of growth will pass and work out for you. I think, however, that you misread me. The real difference is that I've climbed my mountains, slain my dragons, and am content to advise."

"Really?"

Harry merely smiled at the question. He paid and they left the restaurant. The sun bathed them both as they stood facing each other.

"Harry, I have to thank you for helping us conclude a great deal. Your counsel was invaluable. And, I truly hope you find something, beyond your son, about which you can be passionate. You deserve that."

She offered him her cheek as they parted on the sidewalk. "This might really be goodbye, Harry," she said as she adjusted her glasses and walked back across the street.

He stood in front of the restaurant and watched her disappear into the bustling crowd. He wasn't sure how precisely to interpret his feelings, but he knew he had to block them out in order to prepare for his afternoon meeting back at the *Peninsula*.

"Good afternoon, Mr. Morton," said the doorman, nodding slightly as he held the heavy-duty chrome trimmed door for Harry.

"Mr. Ding. It's always a pleasure to see you."

"The pleasure is ours, Mr. Morton. I believe an elderly gentleman left a message for you at the desk about a half hour ago."

Harry crossed the crowded lobby to the main desk. As he approached, the concierge pulled a sealed envelope from his middle drawer.

"Good afternoon, Mr. Morton."

"Thank you, Mr. Ho." He took the envelope and headed for the elevator bank, thinking, "They need to attract more people of color here. I'm way too recognizable."

Harry read the note on his way up to the penthouse floor: *Mr. Morton. Shall we meet in the bar of the Marco Polo Hotel off of Canton Road at 6PM? If that is not convenient, please suggest a time and dial the number below. We look forward to seeing you. CTRED.*

He decided to catch up on phone messages and go back over the briefings prepared by Ellen Kwan. He called down to the front desk to see if any message had come from the U.S. Consulate.

Nothing. Then, he took a shower. Refreshed and tingling after dousing some faintly scented orchid cologne, Harry positioned himself erectly in an arm chair and meditated for a half hour. He did not emerge from his semi- trance until the afternoon mist began to negotiate its way across the harbor.

Harry emerged from the Peninsula at 5:45 PM and walked to the Marco Polo. He registered the shock on the bar maitre d's face when Harry addressed him in flawless Cantonese, asking if any visitors had enquired for "Mr. Morton." The red-jacketed employee recovered and ushered Harry to a table at the far end of the darkening room, where a balding Chinese man dressed in a Western suit rose to greet him.

"Welcome, and thank you for coming, Mr. Morton."

It was Harry's turn to be surprised, for standing before him was Bao Li, Xi's husband.

"Please, be seated. I've taken the liberty to order you scotch on the rocks. I believe that is a favorite of yours, is it not?"

"Perfect. Thank you, Mr. Bao."

"Oh, I believe you should continue to address me by my first name, under the circumstances."

"No offense, but I'm not quite sure of the circumstances of which you speak. In calling you Mr., I only wish to respect your stature, and your superior achievement and knowledge."

"As you will. I am appreciative of your consideration. I trust you had a pleasant flight."

"Yes, thank you. It was quite restful." Harry tried to relax and decipher the older man's words, body language, and now his silence.

A waiter brought bourbon and a scotch.

"Ah, the drinks," said Bao. He raised his whiskey tumbler and offered to clink Harry's glass. "Here's to business."

"Yes, to business, particularly to real estate deals," Harry returned.

They sat and sipped in silence for a few moments. In his head, Harry ran through several scenarios that placed Bao Li in the CTRED deal. Nothing quite fit.

"Are you puzzled about my presence, Mr. Morton?"

"I must admit that I don't yet see the obvious connection between you and CTRED. But I'm quite pleased at the prospect of doing business with you, and this is certainly a pleasant spot to initiate our conversation."

"Flexibility. Indeed, one of your many business virtues, Mr. Morton," the older man spoke more slowly, now. "This time, however, your admirable collection of business skills will prove inadequate. You see, this CTRED deal will fail, and our company will request its money back. And you, Mr. Morton, will have to explain to the Bank of England, and to Masterfield Consulting, of course, the reason why the deal failed."

Harry revealed no outer recognition of the impact of Mr. Bao's words. He didn't change expression, calmly maintaining the other man's gaze. He knew immediately, however, why the deal would not close. He just didn't yet know how unpleasant Xi's husband intended to make it.

"Expensive retribution, but necessary. You see, Mr. Morton, I'm from the old school."

"Is that pistols or swords at dawn?"

"No. The old school in China wasn't uncivilized. It simply meant one had to maintain appropriate dignity, even in the face of outlandish insult."

"I wasn't aware that I had insulted you, Mr. Bao."

"Oh, really, Mr. Morton? Do not take me for a fool. I am an old man, but I am not unobservant."

"Then, I must offer my apologies, sir, for my conduct." Harry saw no choice. No need to claim some appeal to consenting adults. No need to assert that Xi had been the aggressor. He had to apologize.

"I suppose, in some modern Western context, I should be flattered that a man of your sophistication finds my wife so attractive that you would risk---"

"We both know that no such context exists. I'm curious, Mr. Bao. Why not simply have me killed? After all, there were other victims in the South China deal." Harry looked down only long enough to set his glass on the table.

"That was *South China* and that stupid adolescent cousin. The Xiaobin crew has yet to endorse several essential elements of civilized business behavior. I see no need to risk divulging the details of 'the relationship' and embarrassing my family. Even to a hit man. I should think the loss of face for losing this deal and your having to create a tenable explanation will indeed be payment enough for me."

"I must say, you are a most generous man. By the way, how did you create this real estate ruse in the first place?"

"Let us say that I have adequate influence in the company."

Bao began to push back from the table, leaving money on the ashtray.

"Under the circumstances, Mr. Bao, I believe I should pay for the drinks."

"As you will. Good evening, Mr. Morton."

"May I ask you one more thing, Li?"

Bao Li nodded consent.

"Does your wife know that you know?"

Bao stood for a moment. He looked toward the bar, at the tapestry framing the open door to the lobby, then back at Harry.

"Mr. Morton, you are an educated man. You are a scholar of Chinese custom. This is man's business. It is settled between men. One more thing, Mr. Morton. I may have presented you with some obstacles just now. I have no doubt that you will find a solution and be able to save face. You are remarkably resourceful. But, I sincerely hope you have to struggle in finding a solution. Oh, and I almost forgot that your own wife may have recently gained new insight into your activities while you have been on assignment in Hong Kong. I also believe that a reporter from your *Washington Post* has already inquired of Mr. Bartram about the collapse of the CTRED deal.

Good day, Mr. Morton." Bao smiled, turned once again, and left the room.

Harry sat back down and slowly finished his drink.

Back at his hotel suite, he phoned the airlines and easily changed his flight to one on Singapore Air later that day. Then, Harry spread out his folded clothes on the bed in neat piles, and intermittently walked to the bedside table to jot down notes on different explanations he might present as to why he was returning empty-handed.

He knew that Boa would have already taken all actions necessary to back up his story with respect to CTRED. There was no point in trying to save the deal. Bao would have made absolutely sure that it was squashed. The newspaper might be more vexing; depending on the line it had been fed. Harry had to figure out a legitimate explanation that would be verifiable if his people ever checked. But, he was curious how Bao could have revealed the affair to Mary without besmearing Xi's character. Not Harry's problem. He feared this episode could doom his marriage regardless of the Max Dupree affair. His neck tightened and his stomach knotted.

In the lobby, Harry paid his bill and headed for the door to get a taxi.

"Going home, Mr. Morton?" the doorman asked. "Valuable trip?"

"Valuable? Yes, quite valuable, Mr. Ding. See you next time."

Harry watched the early evening street life pass as the taxi raced towards the old Kai Tak airport. Along the way, the tall steel and glass structures that were embraced by tightly laced bamboo scaffolding reflected shades of sunset, lending an explosive sparkle to the end of the day. As he pondered his latest predicament, Harry reflected first on Xi's wish that he discover his "passion." He winced ever so slightly. Then, he thought about his encounter with David Lee and his description about playing the game of life. As if speaking to David again, Harry thought, "I have enjoyed playing the game, but I certainly didn't win. And, for once, I don't know that I've ever really understood the meaning of the game within the game."

Approaching the airport, the driver looked in his mirror and in broken English asked Harry which airlines his flight was on. Harry reached inside his coat breast pocket, fingered his old cancelled Washington, D.C. *United Airlines* ticket, and closed his eyes.

"Sir, can you tell me the airlines?" the cabbie said in urgent Cantonese.

After another moment or two, in broken English, the driver spoke again, "Sir, perhaps you tell me destination?"

Another minute passed before Harry opened his eyes and said, "Sorry. Drop me here, please. I…I just don't know, yet."

ABOUT THE AUTHOR

John "Skip" McKoy has spent most of his life leading major public, private and non-profit organizations. He is currently Director of Programs for Fight For Children, an organization based in Washington, DC which works to improve the quality of life for underserved children and youth. Previously, McKoy was an executive with the Anacostia Waterfront Corporation (a group dedicated to revitalizing riverfront communities), CEO of DC Agenda, Director of the District's City Planning Agency, Vice President in Lockheed Martin Corporation, and a private management consultant.

Born and raised in Philadelphia, McKoy has lived in Boston, San Francisco, and Washington, DC and traveled extensively in Latin America, Africa, Europe and Asia. Fluent in Spanish, he worked as a community organizer in Guatemala for two years. He currently resides in Washington, DC with his wife, Andrea Gay.

McKoy's volunteer activity has included board membership on a wide range of causes: Humanities Council of Washington; Leadership Greater Washington, DC; Mentors Inc.; Communities and Schools of the Nation's Capital; the Corporation of Haverford College; the DC Public Charter School Board; and the DC Chamber of Commerce.

He earned his Masters of Public Administration at Harvard University's John F. Kennedy School of Government and his Masters Degree in City Planning at the University of Pennsylvania. He received his Bachelors Degree at Hamilton College.